PRAISE FOR THOMAS KIES

RANDOM ROAD

The First Geneva Chase Mystery

Library Journal Book of the Month

"Kies's debut mystery introduces a reporter with a compelling voice, a damaged woman who recounts her own bittersweet story as she hunts down clues. This suspenseful story will appeal to readers who enjoy hard-nosed investigative reporters such as Brad Parks's Carter Ross."

—*Library Journal,* Starred Review

"Kies tells a taut, fast-paced tale, imbuing each character with memorable, compelling traits that help readers connect with them."

—*Booklist*

"Kies's fiction debut lays the groundwork for an entertaining series."

—*Kirkus Reviews*

DARKNESS LANE

The Second Geneva Chase Mystery

"Multiple murders and shocking twists are key components in Geneva's ultimate uncovering of the truth. The flawed but dedicated heroine anchors Kies's second mystery with a compassion that compels readers to root for both justice and redemption."

—*Kirkus Reviews*

"Kies neatly balances breathless action with Geneva Chase's introspection and sleuthing savvy."

—*Publishers Weekly*

"There's a solid thriller here—the key is sex trafficking—but the real pleasure is watching Geneva work. Cheer her on as she wrestles with that vodka bottle and trembles with fear as she confronts the monster behind the child-slavery ring. She's also pretty good at standing up to a newspaper publisher about to screw the help into the ground."

—*Booklist*

GRAVEYARD BAY

Also by Thomas Kies

The Geneva Chase Mysteries

Random Road

Darkness Lane

GRAVEYARD BAY

A GENEVA CHASE MYSTERY

THOMAS KIES

Cover design by The Book Designers
Cover images © ARENA Creative/Shutterstock, Ambar Saha/Shutterstock

Published by Poisoned Pen Press, an imprint of Sourcebooks
P.O. Box 4410, Naperville, Illinois 60567-4410
(630) 961-3900
sourcebooks.com

Library of Congress Cataloging-in-Publication Data

Names: Kies, Thomas, author.
Title: Graveyard bay / Thomas Kies.
Description: Naperville, IL : Poisoned Pen Press, [2019]
Identifiers: LCCN 2019021342 | (hardcover : alk. paper)
Subjects: | GSAFD: Suspense fiction.
Classification: LCC PS3611.I3993 G73 2019 | DDC 813/.6--dc23 LC record available at https://lccn.loc.gov/2019021342

Printed and bound in the United States of America.
SB 10 9 8 7 6 5 4 3 2 1

Chapter One

Overkill.

That was the word that immediately came to mind when I saw the crime scene.

It was bitterly cold. I had on a bulky sweater, stocking cap, long underwear, jeans, calf-length leather boots, and insulated, full-length parka. I should have been warm enough, but I couldn't stop shivering. What froze my bones to ice wasn't the temperature. It was the gruesome way the man and woman had been put to death.

The sun was a pale smudge sliding up over the frigid horizon of Long Island Sound. The growing illumination washed pink highlights over the choppy, ash-gray water. Stuttering blue and white lights from the police cruisers flashed behind me onto the pier and the sides of the mammoth aluminum dry-stack building to my left. Crackling, disembodied voices came and went from dashboard radios.

Blustering gusts of wind hurled stinging bits of grit and tiny crystals of ice against my exposed cheeks. I stamped my boots against the snowy asphalt of the parking lot to ward off the creeping chill working its way into my feet and calves.

A swift, repetitive metallic clanging rang out in the giant open lot where the larger boats were stored, some on trailers, some on low jack stands propped under their hulls. Every time a burst of icy air blasted us from the Sound, the riggings of the sailboats beat like multiple fire alarms against aluminum masts.

When the alert came in that morning, I was in my warm ten-year-old Sebring en route to the office, travel mug filled with steaming coffee tucked into the center console. The scanner app on my phone pinged and said simply that bodies had been found at the Groward Bay Marina. Not how many and certainly not how they'd died.

I wished I'd been tipped off before I arrived.

Groward Bay was the largest marina in Sheffield, Connecticut. Only forty-five minutes by boat from Manhattan, it drew wealthy mariners from all over the East Coast. The marina boasted four hundred in-water slips, a massive dry-stack facility, a fully stocked ship's store, fueling facilities, private showers, and marina-wide cable and Wi-Fi.

But at that time of year, the floating docks were mostly empty. With a few exceptions, the boats had been hauled out and put into storage for winter. Christmas was less than a week away, and this was a quiet, lonely place, windswept and isolated, far from curious eyes.

The perfect place for torture and murder.

Standing on my side of the police tape, I watched a marina employee, wearing a blue hooded work coat over dark brown overalls, a ski cap, and leather work gloves, lying on his stomach, seven feet in the air, on the floor of the cockpit of the gargantuan forklift. He was tinkering with the ignition wires of the massive machine perched on the side of the concrete pier. Its sheer size was impressive—a gantry in the front that was forty feet high, eight tires that were nearly as tall as me.

Overkill.

The wheels were pressed against metal stops at the edge of the concrete pier. The prongs of the huge machine rested under the dark surface of the bay. Over and over, the marina employee took off his gloves, reached into the guts of the machine, pulled on some wires, and then put the gloves back on, frustration etched onto his craggy face.

A group of cops and EMTs stood in a small knot, talking, steam rising with their words, bodies moving from side to side, working to stay warm. Temporary powerful halogen lamps had been set up on the pier. One was focused on the stubborn engine as the workman tinkered. The other two bright lamps were aimed at the swirling water below.

Mike Dillon, deputy chief of police, crossed his arms with an impatient expression on his face. He wore a reflective black-and-yellow coat marked SPD, its black hood pulled over his head and ears. Every once in a while, he stamped his feet to ward off the cold. He was standing off to one side with Dr. Foley, the medical examiner also wearing an SPD coat, the two of them talking quietly. Doc Foley's jacket bulged under his pot belly. His red-cheeked cherubic face was accented by a drooping gray mustache that bristled in the wind. He reminded me of a walrus.

Mike hadn't acknowledged my presence yet. I wasn't even sure he knew I was there.

When I arrived, I discovered that the investigation had stalled before it began. There was little to do until the bodies were recovered. They'd already photographed and measured the footprints and tire tread marks on the parking lot and the pier and gathered what little physical evidence there was.

I pulled the scarf up around my face as another gust of bitterly cold wind blew in, and I sensed that someone was close behind me.

Glancing back, I saw a tall man in his sixties wearing a heavy brown coat with the collar turned up, green rubber boots, baseball cap, and earmuffs. His hat was emblazoned with the red-and-blue Groward Bay Marina logo. His face was weathered, his skin resembling the leather of a worn catcher's mitt, webs of deep lines radiating around his green eyes and the corners of his mouth. A two-day growth of gray stubble dirtied his cheeks and chin.

I pulled the scarf down away from my lips. "Do you work here?"

He nodded. "I'm the general manager." He held out a gloved hand. "Rick Guthrie."

"I'm Geneva Chase with the *Sheffield Post.*" We shook hands, and I motioned toward the employee tinkering with the guts of the forklift. "What's your guy doing?"

He tossed a glance to where the cops were standing. "Whoever did this either took the keys with 'em or tossed them into the water. Kenny's trying to hot-wire the damn thing."

"That's one big machine." The huge blue-and-white forklift reminded me of the massive construction vehicles I'd recently seen on the south side of Sheffield.

He grinned and showed me stained teeth that hadn't seen a dentist in a long time. "It's a Wiggins Marina Bull, one of the biggest they make. It can reach down eleven feet under the surface of the water and haul up a forty-thousand-pound boat, lift it up, carry it into the dry-stack over there, then hoist it thirty-seven feet into the air. The two forks are forty-seven feet long. Machine weighs a hundred and thirty-four thousand pounds." He jerked his thumb in the direction of the dry stack building. "The floor in there is a foot thick to withstand the weight of that beast."

I frowned. "How does it do all that?"

"The way it's counterbalanced." He held his gloved hands up, moving one up and the other one down as if he were showing me something. "All the weight of the Bull is in the back. It took three trucks to ship it to us. One of the trucks just for the weights." Then his face turned deadly serious and his eyes studied the dark water below. His voice was little more than a whisper. "It's what you can't see—the prongs of the forklift that brings up the boats. Right now, they're about six feet underwater. It's where the bodies are."

I felt a spinning lurch in the pit of my stomach. It was a cold stew of fear, dread, and the thrill of getting a great story all rolled up into one. "How many bodies?"

He cocked his head. "All I saw were two. Could be more, I reckon. Hard to see in the dark."

I glanced at the water, then back at Rick. "How did you find them?"

"I got here 'bout an hour ago and the first thing I noticed was the Bull sitting out on the pier. It shouldn't be here. It's supposed to be locked up in the dry-stack building."

He pointed behind us. I could see through a yawning three-story open doorway into the cavernous metal building where easily two hundred boats were warehoused on shelves, bows against the wall, sterns pointed toward the middle of the room, stacked one on top of another, five deep. "That's where the smaller boats are stored for winter. Bigger boats are in the lot." He jerked his thumb behind him.

I could easily see the larger boats. They were parked outside, winterized—drained of fluids, shrink-wrapped in white plastic, held off the ground by huge wooden blocks under their hulls, braced against the wind on multilegged, metal jack stands. There must have been at least three hundred vessels. Long, sleek powerboats and magnificent sailboats were lined up in neat rows leaving just enough room for a car or truck to drive along. They were monuments to affluence, like snow-covered markers in a lonely, exclusive graveyard.

Rick's voice was low. When he spoke, his words emerged as a rusty growl. "I saw it and wondered what the hell it was doing there. Why were the Bull's forks underwater? I went to the side of the pier and aimed my flashlight into the bay." He held the big, black light up for emphasis. "I could see there was something attached to both prongs, something pale in the beam of the light. I took me a minute because the water was movin' and it was still dark. When I finally figured out what I was lookin' at, I thought my heart would seize up. There are people tied to them forks."

Overkill.

The skin on the back of my neck crawled when I heard him say that. An engine suddenly belched and rumbled to life. Startled, we both turned and stared at the machine. Kenny had gotten the forklift started. He swung himself up and hopped into the black plastic seat of the cab, then pulled a lever back, and the water began to roil.

The cops all moved closer to the side of the pier as the rubber-covered metal forks broke the surface of the icy bay.

My breath caught in my throat, and my eyes struggled to make sense of what I was seeing.

Two bodies tied to the prongs, wrapped tightly with chains.

A man and a woman.

Water sluiced off the glistening corpses as they emerged into the stark glare of the halogen lamplight. Taking off my mittens, I brought the camera up to my eye and adjusted the telephoto lens. The chains glinted in the illumination. Through my lens, I could see the male was Caucasian, had a full head of sopping salt-and-pepper hair, and was most likely in his late fifties or early sixties.

The woman, also Caucasian, appeared much younger, in her thirties, with long, waterlogged auburn hair.

Dear God, I think they're both stark naked.

For a moment I wondered if they'd died of hypothermia or drowning. What would be worse? I took a deep breath of frigid air and took my photos.

I turned back to Rick Guthrie, gesturing to the open space in the dry-stack where the forklift should have been. "Who has access to that building?"

He was staring, transfixed, mouth open at the macabre scene unfolding on his pier. The forklift was backing up, its human cargo chained tightly to the jutting prongs.

I tried again. "Mr. Guthrie? Who has access to that building?"

His attention snapped back to me. "Me, Kenny...couple of the other employees. But it wasn't any of them. Someone busted in." He pointed to the entrance off to the side where the door was hanging at an odd angle. "Looks like they mighta used a crowbar."

"No alarm?"

"Someone was smart enough to cut the alarm, but we got closed-circuit cameras all over the place." He waved his hands. "Motion-activated, the video is saved on the computer in my office."

"Have you looked at it yet?"

"I ran it for the cops when they got here. They copied it onto a thumb drive. They said they'd have to take my computer too."

"But it's still in your office?"

He nodded, staring at the bodies chained to his forklift.

"And the video is still loaded onto your computer?"

"Yes, ma'am."

Holy crap.

I smiled at him coquettishly. "Can I see it?"

—

Rick's office was tucked away in the back of the dry-stack building in a small one-story metal annex. We walked through the massive open doorway, across the concrete floor where the Bull should have been parked for safekeeping, past the shelves of powerboats stacked impossibly on top of one another.

I glanced back to where the cops were snapping off the locks with a set of bolt cutters. Nobody was paying any attention to us.

At the back of the building we came to a doorway with a sign saying Marina Offices. He unlocked the door, letting us into a narrow hallway. His office was the first door on the right. After he flipped on the fluorescent lights I went in and distinctly felt the rise in temperature.

"Oh, this feels so good," I told him, taking off my mittens and shoving them into the pockets of my parka.

The office was little more than a large closet. It smelled vaguely of sawdust and aftershave. There was a single window that looked out over the floating docks. Sea charts of the immediate coastline were tacked onto the wood paneling alongside a bookcase. His metal desk was pushed up against a wall, piles of folders sitting next to a large computer monitor.

Rick took off his earmuffs, leaving on his Groward Bay Marina cap, and slipped out of his coat, draping it on the back of his chair. He sat down and brought his sleeping computer to life. "This won't take long," he said. "It's always the first thing I check when I get here in the morning. We have a dozen motion-activated cameras around the boatyard and this here building. Usually, there's nothin' to see. But once in a while I catch a homeless guy who's climbed over the fence, trying to sneak under the shrink-wrap of one of them boats, lookin' for a place to sleep."

Suddenly, the screen showed the front entrance of the marina. Under the bright boatyard lights, the video appeared black and white. There was no audio. The front gate was rolling to the side.

I pointed to the screen. "Do you need a card to activate the gate?"

Rick nodded. "Yeah, anybody with a boat down here has one. Truth be told, they ain't that hard to get hold of."

We watched as a white, unmarked cargo van, headlights on, drove slowly through the entrance. I got up close to the monitor, eyes straining to see the license plate on the front of the van.

They've put something over it. Black plastic and duct tape?

As the vehicle rolled through the marina, it activated new cameras, one after another. Finally, we watched as it pulled up and parked in front of the dry-stack building, just at the foot of the concrete pier. Five men got out, all dressed the same: black jeans, black quilted parkas, leather gloves, and black balaclavas—knit ski caps, pulled down over their faces. Only their eyes, noses, and mouths were exposed to the frigid night air. They reminded me of terrorists I've seen in photos.

I checked the time stamp on the screen: 2:37 a.m.

The tallest one, a big man, broad in the shoulders, carrying a crowbar, lumbered out of the video but another camera, just outside the door, caught up with him. We watched as he shoved the metal rod into the jam near the lock and, in one impossibly strong motion, yanked the door open.

Adrenaline suddenly ripped through my veins.

Could that be Bogdan Tolbonov?

The man on the screen was certainly the right body type. Bogdan was one of the biggest men I'd ever been frightened by. He was a Russian gangster who'd scared the hell out of me back in October. The man was a living, breathing Halloween monster.

The action came up again as a camera captured the man inside the dry-stack building when he flipped on the lights. He had to be at least six foot nine and his shoulders were massive, his parka straining from the musculature underneath. When he moved, it was deliberate with a restrained sense of power.

The man slowly turned toward the camera, staring into it, intentionally letting us see his face.

Is he mocking the cops?

He wasn't wearing a ski mask like the others. His parka hood had been up over his head, making it difficult to get a good look. But while he stared up at the camera, he pulled the hood back. The man had on a black leather, form-fitting mask with slits for his eyes, nose, and mouth, around which were silver metal studs.

Like something out of an S&M porn flick.

Staring at him, my fingers and hands went cold again. I involuntarily recalled Bogdan's deep, creepy voice, his tiny pig's eyes, his thin lips, the way he'd threatened me and Caroline.

You don't know if it's him, Genie.

He went straight to where dozens of keys were hung from hooks on the wall. Without hesitating, he picked one out.

Rick whispered. "Son of a bitch knew right where we kept the key."

"Who all would know that?"

He shrugged and chewed at his lower lip. "Anyone who's watched us haul their boat out of the water, I guess."

Then we watched as the man in black trod to the bay door and pressed a button. Soundlessly, the huge door slid open and he went back and got into the cab of the forklift.

Rick clicked on his mouse and the scene changed to outside the dry-stack building again. As the massive forklift slowly rolled out onto the pier, the other four men reached into the back of the van in a frenzy of activity.

My stomach dropped when a male with a thicket of salt-and-pepper hair, blowing wildly in the wind, and a slim female were dragged out, struggling, hands tied behind their backs, completely naked, cruelly exposed to the frigid temperatures. Held in the grip of their captors, they both shivered uncontrollably.

Shaking from the cold? From terror?

Both.

I knew that overnight, the air temp had dropped to eighteen degrees. Even with the sun coming up, it was barely reaching the low twenties.

The big man braked, parked the lift, and jumped out. He pointed to the concrete surface of the pier.

Gun barrels held tight to their heads, rough hands on their shoulders, the two captives were forced to their knees. They were facing the camera. The male captive seemed familiar to me. He had a square jaw that quivered in the video, his eyes closed against the dangerous chill.

I didn't recognize the woman at all. In her thirties, she was athletically trim, her chest heaving from fear and exposure, her long, windswept hair twirled and wound around her head as if it had a life of its own.

The big man in the mask pointed at them and appeared to be shouting. With no audio, it was silent theater on our computer screen.

The deathly quiet in Rick's claustrophobic office thickened the air. We were holding our breath, guessing at what was being said.

Both captives quickly shook their heads in response. I thought I could see tears glistening on their faces.

The man shouted again and angrily waved his gloved hands in the air.

The male captive shouted in return, his head shaking wildly.

Denying something? Pleading for his life?

The man in the leather hood shrugged and pointed to the prongs of the lift. The four black-clad thugs wrestled both struggling captives onto the forklift prongs, laying them on their backs and wrapping heavy chains around their chests, arms tight to their bodies, locking them in place.

They look so tiny on those huge forks.

I heard Rick whisper, "Dear God, they musta been cold."

"Stop the video."

He glanced at me but then hit the Pause button.

I got closer to the screen. The resolution of the video was fuzzy at best. I stared at the face of the male. Salt-and-pepper hair, lantern jaw, early sixties.

Is that Judge Niles Preston?

I stared harder. Try as I might, I couldn't positively say for sure.

I took a breath and put my hand on Rick's shoulder, as much to steady myself as to tell him to hit the Play button. "Okay, let's see the rest."

We saw Leather Mask climb back into the cab of the lift and power it slowly forward until it reached the metal stays at the edge of the pier. Then he pushed a lever forward and lowered the man and woman, their mouths open in silent screams. Just before being submerged, they both took a last gulp of air and sank into the icy, breathtakingly cold water until they'd completely vanished beneath the black surface of the bay.

Rick and I both held our breath.

Ten seconds.

I knew from a piece I wrote a few years ago that if a human

is immersed in water between fifty and forty degrees, while it doesn't sound like it's horribly cold, they go into cold shock.

Twenty seconds.

Any colder than that, the water feels like it's burning your skin. Your body suffers from severe pain, and any clear thinking becomes impossible.

Thirty seconds.

You begin to lose control of voluntary functions, hypothermia is creeping in. You become lethargic.

Forty-five seconds.

The prongs of the forklift emerged from the water, and the two captives broke the surface. Once the forks were level with the pier, Leather Mask, still sitting in the cab, began shouting again, his gloved hands pointing and gesturing.

The two captives, gasping for air, hyperventilating, chests heaving, shook their heads back and forth, their mouths open, screaming, sobbing uncontrollably, wailing, begging for mercy.

Even though the video was soundless, I could hear them in my head.

After a few more moments, Leather Mask shook his head in disgust. He dismissed the two of them with a wave of his hand. The forks were lowered again.

Permanently.

"Geneva!"

My stomach lurched. Turning, I saw Mike Dillon in the doorway.

"What the hell are you doing?" His voice sounded seriously pissed off.

I folded my arms across my chest. "My job."

He turned his attention to Rick. "Turn that off right now."

The marina manager hit a button and the screen went black.

"You and me, outside. We need to talk."

Up until a couple of months ago, Mike Dillon and I had been in a relationship. We'd made a very handsome couple. He's in his early forties—a six-foot tall, good-looking guy with a face that's angular, cunning, with expressive brown eyes and an easy smile. Plus, he's smart and a hell of a cop.

I'm nearly as tall, five-ten, blond, blue eyes, and I keep my weight in check and my muscles toned by working out and running on the waterfront as often as I can. I'd like to think that at forty, I'm still attractive with only a minimal application of overpriced cosmetics.

For about ten months, Mike and I were dating, seeing each other for dinners, movies, and we even had sex a few times. We were friends with infrequent benefits.

Then, in October, he'd abruptly called it off. Mike wanted more of a commitment.

I didn't know what the hell I wanted.

He and I walked out of the general manager's office and into the small hallway. Mike glared at me. "You know this isn't how we do things. This is my investigation and I'll give you a full report when *I'm* ready."

I hate to wait.

"Who are the victims?"

He gave me a look.

I jerked my head toward Rick's office door. "You saw the video?" He nodded.

"Like watching a horror movie," I offered.

Mike turned his gaze toward the office doorway, recalling what he'd seen. "Yeah."

"And what's with that guy's mask?"

He shook his head. "Trying to scare the victims?"

"I'm not sure how much scarier it could get. It was like he was mugging for the camera." Then I asked the question again. "You know who the victims are?"

Mike eyed me. "No IDs yet."

I moved closer to him and whispered. "The male looks a little like Judge Preston."

He glanced away from me. "We don't have an ID on either one of them."

Mike knew Judge Preston. He'd testified plenty of times in his courtroom. If it wasn't him, he could have simply stated that it wasn't the judge, but he didn't. Without actually saying it, he'd just told me that the male murder victim was indeed Preston. But there was no way I could use it in my story. When I wrote this up, it would be two unknown victims. "Any idea at all who the killers are?"

"Nope."

Mike wasn't saying much. He was still pissed off at me for sneaking a look at the video.

I pulled my mittens out of my pockets, preparing to go back out into the cold. "Call me when you find out who they are?

"Yeah." He put his hand on my wrist. "I'd appreciate it if you don't make mention of the video just yet. The tall guy, the one in the mask, he deliberately looked into one of the cameras. He did that for a reason, and I want to know what it is before it goes public."

"Yeah, I'll sit on it, but when you ID the victims, you got to give me the names before you give them to anyone else."

He nodded and smiled at me for the first time that morning. "Deal."

I knew Mike. I wasn't entirely certain he meant it. But I had to give him the benefit of the doubt.

I bundled back up and headed outside, glancing at the two bodies, now on gurneys, under gray sheets that had to be tied down to prevent being blown away by the wind. Dr. Foley was examining the dead woman's fingernails.

Slipping and sliding back to my car, I pulled the scarf back over my face and thought about what it must have been like to be lowered into that water, trying to hold your breath, your body screaming from the cold.

I began to shiver again.

Chapter Two

As I put together the piece about the murders, I found it difficult not to steal glances at the digital clock on my computer screen. Nine-thirty—a half hour still to go before my meeting with Robert Vogel.

The *Sheffield Post* was getting new owners. The sale would be final on January 1, but the transition had been ongoing for weeks.

It hadn't come as a surprise. Fairfield County was an extremely competitive media market. Outrageously affluent, the region was a ripe target for advertisers. Stamford, Norwalk, Danbury, and Bridgeport all had their own daily newspapers, and they were all owned by the same company, Hearst Media Services Connecticut, as were most of the weekly newspapers in the county.

The *Sheffield Post* was the last of the independent dailies, solely owned by our publisher, Ben Sumner. He was in his late fifties and had been running the newspaper most of his adult life. Recently, two of our largest advertisers abandoned the *Post* for digital and broadcast options.

We were hemorrhaging red ink, and Ben was burned out. He was throwing in the towel.

No, the only surprise was that Hearst wasn't adding us to their roster.

As of the first of the new year, we were going to be owned by Galley Media, a publicly traded company with a profitable stable of twelve televisions stations, ten radio outlets, four magazines, and twenty-seven newspapers.

Soon to be twenty-eight.

The puzzler was why Galley wanted us at all. We didn't fit their profile of acquisitions. They liked to buy newspapers in a geographic cluster and combine staffs to save money and squeeze nickels out of economies of scale.

The nearest Galley property to Sheffield was over a hundred miles away.

They were also reluctant to pursue properties in a competitive market. Fairfield County was overpopulated with newspapers. Add to that the newspapers out of New York and the news services over the internet. Our market was downright cutthroat.

The official announcement had been made just before Halloween. Since then, not much had changed in our office, other than representatives from Galley visiting Ben almost daily and, one by one, interviewing all the employees.

When Ben signed the deal with Galley, he'd made them promise to keep us all on staff for at least a year. The twist in that devil's bargain was that it didn't stipulate we'd all stay at the *same* job or at the *same* level of pay.

As I sat in my office, one of the few glass cubicles in the newsroom, I couldn't help but watch the clock. In less than thirty minutes, it would be my turn to be interviewed and analyzed, squirming under the Galley Media microscope. Although I was primarily working the crime beat again, I was still making an editor's salary and working out of an editor's office.

I glanced out at the newsroom. A half dozen reporters were either on the phones or pounding out stories at mismatched desks and chairs. Some of the staff writers worked with laptops, and some had the old-style desktop monitors and keyboards. All of them had stacks of manila folders and newspapers on their desks and piled around them on the threadbare, coffee-stained carpet.

Will I be back out there again? Will they cut my salary? How am I going to pay the bills? I'm barely getting by as it is.

I'd been the daytime news editor for *the Sheffield Post* for over a year, right up until October. That was the time that Darcie Miller, my crime beat reporter, informed us that she was pregnant. It was also the same week that Ben put us up for sale.

Ben thought it would be best to move Darcie to features and me to go back to working the cop shop. He'd take up the slack as temporary editor until Galley made their move.

In preparation for my interview with Robert Vogel, I'd called some of my old friends who I'd worked with in the past and were currently employed at various Galley publications. I asked them about Vogel. He was described as a bloodless hatchet man, an empty suit, and a self-centered, corporate drone.

Gulp.

He'd be the one to decide my fate.

I became queasier as the minutes ticked by. Almost to a person, every *Post* employee who had already gone through the interviewing process described Vogel as an evil little weasel.

I took a deep breath, sipped my lukewarm Starbucks latte, and tried to put it out of my mind. Instead of dwelling on my meeting with Vogel, I worked on the piece about the double homicide at the Groward Bay Marina. It didn't take me long, since officially there weren't any IDs on the victims and I had promised Mike that I'd sit on anything I'd seen in the video.

"Hey, I heard about the murders out at Groward Bay." Looking up, I saw Bill McNamara—tall, thin, lanky—leaning up against the doorway. In his early fifties, he had a full head of prematurely gray hair and a silver handlebar mustache that I found very handsome and distinguished. He was wearing his usual natty attire of tan slacks, a white button-down shirt, and a green bow tie. If Bill were cast in a movie, he'd surely play an Englishman.

I liked Bill. He'd been working at the *Post* for thirty years in ad sales, had an infectious sense of humor, and was our unofficial historian. He leaned forward and said in a conspiratorial voice, "It sounded grim."

I recalled the video. "Most murders are."

Without waiting for an invitation, he came in and slid onto one of my beat-up office chairs. "Groward Bay has a history. Want to hear? It might add a little color to your story."

"It's a double homicide. That's pretty colorful all on its own." I took another sip of my latte and rested my chin in the palm of my hand, elbow on the desk. "But, sure. Dazzle me."

Bill leaned forward, glancing around to see if anyone was listening. When he talked to you, you had to be patient and expect a bit of theater. "On July 17, 1779, Sheffield was nearly burned to the ground by English troops commanded by Major General William Tryon. It was one of a series of raids on the Connecticut coastline meant to draw Colonial troops away from the Hudson River."

I wondered where he was going with this. "Yeah, I grew up here. I heard about it in school."

He held up a finger, indicating patience. "Yes, but did you know that while the English were torching over eighty houses, two churches, fifteen shops, and seventy-five barns, our local militia rowed out to the two British ships anchored in Groward Bay?"

"Oh?" I eyed the screen of my computer, watching the time. "I don't recall reading about that."

"They were hoping that while the British troops were busy putting Sheffield to the torch, the ships would be undermanned. The plan was to board them, take possession of the vessels, and when the English troops rowed back to their boats, the militia would cut them down with their own cannon."

Nope, I didn't recall reading about that in history class. Maybe I'd been out smoking in the girl's room when the teacher had been covering that.

"Unfortunately for the thirty Colonial militiamen in the two longboats, they somehow lost the element of surprise and were met with withering cannon shot and gunfire. It was a massacre. Every one of them was killed."

"Yikes." I hoped that I'd kept my disinterest out of my voice. History had never been a passion for me and I wasn't sure if this would have any relevance to my piece on the two murder victims.

"For weeks, well after the English had left for other towns to raid and the fires in Sheffield were out, one by one, the bodies of those poor, brave militiamen washed ashore. Or to put it more succinctly, the body pieces. The cannons had made a real mess." Bill scrunched up his face. "Finding arms or legs or torsos became such a regular occurrence that the townspeople temporarily changed the name from Groward Bay to Graveyard Bay."

I smiled.

Two bodies found in Graveyard Bay.

There's no way I'd let that be my headline, but Bill was right. It would add a little color to the story.

Before I could say anything, my landline rang. Caller ID told me it was Mike Dillon. "Sorry, Bill, I've got to take this. I might use that Graveyard Bay thing in my story."

He gave me a thumbs-up and left my cube.

"Hey, Mike, what's up?"

"I thought I'd let you know that we have a positive ID on one of the victims."

I took another look at the clock. "That didn't take you long."

"You were right. He was identified by his wife. It's Judge Niles Preston."

I knew Preston from covering the courthouse. I liked him. He was in his early sixties and had been on the bench for twenty years. Preston had the reputation for being tough but fair, and often during sentencing he'd say something that would make a decent quote for a story. I thought he enjoyed seeing his name in print. I'd do some more background checking on him but recalled that he was a gourmand, enjoying extravagant dinners and fine wines and expensive scotch. He also enjoyed art, foreign films, and exotic vacations.

The judge liked nice things, made glaringly obvious by his young trophy wife.

I couldn't recall what happened to his first wife, but everyone was surprised when the judge started dating this one and was shocked when they got married. Eva Preston was easily thirty years younger than the judge.

And drop-dead supermodel gorgeous.

The judge was a good-looking guy, but he was no George Clooney and, let's be honest, I'd say he was past his sell-by date.

"How about the Jane Doe?"

I heard Mike hesitate. "We don't know who she is yet. We asked Eva Preston if she could identify her. Mrs. Preston looked at the body but said she'd never seen her before. I hated to be the one to tell the judge's wife that her husband had been murdered alongside an unknown female." Mike stopped talking, but I could feel that he had more to say. He continued. "Then Mrs. Preston told me that she thought her husband might have been having an affair."

Would the judge have cheated on his gorgeous wife? Really?

I glanced up and saw Robert Vogel, briefcase in hand, walking up the hallway from the main entrance, striding between the five-foot-high dividers that separated the editorial department and advertising. He was a little over six feet tall and thin to the point of being nearly skeletal. When he walked, he leaned slightly forward as if pressing against a stiff wind. He had on a light-blue shirt, red tie, gray suit, and carried his beige trench coat over his arm. Vogel had red-rimmed brown eyes that peered through wire-frame glasses. His cheeks were drawn and covered by a brown-and-gray goatee and mustache.

He was heading for Ben's office, where he'd been conducting his interviews. This would be his third day in a row at deciding the fate of *Post* employees.

I turned my attention back to Mike. "Was the Jane Doe wearing a wedding ring?"

"No."

I tapped the top of my desk with my pen. "Do you think Preston and this woman were having an affair?"

"Off the record?"

"Sure."

"Off the record, Niles Preston had an eye for the ladies. Maybe he pissed off the wrong husband. But more than likely, if I had to take a guess, I'd bet someone he'd sent to jail came back for revenge. Remember that guy who escaped from the Lockport Correctional Facility two weeks ago?"

I watched as Robert Vogel knocked on Ben's door. It opened, and Ben ushered the Galley representative in, closing the door behind them. I glanced back at the clock on my computer. Then I Googled "Lockport Correctional Facility Escape."

Up popped a mug shot of Merlin James Finn dressed in an orange jumpsuit. Scalp cleanly shaven, dark eyes under heavy brows. He had a thin-lipped expression, more a snarl than a smile, square jaw, and pronounced ears with heavy lobes. Most eye-catching, however, were a pair of tiny tattoos, one on each cheekbone. On the left side of his face were two crossed hammers superimposed over a cogwheel. The other was the head of a pit bull.

White supremacist symbols.

Mug shots are never complimentary, but this guy looked like a true badass.

I scanned the story. Merlin Finn had somehow managed to punch through a concrete wall, climb up through a narrow air vent using ripped bedsheets as rope, and then impossibly cut through four layers of metal grating to reach the roof. He climbed down the outside of the building, chopped through the perimeter fence, and disappeared into the night.

According to the news story posted by the *New Haven Register* online, he was six foot eight, weighed two-eighty pounds, and worked out every day in the prison gym. He was still at large and considered extremely dangerous.

He certainly could be the guy wearing the leather mask in the video.

I whistled. "You think it's Merlin Finn?"

I heard Mike take a breath. "Don't know. Judge Preston was the one who sentenced him to two consecutive life sentences. Clearly, Finn had motive."

"And opportunity?"

Mike didn't answer for a moment. "We don't know where he is."

"No chance the killer was Bogdan Tolbonov?"

I could almost hear Mike smiling over the phone. "What a surprise. Now why do you think it was Tolbonov?"

"Because the leather mask guy in the video is Bogdan Tolbonov-huge."

"So is Merlin Finn."

It was my turn to hesitate, realizing how weak my theory was.

"Look, Genie, you're fixated on the Tolbonov brothers. Let it go. State and federal investigators are all over those guys. They can't breathe, let alone commit any more crimes. Leave it to the FBI."

Mike was right, of course. Ever since I'd gotten a taste of how evil the two men—Valentin and Bogdan Tolbonov—were and how extensive their web of criminal activities was, I wanted to see them behind bars.

Or dead.

He was also correct when he advised me to let it go. They were dangerous men. "You're right, Mike. I'll leave it to the experts. Hey, thanks for the heads-up on the ID. How about I repay you with a drink sometime?"

I heard his nervous silence. One of the reasons Mike had kicked me to the curb had been my excessive drinking. The quiet was awkward.

Poor Mike. I must have spooked him.

I broke the silence. "Or coffee. We can do coffee."

Finally, he answered. "Yeah, sure, I'd like that, when the time's right."

Hanging up, I finished reading about Merlin Finn. He'd headed up a crew of biker-skinhead supremacists who trafficked in drugs, guns, and prostitutes. They'd had a strong influence in western Massachusetts, Connecticut, Long Island, and Westchester County, New York. The gang seemed to go dormant after Finn was arrested for the murders of two rival gang members, then convicted and sentenced to the Lockport Correctional Facility.

Glancing back at the clock and seeing I still had a few minutes, I punched up Niles Preston's name. Sixty-two years old at the time of death, he'd come straight out of law school in his twenties and founded his own law practice in Stamford. When he was thirty-two, he formed a partnership with another attorney by the name of Terrance Fuller. At the age of forty, Preston was named a state supreme court judge by the governor.

While still in his early thirties, he married Claudia Hardesty of Greenwich, Connecticut. They never had children. Claudia was killed in a tragic auto accident on I-95 just north of Westport a little over two years ago. Six months after the accident, Preston married Eva Novak, who was twenty-nine at the time.

I called the office of State Supreme Court Justice Donald Whitaker to get a quote. I got his administrative assistant, who was shocked to hear about Judge Preston's untimely death and promised to pass along my request. Less than five minutes later I received an email from the Honorable Donald Whitaker. It said simply, "Judge Niles Preston was a judge's judge. A man who made his district a better place, and as a result, he made the world a better place."

Finished, I sent the story to Ben, still behind the closed door of his office. When Ben had a chance to edit the piece, he'd have it uploaded onto our website. I'd continue to add to it as I got more facts, right up until we hit our press deadline. I was confident that it would be a six-column headline on the front page of tomorrow's newspaper.

A murdered judge is big news.

Chapter Three

"You've worked at *Time* magazine, the *Boston Globe,* and the *Democrat & Chronicle* in Rochester." Robert Vogel glanced up from my résumé and offered up a cold grin, all teeth, no warmth. "That's a Gannett newspaper, isn't it?"

I nodded and did my best to smile back. There was a chill in the room, but it didn't come from the icy wind beating against the office window. I cupped my latte in both hands, wishing I'd taken a minute to heat it up in the lunchroom microwave.

When I first met Vogel earlier in the month, I'd made the mistake of calling him Bob. He was quick to tell me, in a condescending voice, that his name was Robert.

He sniffed and glanced back down at the life story of my career. "You've written for the *New York Daily News,* the *Hill, Huffington Post,* and for a very short period, Fox News. You've worked the crime beat for some very impressive news outlets." He fixed me in his sight again. "So, Geneva Chase, what god-awful crime did you commit to end up here in this shithole?"

My stomach twisted. "What, the *Sheffield Post?"*

He nodded and studied me with his unblinking eyes. "Yeah, the *Sheffield Post."* It came out more of a sneer than an answer.

I avoided his offending stare and focused instead just above his gray-and-brown mustache, where a cluster of nose hairs peeked out from the entrance of each of his oversized nostrils.

"Well, this is my hometown."

Really? That's the best you can do?

Robert flashed me another sour grin. "I think we both know the real reason, don't we?"

I did, of course. I'd drunk myself out of every other good job I've ever had.

I didn't answer him, but I didn't lower my eyes either. I wasn't going to let him see how anxiety was creating an ice ball of fear inside of me.

We sat in Ben Sumner's office, but once I'd been summoned, Ben had left to go home. Almost daily he abandoned his office to the soulless Robert Vogel.

While Ben had been putting on his coat, he leaned over and murmured into my ear, "Good job on the murders out at the marina. Don't let this asshole intimidate you, okay?"

Easy for you to say, Ben. You're bailing with a huge paycheck.

Robert sat at Ben's desk, the big window behind him overlooking the employee parking lot and the tree line beyond, bordering the Merritt Parkway. With Christmas a week away, the oak and maple trees were denuded, leafless, their black limbs scratching against the steel-gray snow clouds.

Entering Ben's office, I noticed that the photographs of him sailing in various locales around the world had been removed and packed away in cardboard boxes that sat on the carpet against the wall. The books from his shelves were also missing.

It was as if the life had been sucked out of the room.

Robert picked up a clear plastic cup of iced coffee, took a sip, and placed it back onto the desk. "We have a number of Galley Media employees who have worked with you at other properties. You have a colorful reputation."

Oh, I know how to party.

He glanced back down at the file in front of him. "Ben assures me that the past is the past. That whatever problems that might have plagued you are in the rearview mirror."

I nodded but remained silent.

He continued. "You've done some very good work here at the *Post.* I'm trying to match the right people with the right job. I think we both know that your strength lies with being on the street, as a beat reporter, not in-house correcting typos."

I felt my stomach clench.

"When I tell you what I want to do, know that I'm coming at it from a good place."

Such bullshit.

I managed to squeak out a reply. "Okay."

He pulled at his goatee and studied me. "I need you back on the crime beat full time. I'm going to bring in Lorraine Moretti to edit. She's helped transition a half dozen other editorial departments at properties we've acquired. You'll like her. She knows how to build a team."

I cleared my throat. "I don't want to sound mercenary, but what does that do to my salary?"

He nodded as if he understood my trepidation. "Well, as you can well understand, we can't pay a reporter the same salary as an editor." He leaned back in Ben's chair. "However, in the spirit of Christmas, we'll keep your pay grade the same until the first of January."

I tried hard to keep my voice steady and not let my instantaneous hatred spill out. "When is Lorraine Moretti's first day?"

He smiled at me again. "Tomorrow morning. So with all due respect, if you can find another desk in the newsroom to move to, that would be great."

"Of course." It came out more of a sarcastic growl than I had intended.

Kiss my ass.

He added, "And it goes without saying that if you can maintain the high standard of professionalism you've shown us over the last month, it would be greatly appreciated."

Kiss my ass twice.

—

I spent the rest of the day alternately moving my things from the editor's cubicle to Zach Meyer's old desk and editing stories that were still coming through the pipeline.

All while sympathetic eyes in the newsroom were surreptitiously watching me.

The last thing I want is pity.

Zach Meyer had been our city reporter specializing in local and state politics. He'd written for the *Post* for over twenty years. Once the sale to Galley had been officially announced, he opted to retire. Zach bitched that he didn't need the bullshit anymore, especially the corporate kind. Checking the drawers of the old gray metal desk, I found that he'd left pencils, paper clips, and a ton of unopened cellophane packages of plastic spoons, forks, and paper napkins—the kind you get when you buy fast-food takeout. He'd never used them.

What did he do, eat everything with his fingers?

When I had a moment, I sat back down in the editor's cube and took a thumb drive out of my oversized bag. Plugging it into the computer, I opened a file called "Tucker's Veterinarian Records."

Tucker is my Yorkshire terrier. When I named this file, I chose the most innocuous title I could think of, something so banal that if I lost the thumb drive or someone stole it, nobody would care to open. Or so I hoped.

Who wants to read about my dog's stool sample?

Actually, it was a page-by-page photo-recording of a criminal's notebook.

Last October, a woman killed her sadistic, abusive husband by waiting until he was drunk and passed out, pouring gasoline on him, and lighting a match. The husband, Jim Caviness, had been

a low-level enforcer for Wolfline Contractin
that engaged in a dangerous web of illegal
gambling, drugs, guns, extortion, blackma
sex trafficking. Betsy Caviness lost everythi
little money she had, and her freedom. She was cu
time at the Hampton Correctional Facility.

More secure than Lockport?

The only thing she owned was her husband's notebook. A reward for all the drugs and alcohol he'd consumed was a Swiss cheese memory filled with holes and gaps. To keep track of what he was supposed to do next, he kept a neat notebook, filled with cryptic initials, dates, places, and tasks.

Valentin Tolbonov, the alleged mastermind behind Wolfline, and his brother, Bogdan, had tried mightily to get that notebook from Betsy. She created a stand-off with the two murderous brothers by sending it to an anonymous third party with instructions that if something bad happened to her, the notebook would be turned over to the police.

Everyone assumed that she had sent it to her attorney.

Nope, I have it hidden in my house, in the freezer in a plastic bag under a pile of ice cubes in the plastic icemaker bin.

Betsy Caviness had sent the notebook to me with the message, "You'll know what to do with it."

Truth is, I didn't. I couldn't take it to the cops. Even with Betsy Caviness in prison, she'd be dead within twenty-four hours. I couldn't use it in a news story—same result.

Most of the entries were in weird shorthand, an unfathomable code so that only Jim Caviness knew what the hell he was writing. I could decipher very little of it.

On the computer terminal in the editor's cube, I scrolled through the copied pages. Cryptic notes with dates and times and an occasional address.

There had been that one that I was able to crack:

...t 10, l.am., pu $ TMs Cad, 113 Edison Ave, Shef, drop @ Ivans

That was on page thirty-two. It was also on three, four, five, six, and a dozen other pages, but all with different dates. But it seemed to be the same task—pick up money from someone with the initials T.M. at 113 Edison Avenue, Sheffield, at one o'clock in the morning, and drop it off at Ivan's, wherever that was. It was a task that Jim Caviness had performed often.

Late in November, I staked out 113 Edison Avenue. It was in a part of Sheffield that had been missed in the gentrification process of the rest of the city. Many of the old Victorian homes on that block had been chopped up into cheap apartments while others were dark and empty, their windows covered with boards and graffiti. Yards were strewn with leaves, weeds, fast-food wrappers, and plastic bags. It was rumored that a development company was buying up property in the neighborhood, but nobody seemed sure who it was or what for.

A few beat-up cars were parked on the street at the curb, but there wasn't a soul walking along the sidewalk. This part of town was dangerous. Better to stay inside—best to not be there at all.

I'd found a trash-cluttered alleyway between a shuttered single-story brick building that once held a beauty salon and an abandoned two-story structure that, in another life, had been a barbeque joint. Now they were both empty, silent monuments to better days. Backing my Sebring into the narrow space, I sat in the shadows, away from the streetlights. I was well hidden and yet had a reasonably good view of the street, including 113 Edison Avenue, the address of a vacant two-story Cape Cod at the end of the block. Before the daylight completely faded, I saw that the front porch of the Cape Cod had nearly collapsed under its own weight. Paint was peeling from the home's faded facade, and the tiny yard was occupied by a torn mattress and a rusty washing machine someone had left behind.

Even though the heater in my car was cranking, I shivered.

I just know that house is crawling with cockroaches, rats, and ghosts.

I glanced at my watch. It was a little after ten when a brand-new, polished black Cadillac Escalade rolled slowly by and pulled over to the curb in front of the dilapidated old home. Brake lights came on, then extinguished, and the vehicle was parked and ready for business. The streetlight above the SUV was conveniently dark.

Purposely broken? Shot out?

I was gratified to see that the SUV was parked facing away from me, lessening my chances of being spotted by the driver.

From the front seat of my car, I watched as a steady stream of cars, pickup trucks, vans, and SUVs turned the corner from South Sheffield, drove slowly up Edison Avenue in my direction, pulling up parallel with the Escalade. Brake lights would go on while the driver's side window in the customer's vehicle slid down. The Escalade's window would do the same, and the transaction would take place.

Fast, quiet, unobtrusive. I didn't know what kind of drugs the Cadillac was dispensing, but I had a pretty good idea. Grass, cocaine, oxycodone, meth, and, for sure, fentanyl-laced heroin. The opioid was a cheap way to increase the high and decrease the cost of production and seemed to be wildly out of control in Sheffield.

It was also deadly as hell.

I took photos of each vehicle. I used the *Post*'s night-vision telephoto lens to take the shots and was able to get clear pictures that included their front tags—Connecticut, New York, and New Jersey. This guy might be a low-level drug dealer, but he had a tristate clientele.

I took a few sips of the vodka I had stashed in my commuter cup, felt the love spread through my core, and relaxed as the rhythm of the night took over, watching the repetition of car after car cozying up close to the black SUV, the driver handing over a wad of cash, taking a baggie, rolling up their window, and driving away. Every single time they rolled past where I was hidden, I slid down a little, making myself more of a shadow in my seat.

I glanced at my watch. It was nearly one in the morning. Almost time for the bag man to pick up the cash from the Escalade…if I'd read the notebook correctly.

A hand slapped my window.

My heart froze, air caught in my throat. I turned to look.

A face glared at me, inches away from the glass.

Horror-struck, eyes wide, I leaned into the passenger's seat, staring at the man standing just outside my car, the filthy palm of his hand still pressed against the window. His face was deeply lined, a heavy gray beard covered the bottom half of his face, a baseball cap barely kept his long, greasy hair at bay. He was wearing a camouflage jacket.

He grinned, showing me a mixed grill of yellowed and missing teeth.

My heart slamming hard against my ribs, I shot a worried glance at the business going on down the street. The last thing I needed was wary, curious eyes looking my way.

Rolling down my window, my stomach twisted when a sour odor of alcohol, tobacco, and vomit immediately flooded into my car. "What?" I growled.

"Got any spare change?" His voice was much too loud.

I glanced back at the Escalade. A black Ford pickup truck sat next to the drug dealer. The truck's powerful headlights bathed the road in front of me in bright illumination. My fear grew exponentially.

Bogdan Tolbonov drives a black Ford F-150 pickup truck.

I tore through my bag and found a couple of wadded-up singles. "Hold out your hand."

He did as I'd ordered, his right palm facing up, shaking, tremor ridden. Without touching him, I dropped the cash onto his hand. "Now beat it," I hissed.

The man grinned again and doffed his baseball cap. "Bless you."

He disappeared behind me, into the shadows, and I glanced back at the Cadillac SUV.

My stomach dropped.

It was gone.

But the pickup wasn't. The truck slid slowly, too slowly, past where I sat in the shadows. Then it accelerated and disappeared around the corner.

Dammit. I got made. Please God, don't let that be Bogdan Tolbonov.

Paranoia wrapped around my gut like a snake.

Was the homeless guy a plant? A scout? Did the driver of the pickup get a look at my car? What if it really had been Bogdan? He kills people.

And he already knows where I live.

My plan had been to tail whoever picked up the cash and follow him to see where the money was dropped—the notebook had called it Ivan's. There was a strip club in Bridgeport called Ivan's. That could be where the black pickup was heading.

But hell, I was dealing with a crew of crazy Russians. It could be any damned place.

All I knew was that it was prudent to get as far away from Edison Avenue as I could, and as quickly as possible. I had a feeling this was about to become a very precarious place to be.

I waited a week before I had the nerve to go back. I knew that someone would be watching the alleyway where I'd hidden, so I didn't try to stake out the drug dealer again. Instead, I did a drive-by to see if the Escalade, or a replacement, was parked in front of the spooky old Cape Cod.

The street was empty.

I went back the next night and the next after that.

For the time being, Edison Avenue was drug-free.

I couldn't tell Mike Dillon that I had staked out a drug dealer using Betsy Caviness's notebook without putting her in danger. So I sent the photos I'd taken to the police using a fake Gmail account. I was able to trace the Escalade's owner by the license plate. It belonged to a Travis Monk, twenty-seven years old, five eight, one hundred seventy pounds—according to his DMV info. Last known residence was in Millport, Connecticut. I checked it out. The address was an empty lot.

For weeks, I watched the arrest reports to see if his name showed up. It never did.

Having been caught staking him out, my anxiety level ramped up and I kept my eye out for anyone who might be tailing me. When I was home, I watched to see if cars I didn't recognize were parked out on the street. At work, I kept worrying I'd be approached in the parking lot.

I remembered the dominatrix Shana Neese's warning.

You can't be too paranoid.

I shoved that out of my mind and scanned the contents of the notebook on the screen of my monitor. Hearing that Judge Niles Preston had been positively identified as one of the homicide victims, something had jogged my memory. Since Betsy had sent it to me, I'd studied that notebook for hours, days, looking for a way it could be useful.

On that morning in the newspaper office, it took me a few seconds, but I found what I was looking for.

A single entry, dated early October.

Starbucks, Wilton, Rt.7, Wed, Oct 3, 8 am, drop $, Judge P.

Judge P…Judge Preston? Was that an entry for Jim Caviness to pay off the judge?

Was Judge Preston dirty?

Before I went to DaVinci's to pick up some takeout food for Caroline and me, I made two stops. One was at Al's Liquors for a bottle of Absolut. The one I had hidden at home was nearly empty.

And then I dropped into the Starbucks in Wilton on Route 7. Smooth jazz discreetly floated in the air and the scent of strong brew hugged me like a long lost relative. If it hadn't been so close to the dinner hour, I suspected the coffee shop would have been packed. But as it was, I was nearly the only one there who wasn't wearing a green barista apron. A tall man stood attentively behind the counter. In his twenties, his dark hair was propped up in random spikes with gel. The name tag on his chest told me his name was Chuck.

"Hey, Chuck."

He had a pleasant smile. "Hi, can I help you?"

I almost asked for a latte, but then remembered I had vodka in the car that was seductively whispering my name. I pulled a photo out of my bag and held it up for the barista to look at. "Do you know this man?"

Chuck's smile faltered. "That's the judge. Are you a cop?"

I cocked my head. "I'm sorry, I should have introduced myself. I'm Geneva Chase with the *Sheffield Post.*"

He held up a smartphone. Chuck's voice went low. "Oh, I read about it online. It was awful what somebody did to him."

I nodded. "Did Judge Preston come in here a lot?"

"Should I be talking to you?"

I frowned. "I'm not looking for dirt, Chuck." I lied. I'm always looking for dirt. "I'd just like to know if the judge was a regular here."

Chuck appraised me with squinty eyes for a moment but must have figured I was okay. "He was in here all the time."

"He ever meet anyone here?"

The boy nodded. "The judge used to joke that this was his second office."

I pulled another photo out of my bag. This one was the mug shot of Jim Caviness when he'd been arrested for trafficking in underage girls. "How about this guy? Recognize him?"

Chuck concentrated. Then he slowly shook his head. "Nope, sorry. A lot of people come and go here." He turned to a young woman standing behind the counter who had been staring at the screen of her smartphone. "Hey, Deb. You ever seen this guy before?"

A woman in her early twenties dropped her phone into the pocket of her barista apron and stared at the photo I held in the air. She ran her hand through her mop of brown hair and pursed her lips. Finally, she said, "Could be. A guy who looks something like that used to come in now and then and sit down with the judge." She pointed to an empty table in the corner. "If it's the same guy I'm thinking of, he'd drop by where the judge was sitting for a couple of seconds and then leave. I noticed him because he'd come in but never buy anything."

Walking back out to my car, I pulled my scarf up around my face and thought about what I'd just learned. Judge Preston was a regular at Starbucks and he might or might not have met with someone who bore a resemblance to Jim Caviness.

That's a whole lot of nothin'.

Chapter Four

I dropped the plastic bag holding the takeout dinner onto the kitchen counter. Tucker looked up at me expectantly, tail wagging so hard, his tiny butt was shaking. I leaned down and picked the little guy up into my arms, still wearing my parka.

"I thought I heard the car pull into the driveway."

Turning around, I saw Caroline standing in the doorway. She's fifteen, long blond hair cascading over her shoulders, about five-foot-seven, and trim as a ferret, even though she can eat like a horse. When I look at her, I see Kevin. She has her father's sparkling blue eyes and pretty smile. That evening, she was wearing her ratty, gray UCONN sweatshirt, pink sweatpants, and black, fluffy slippers. Around the house, she ain't a fashion plate.

But then again, neither am I.

I was Caroline's guardian. I'd made a promise to Kevin Bell that I'd take care of his daughter if anything ever happened to him. Way too soon, it did. Now she's my responsibility and Kevin's legacy to me.

I smiled back at her, put the dog down, and shimmied out of my coat. "Hey, sweetie, how was your day?"

She glided to the counter and opened the plastic bag, sniffing the air. Then Caroline grinned at me. "I'm on Christmas vacation."

She'd answered like I should have had a clue. "I slept late, read a little, watched some videos, and I finished packing." She pointed to the takeout on the counter. "This smells really good. What did you get?"

"Lasagna from DaVinci's."

"Yum." She looked up at me. "Hey, are you sure you're okay with my going to Aspen with Aunt Ruth?"

I wasn't, but I was determined not to let Caroline see it. "Of course I'm okay with it. Heck, if Aunt Ruth offered to take me skiing over the holidays, I'd jump at the chance. When's the last time Tucker went out?"

She grinned. "Just before you got here. Tucker's good. Want me to ask Aunt Ruth to bring you too?"

Oh God, no.

Caroline's Aunt Ruth and I barely tolerated each other. Ruth was the sister of Kevin's late wife. When I came onto the scene, it was easy to see that she had eyes for her widower brother-in-law. Then Kevin fell in love with me, and Ruth became downright hostile.

After Kevin died and Caroline came to live with me, Ruth's attitude softened...a little.

In my head, I knew that Ruth's offer to take Caroline and her best friend, Jessica Oberon, skiing had been incredibly generous. On my meager newspaper salary, soon to be cut even further, there wasn't a snowball's chance in hell that I'd ever be able to afford a ski vacation in Aspen.

Yes, in my head, I knew rich Aunt Ruth was doing something really nice.

But in my heart, I strongly suspect that Ruth wants me to be alone at Christmas.

I held up my hand. "I have to work, sweetie. I couldn't go with you if I wanted to. Is Jessica excited?"

"God, yes. Jessica's gone nuts. Almost overnight, she's gone from Goth to full-blown snow bunny. You should see all the crap she's packing."

I was suddenly struck by the fact that we hadn't done any shopping for Caroline. "Do *you* have what you need to hit the slopes?"

She gave me a confident smile. "I've got long undies, jeans, sweaters, my heavy coat, mittens, extra socks, and snow overalls. I'm good. I'm worried about *you*, Genie. You're going to be here all by yourself."

Alone for Christmas.

I waved it off. "It won't be the first time. Tucker's pretty good company."

I said that, but I knew how depressing it can be to spend the holidays alone. That, on top of the unfortunate events unfolding at the newspaper, meant I was going to have to work hard to stay out of a black pit of despair.

Caroline leaned against the refrigerator and crossed her arms. "Being alone during the holidays can be pretty awful. Promise me you won't do something stupid?"

Like drinking myself into a DUI? Or the hospital? Or to death?

For an angry flashing moment, I took exception at her implication. But I counted to five before I answered, because deep down, I knew she was genuinely concerned for me. "Baby, don't you worry about me. The only thing I want you to think about is not breaking any bones."

On the one hand, it pissed me off that Caroline thought she was the adult in that conversation. But on the other hand, I welcomed her concern. Only a couple of months before, Caroline was cycling through periods of sarcasm, belligerence, and insecurity with occasional annoying streaks of meanness. Then, over the last month, she seemed serene, more like a normal teenager, if there is such a thing.

I wonder if she's smoking pot?

Her grades, when her father was alive, were always good. After he passed away, she struggled in school. Barely passing. Recently, however, her scores had ticked upward again.

Nah, smoking dope never made me any smarter.

She hadn't even mentioned my drinking since last October. Of course, I kept it closeted. And I've tried to ratchet it back. I'm certain Caroline knows that when I'm in my bedroom, I have a couple of pops before I go to bed. And if she's going to stay after school for a club project, I might stop at Brick's for a glass or two of Absolut over ice and cover my tracks with a mouthful of breath mints.

It's all under control.

I smiled at her. "I'm going upstairs to change clothes. If you can set the table, we'll eat when I come back down." As I exited the kitchen, I glanced back. She was already leaning against the counter, texting someone on her phone. No denying that she was a teenager.

Before I stripped off my sweater, slacks, and bra, I took a glass sitting on the headboard of my bed, rinsed it out in the bathroom, then plucked out the nearly empty bottle of vodka hidden in my panty drawer. I poured a liberal amount and took a healthy swallow. The familiar heat drizzled down into my chest and tummy. Thinking about the pain of being on a reporter's salary again, I upended the glass and polished it off.

I poured another and fished the full bottle out of my bag and hid it in the drawer beneath my underwear.

Robert Vogel, the evil weasel, was right. I'd drunk myself out of every good job I've ever had. But this time, he wasn't punishing me for being a drinker. He was punishing me because I had the *history* of being a drinker.

I took the phone out of my bag and checked the screen. According to the time stamp, while I'd been driving, someone had tried to call me. It was a New York number.

They'd left a message on my phone voicemail. In a low range but with crisp diction, a male voice stated, "Hi, this message is for Geneva Chase. My name's Nathaniel Rubin. I'm the CEO for a company called Lodestar Analytics. I wonder if you and I could chat about a possible career opportunity? Perhaps you can give me a call tomorrow morning?"

Lodestar.

Isn't that the star sailors used to guide their ships?

He left a number that I entered into my contact list. Glass in hand, still in my work clothes, I sat down at my desk and punched Lodestar Analytics into my laptop. The company was listed as a commercial research and strategic intelligence firm based in New York. According to its website, "Lodestar Analytics conducts open-source investigations and provides research and strategic advice for businesses, law firms, and investors as well as for political inquiries, such as opposition research. Lodestar employs a diverse range of experts including scientists, retired FBI agents, private detectives, and journalists."

I looked up Nathaniel Rubin. Like me, he'd worked at a number of top media outlets—*New York Times, Washington Post, Philadelphia Inquirer*. Then, five years ago, he created Lodestar.

I sat back in my chair, intrigued.

The timing of Mr. Rubin's call could not have been better.

Chapter Five

I got up early and made us scrambled eggs and bacon. Well, it was that precooked bacon that you stick in the microwave. I'm sure it's mostly preservatives, but it smells and tastes a lot like the real deal, even though it has the texture of cardboard.

On a regular school day, Caroline would fix herself a bowl of cereal and I'd eat a couple of slices of whole wheat toast and a banana. But she was starting her Christmas vacation.

I'm not going to see her again until after first of the year.

Aunt Ruth would be picking up Caroline and her best friend, Jessica, at about 8:30 and driving to LaGuardia, then they'd fly out to Colorado.

Running the spatula through the hot eggs in the pan, I almost started crying.

I'm going to miss her so much.

This was the first time we'd been apart since Kevin had died. I'd never wanted children. I could barely take care of myself, let alone someone else. But parenting Caroline was a game changer. It was sometimes aggravating, often frightening, occasionally sad, but mostly the best thing that had ever happened to me.

As we dug into breakfast at the kitchen table, I did my best to keep my side of the conversation positive and bright. I didn't have to work too hard, though. Caroline chattered nonstop about how much she was looking forward to getting away and hitting the slopes.

When we'd finished eating, I went into the living room and came back with a wrapped present the size of a jewelry box. I handed it to her. "Now, you can't open that until Christmas."

She smiled. "Okay, wait right here."

I heard her as she trotted through the living room and pounded up the steps to her bedroom. Minutes later, she was rushing back into the kitchen with a gift of her own. Wrapped in bright red-and-green paper, it was about the size of a book. She smiled and handed it to me. "Here, but you have to wait until Christmas too."

I took the gift and hugged her tight. "Call me as often as you can, okay?"

In my arms, Caroline looked up at me and gave me a crooked grin. "We can FaceTime, Genie, whenever you want. I'll always have my phone with me."

"Watch out for those ski bum rich boys."

Still holding her, I felt her chuckle. "We got rich boys right here in Fairfield County. I'm not impressed. Hey, are you going to decorate at all?"

I glanced back into the living room. Last year, our first Christmas after her father had died, I did my best to make the holiday festive. I bought a real tree, hung ornaments and tinsel, and put lights up around the windows. I loved the smell of fresh pine, and the decorations actually made me feel a little like a kid again.

This year, with Caroline jetting off to Aspen, my heart wasn't in it. The living room was dark.

I lied, "I just haven't gotten around to it yet. I will."

Still hugging me, she said, "I love you."

"Love you back, baby."

—

Sliding into my cold Sebring, I could feel the burn of my tears as they trailed down my cheeks.

I'm going to miss her so damned much.

I wiped them away with a wad of tissue I found in my bag, turned on the engine, and cranked up the heater. I took a couple of deep breaths, and when I was confident that my voice wouldn't crack, I called Ben Sumner.

"Genie?"

"Hey, Ben. Look, I'm going to be a few minutes late. I'm going to stop by SPD to pick up last night's incident reports and see if there's anything new on the Groward Bay homicides."

"Just a heads-up, Genie, the new managing editor is in your old office."

I exhaled a heavy sigh. "And so it begins, Ben."

"It's all going to be okay. By the way, I liked the reference to Graveyard Bay in the piece you wrote. I kept it in the story. The new editor actually worked it into the headline. Not sure I would have done that."

I frowned. I'd written the headline before I'd left the office. That's what editors do. And the words "Graveyard Bay" weren't in it.

That bitch must have come in last night after I'd left and changed it.

I shook my head and exhaled. "Is it at the top of the front page?"

"Six columns, Genie."

"Okay, do me a favor and let the new managing editor know I'm stopping off at SPD for the reports. I'll be in the office as soon as I can." I let sarcasm drip from my lips when I pronounced the words *new managing editor.*

—

The heater in my car was percolating nicely as I pulled into the SPD parking lot. Getting out and into the bitter cold, I pulled my scarf over my face, hoisted my oversized bag onto my shoulder and, thankful for the tread on my boots, trudged across the ice-slick asphalt and into the nondescript two-story brick building. I was mildly surprised to note that the sparse lobby wasn't much warmer than the outside.

I approached the sliding glass window and pressed a button.

Cathy Sloan was dressed much like I was: wool hat, scarf, parka. Recognizing me, she slid open the window. "Hey, Genie. Here to see Mike?"

"If he's available. If he's not, I'll just grab the reports and scoot."

"I'll give him a call."

I rubbed my gloved hands together. "What's with the heat?"

"Old building. The heating unit just can't keep up with this cold snap. City says they got their guys coming over to see what's wrong." I watched her as she picked up her phone and punched in a two-digit number. Then she nodded. "I'll buzz you in. He's in his office."

It was slightly warmer in Mike's office, thanks to a small space heater humming away on the floor next to his chair. He was wearing a navy-blue cardigan that Caroline would have called an "old man" sweater. When he saw me walk through the door, he smiled and stood up, gesturing to one of his plastic office chairs.

In the old days, he would have come around his desk and given me a hug.

I kept my coat on as I sat down. "You guys too cheap to pay the heating bill?"

He rolled his eyes and sat back down, partially hidden by his open laptop. "Half my staff will be off work with head colds and the flu before this is over."

"Anything new on the Groward Marina homicides?"

Mike grinned. "You mean the Graveyard Bay homicides?" He picked up a copy of the paper from his desktop and held it aloft for me to see.

I read aloud the headline that screamed at me. "Two bodies

found in 'Graveyard Bay.'" I felt my face redden and cocked my head to the side. "We have a new editor."

Mike glanced at the headline again and then dropped the newspaper back on his desk. "Nope, nothing new. Foley is supposed to do the autopsies today, and we're reviewing the closed-circuit video one frame at a time. Yesterday, we interviewed the judge's staff but didn't get anything helpful."

"Any idea at all who the Jane Doe is?"

"Running her prints, but we haven't gotten a match yet. And we're looking at all missing person reports, starting with the tristate area."

I couldn't think of any polite way to ask my next question, so I blurted it out. "Was Judge Preston dirty?"

Mike's eyes widened. "What?"

I shrugged. "Just asking. He got whacked in a very unusual way. Must be a reason."

He frowned. "I've known Judge Preston for over ten years. He was smart, fair, and compassionate." He hesitated. "Maybe a little too compassionate from time to time."

"Oh?"

"I've seen some bad actors walk out of his courtroom because Preston thought the evidence was weak. Case in point, do you remember Del Randall?"

Del Randall was also known as Lucifer because of the Satan tattoo on his forearm. Nicknamed Loose, he was a pimp who trafficked underage girls. I was there when two vigilantes, Shana Neese and John Stillwater, members of a shadowy group called Friends of Lydia, freed four girls, all smuggled into the country illegally and forced into prostitution. Shana and John drove the girls to Hartford for shelter and new identities. Del Randall we left tied up on the dirty floor of the ramshackle house he was using as the girls' prison.

That had been one scary afternoon. Now and then, I still feel a twinge of pain in my shoulder where I'd gotten thrown into a wall...and recall the cattle prod the pimp used on the girls if they got out of line.

"I remember."

"I thought the cops in Bridgeport put together a good case against Randall. They found evidence he'd imprisoned individuals inside that house. They found implements of torture. They found personal items left behind after the girls had been spirited away by *your friends.*"

I detected the hint of snark in his voice and replied, "I happened to be there when two members of FOL freed those girls from a life of sexual slavery."

"Point taken. The piece you wrote and the photos you ran gave this county a wake-up call. It showed the world that even Fairfield County has a human trafficking problem." His voice had become conciliatory.

"Thank you."

Mike leaned forward. "But you were never called as an eyewitness to Randall's trial because Judge Preston threw the case out, ruling insufficient evidence."

"Why?"

He pointed toward me. "He said that whatever evidence the prosecution had was the fruit of a poisonous tree. It was gathered as a result of a home invasion. The evidence was tainted. If Del Randall's lawyer had been of a mind, you and the two members of FOL could have been accused of breaking-and-entering and assault. If the pimp had admitted that there were four girls there, you might have been arrested for kidnapping as well."

I felt a slow burn. "Four underage girls were being pimped out for sex every night against their will."

Mike held up his hand. "The judge dropped the case."

I took a deep breath. "How often did Preston do that?"

He shook his head, thinking. "Once in a blue moon, maybe. He'd toss a case I thought had merit and it would leave me scratching my head. Wasn't often."

"So, back to my original question."

Mike stared at me. "What, do I think he was dirty? If anything, I think someone killed him because he *didn't* toss a case. Maybe someone he put away went to prison and recently got out. That's what we're looking into. Now, if you get a line on where we can find Merlin Finn…" His voice drifted. Then he asked, "Are you here for the incident reports?" Clearly, he was done discussing the homicides because he had a file folder in his hand.

I nodded and took the folder. "Busy night?"

"A domestic dispute, a missing person report, a couple of DUIs, someone broke into the laundromat on Queen Street, and three overdoses, one of them fatal."

I frowned. "Seems like there's been a ton of those lately."

"The opioid epidemic has hit here hard over the last couple of months. Wish we could figure out where it's coming from."

"Anything interesting on the missing person?"

He shrugged his shoulders. "Not really. Charlie Tomasso, resides at 81 Indigo Drive, thirty-five years old, six foot six, two hundred and seventy pounds, Caucasian, distinguishing marks are a tattoo of a lion on his right shoulder, a scar on his right cheek, and a gold tooth, one of his front left incisors. His wife reported that he came home from work three days ago, they argued, he left, and hasn't come back."

"Did she say that this has happened before?"

"Apparently, when he's pissed off, he goes off on bender. But she's concerned because this is the longest he's been gone."

I tucked the folder with the incident reports into my bag and fished my mittens out of my coat pockets. "Are you the one who talked to Mrs. Preston when she came in to ID her husband?"

He bobbed his head. "She thinks it's someone who had a grudge against her husband. Or maybe the husband of the woman he's been having the affair with."

"What do you think?"

"I'll tell you when I'm ready."

I sighed. "Guess I'd better get to the office. I have a new boss I need to meet."

He scrunched up his nose. "Sorry, Genie. Is this part of the sale?"

"New owners mean new bosses."

Mike offered up a small smile. "Let me know if you need me to call down there to tell them what a great journalist you are."

I smiled back. "Mike."

He raised an eyebrow. "What?"

I felt a flutter of anxiety as I searched for the words I wanted to say. "Hey, Caroline is flying to Aspen today with her aunt for Christmas vacation. It's going to be pretty quiet around the house with her gone. How about if I pick up some takeout and you drop by for dinner tonight?"

Did I really just ask that? Damn, my heart is racing.

He looked down at his desk, his eyes blinking, clearly flustered.

My anxiety slowly solidified into the cold fear of rejection. What was I thinking? He'd been the one who had kicked me to the curb when I wouldn't commit to a relationship.

Oh, yes, and the drinking, let's not forget about that.

He cleared his throat. "There's no good way to tell you this."

Growing dread burrowed its way into my chest. "Tell me what?"

"I'm seeing someone."

Oh, knife to the heart. "Really, who? Someone I know?" I tried to keep my voice bright, but I was pretty sure I wasn't pulling it off very well.

"Her name is Vicki Smith. We've been seeing each other since Thanksgiving."

Feeling the complete fool. "Well, how about that? Vicki Smith, the Realtor on the billboards out on Route 1?"

He nodded. "Yeah."

All I knew about her was what she looked like. Vicki Smith's smiling face was plastered up on the billboard on Connecticut

Avenue as you were coming into town. I'd also seen her in a couple of television ads, wearing her dark-blue blazer with the Vicki Smith Realty logo over her right breast. Looking straight into the camera, she purred, "I don't want to sell you a house. I want to find you a *home.*" She was petite, had shoulder-length raven-black hair, large, earnest, chocolate-brown eyes, and a lovely smile with the whitest teeth you've ever seen. I'll bet they glowed in the dark.

And she looked like she was at least ten years younger than Mike.

And me.

I stood up, still wearing my coat. I could feel heat spreading through my cheeks, my face flushing with embarrassment. I repeated, "Well, how about that?" I turned and started out the door, then stopped and looked back. "Forgive me for asking, how old is Vicki Smith?"

Mike appeared bemused that I was interested enough to ask. "Don't know. Early thirties, maybe."

"She have any kids?"

He shook his head. "She was married once, but no kids."

I knew that Mike had a fifteen-year-old son, the same age as Caroline. Davy spent most of the time with his mom, Mike's ex-wife. When Mike and I had been dating, he'd told me that his son hadn't taken the divorce well. Davy was acting out, having problems with authority figures, his father, in particular. At one point, Mike admitted that he was glad he'd only had the one child.

"Ya might want to be careful, Mike. Vicki Smith's biological clock is ticking. When they're that age, they want to have kids. Is that something you really want to do again?"

As I turned to walk out the door, I caught sight of him mulling that over, brows knitted together, eyes to the floor.

Catty?

Sure, why the hell not?

Chapter Six

It was disconcerting to walk into the newsroom and see a stranger in my old office. I stripped off my coat, hung it on the department coat tree, and sat down at my new desk in the middle of the newsroom. Glancing over my desktop monitor, I surreptitiously scoped her out and judged that Lorraine Moretti was in her early thirties.

Is everyone younger than I am?

Since she was seated at what used to be my desk, I couldn't guess her height. Her brown hair was a chic, short style with bangs swept across her forehead. She had wide brown eyes, distinctive cheekbones, Cupid's bow lips, and flawless arched eyebrows.

While she pecked at her keyboard and studied the computer monitor, she puckered her lips as if getting ready to kiss the screen. I watched as she pulled up a pair of glasses hanging on a cloth strap around her neck and put them on. They were silver with wide frames, retro—what I'd call old-lady-with-a-cat glasses.

I guess they're back in style? Were they ever in style?

Setting my Starbucks latte down on my desk, I opened up the computer and checked my emails. In open defiance of the company's useless spam filter, there were a dozen emails that ranged from "fake" news stories from unreliable sources to blatant phishing attempts to get my personal information. I quickly deleted them and then scanned the messages from Connecticut and New York authorities on the latest scams, changes in legislation, and notable crimes and arrests.

"Geneva Chase?"

I turned at the sound of the voice behind me. "Yes?"

"I'm Lorraine Moretti." She was studying me from behind her silver cat-lady glasses.

I could see that she was about five six in height and wearing a very professional, long-sleeved white blouse, simple gold necklace and earrings, brown knee-length skirt, black hose, and black flats. It was impeccable office attire but entirely out of place in cold weather.

I, on the other hand, was wearing a sweater, jeans, and my calf-length leather boots.

I noted that she was curvy in the bust and hips. I'd bet that in a few years she'd cross the border from zaftig to obese.

Meow.

I stood up. "It's nice to meet you."

She smiled but it was forced. "Can we talk in my office?"

I sighed and followed Lorraine into the cubicle that, up until twenty-four hours ago, had been mine. She sat behind the desk, and I plopped down on one of the two beat-to-hell leather chairs used for visitors.

She folded her hands on the desktop and began. "First of all, I want to tell you how much I've enjoyed your work over the years. Whenever the Associated Press picked up your stories, we ran it in all our Galley affiliates."

Good start.

"Thank you."

"The work you did on that missing fifteen-year-old high school girl back in October was exceptional. And the series you did on those six people cut to pieces on that island was very impressive."

I repeated myself. "Thank you."

She took her old-lady glasses off and let them hang from her neck. "You've had a very interesting career. A little bit like a roller coaster—a lot of highs and lows. I understand that Robert had a chat with you yesterday."

I felt my face flush. I didn't like the way this fledgling relationship was headed.

The smile on Lorraine's face was gone. "Let me be blunt. I won't stand for any drinking on the job. Period. It'll be grounds for immediate dismissal. What you do on your own time is your business, but I would strongly suggest that you exercise moderation at all times. Oh, yes, I know about the drunken incident in which you were arrested for punching a police officer." Her voice carried a tone of disgust.

My face went from a flush to a total burn. "Is that all?"

She attempted a smile again. "Genie, look, I want us to all be a team. You have talent and instinct. When you're on your A-game, there's no one better. I need you to be part of what we're going to build here at the *Sheffield Post.* I'm willing to work with you, but you have to do the same."

I nodded and felt the searing heat of tears pooling in my eyes and hoped that this bitch couldn't see them.

She put her glasses back on again, all business. "Where are you with the Graveyard Bay murders?"

I cleared my throat. "You mean Groward Bay?"

Her grin broadened, genuine now. "Yes, but Graveyard Bay is so much more colorful, don't you think? So where are we?"

I folded my arms. "Cops are looking at the marina's video footage."

She interrupted. "Video? Have you seen it?"

I sensed a trap. If I told her that I'd seen it but hadn't mentioned it in the story, it was a potential black mark. I'd kept it out of the story, for now, at Mike's request. She'd think I was too cozy with the cops. I lied. "No."

She stared off into space. "We need to get our hands on it."

I nodded wordlessly.

She refocused on me again. "I hear that you have a good relationship with the assistant chief of police."

Not as good as it used to be.

I answered, "If you're on the crime beat for any length of time, you're going to have a relationship with the cops. Depending on what you're writing about, sometimes it's good and sometimes it's bad."

Lorraine arched an eyebrow. "Yes, I know. It's not like you're sleeping with them." She shook her head slightly. "And you're not supposed to be."

How much does she know?

I changed the subject. "The ME is doing the autopsies today. The cops are running the female victim's prints to see if they can ID her. In the meantime, they're reviewing missing-person reports. Mike Dillon told me that they've talked to Judge Preston's wife and his staff. Nobody recalls hearing about any death threats."

"What's *your* next step?"

"I'm heading out to talk with Judge Preston's wife. See if I can get a statement."

She turned her full attention back to her computer screen. "Don't let me keep you."

Am I dismissed?

I stood up and walked out of the cube. I didn't have a warm, fuzzy feeling about the team-builder from Galley Media.

Before I left to interview Eva Preston, I went through the rest of the incident reports I'd gotten from Mike. Nothing warranted anything more than mentions in the Police Log we ran every day on page two, one of our more popular features. Our readers loved looking to see if a friend or neighbor had been arrested for driving while under the influence or busted for indecent exposure.

I did some digging on the overdose fatality from last night. Her name was Holly Dickenson, twenty-two years old. She was a student at the community college and lived with her parents on the east side of town.

I found a photo of her on Facebook. Brown eyes, freckles, auburn hair brushed away from her face, earnest expression, pretty smile. Her last post was, "Ladies night at Lando's, bitches. It's gonna' be kickin'. See y'all there."

Lando's was a nightclub in South Sheffield, the part of town where all the restaurants and trendy bars had settled. That particular club catered to a demographic of twenty-one to thirty. The last time I stopped by, I felt positively ancient.

According to the report, the cops were called around eleven when her friends found Holly comatose in the ladies' room. The EMTs arrived and administered Narcan, the brand name for naloxone, used to block the effect of opioids and reverse an OD.

But Holly was too far gone. She was pronounced DOA at Sheffield General.

Her friends didn't know what she'd taken that night, and the police were awaiting a toxicology report from Doctor Foley.

I mused, sadly, that Holly seemed like a nice holiday name.

That is so goddamn sad. Every Christmas, her parents will be thinking about how their daughter died.

Then I stole a glance at the photo of Caroline I kept on my desk. She was wearing a Boston Red Sox baseball cap and smiling at the camera. I'd taken that photo last summer at Cape Cod where we were vacationing together.

And where I started drinking again.

I glanced at the time on my computer screen and wondered if she'd landed in Colorado yet. Her plane was supposed to have taken off at ten and it was only coming up on noon. Flight time from gate to gate, New York to Aspen, was four and a half hours. She wouldn't be landing until about 2:30 my time.

Out of the corner of my eye, I saw Bill from advertising slide up to my desk and sit down next to me. He straightened his bow tie. "Want to hear something interesting?"

"Always." I rested my chin on my hand. "Whatcha got?"

He glanced around him. "All that property someone's been buying up out by I-95?"

"Yeah?"

"Somebody's building a mall."

"What? I thought malls were as yesterday as newspapers."

He rolled his eyes. "I know, right? I got a phone call from a rep from Nordstrom about an hour ago. They want a rate package. He said they're going to be one of the anchors in an urban mall that should be finished in about two years."

The gears turned. "Wait a minute. Isn't that a game-changer as far as the profitability of this newspaper?"

He cracked his knuckles. "I'm pretty sure that if Ben had known about this, he wouldn't have sold us out."

"Holy shit. Does he know now?"

Bill gave me a toothy smile and shook his head. "I'm on my way to deliver the news."

I glanced at the closed door to his office. "I'd love to be a fly on the wall when you do, Bill." I peeked over at Lorraine, who was watching me. "But I'd better get back to work."

He patted my arm. "This may all have a happy ending after all."

"From your lips to God's ear."

I watched him get up and lope out of the newsroom in Ben's direction.

An urban mall. Who builds malls anymore?

I picked up the phone and punched in Judge Preston's home phone.

To my surprise, Eva Preston answered and said yes when I'd asked if I could come by for a statement. We set the time at 1:30, which gave me time for lunch.

And a quick drink?

I took a glance at the Wicked Witch of the West sitting in my old office.

Okay, coffee instead.

Chapter Seven

Passing on the vodka tonic, I opted for a grilled chicken Caesar salad delivered from Pete's Deli just up the street.

While I picked at my lettuce, I did a little net surfing. Eva, the judge's second wife, was originally from Slovenia, formerly Yugoslavia. There wasn't much about her life before she came to the United States. Once here, she managed to land a job with the Patricia Wallace Modeling Agency. She was best known for her work for SeaNet Swimwear.

I looked at some of her photos wearing some mighty daring bikinis. Bronzed skin, long golden hair, sky-blue eyes, high cheekbones, toned legs, a tummy firm enough you could bounce a quarter off it—she must have been in her twenties when those were taken. Eva was staring into the camera, her rosebud lips slightly apart, a smoky, seductive expression on her face.

She gave new meaning to the term "making love to the camera."

I could easily see what Judge Niles Preston saw in her.

But what did she see in the man who was more than twice her age?

Doing another search, I saw that the judge and his wife owned a home at 13 Branson Ridge Trail in Wilton, only about fifteen minutes from the newspaper office. The judge had purchased the property three years ago for $815,000.

I quickly looked up what a Connecticut Supreme Court judge makes a year—$170,000, on average.

I guess someone with that salary could swing a house with that kind of price tag, but it would be a stretch.

The twenty-five-hundred-square-foot white two-story Colonial was situated on an acre of land on a quiet wooded cul-de-sac. It boasted four bedrooms, four bathrooms, three fireplaces, a gourmet kitchen, nearly two acres of fenced-in backyard, and an in-ground pool.

I studied a series of photos that had been on the Realtor's website from when it was for sale. Ironically, the Realtor of record was Vicki Smith, Mike Dillon's new squeeze.

I did a fast calculation. If she received the full six percent commission, then she earned over forty-eight thousand dollars on just that one sale. That's about what an average newspaper journalist makes in an entire year.

I glanced back at Lorraine Moretti in the editor's cube and silently seethed.

—

Before I drove up to Wilton to meet with Eva Preston, I decided to drop by the house owned by Holly Dickenson's family. I wasn't so much fishing for a statement from them as I wanted to express my condolences. Unfortunately, overdoses like Holly's had become so common that they didn't always warrant a story in the newspaper.

Not unless there was celebrity involved.

A paid obituary. That was what the twenty-two-year-old college student would get, if her parents could afford it.

And if you read the obits carefully, you can generally spot the ODs and the suicides. The age is a giveaway, of course. But the words *died suddenly* or *died at home* were the tell.

Holly died in the filthy bathroom stall of a loud nightclub.

What a waste.

Don and Alyce Dickenson lived on the east side of Sheffield in a neighborhood of small, one-story homes on tiny tracts of land. It was where the teachers, the blue-collar laborers, the nurses, and the people who didn't make six-figure salaries lived. It was kept neat and clean and people took pride in their homes.

That's why I was so surprised when I parked on the curb in front of 148 Norris Street and saw garbage strewn across the front yard. Empty cans, plastic packaging, newspapers, coffee grounds all marred the white-gray snow covering the lawn. A woman in tan slacks, sneakers, and a heavy winter coat was stooped over, gingerly picking up what she could and dropping it into a black trash bag.

I got out of the car and she straightened up, noticing me as I picked my way toward her. "Hi, I'm Genie Chase."

"What can I do for you?" The woman was in her fifties, wore no makeup, had thin lips pressed together, and her expression was one of suspicion.

"I'm looking for Mr. or Mrs. Dickenson. Are you Holly's mother?"

She shook her head slightly. "They're both at Franklin's making arrangements for Holly's funeral."

Her voice caught in her throat and she stared up at the sky for a moment.

"I understand. Are you a neighbor?"

She jutted her chin to the house next door. "I've known the Dickensons since they moved here when Holly was just a baby."

I nodded. "I just wanted to tell them how sorry I am. I can come back another time."

"How did you know Holly?"

I gave the woman a sad look. "I didn't. I'm a staff writer for the *Post.* I saw the incident report this morning. I'm raising a girl not much younger than Holly. I just I wanted to stop by and offer the parents my condolences."

She blinked her eyes. "But not do a story?"

I slowly shook my head. "No. I'm not sure the Dickensons would want one."

"No." The woman looked past me, staring at something she could only see in her mind. "You know, up until a couple of years ago, when she broke her leg, I don't think Holly took so much as an aspirin."

"Oh?"

"Broke her leg playing soccer when she was seventeen. Doctor gave her some pain pills and Holly got hooked." She reached down and picked up an empty Campbell's soup can. Dropping it into the bag, she continued. "Over the last year or so, she got really bad. Stealing money from her folks, getting arrested. Don told me that Holly had moved on to heroin. Half the time, they didn't know where Holly was living. I heard her boyfriend was a junkie too."

The woman stepped closer to where I was standing and glanced up and down the street. "I think she was dealing. When her parents would go off on business or vacation, I'd see car after car drive up here and go inside. They'd leave again a few minutes later."

Old story. Pain pills to heroin to dealer. Often that was the only way to pay for the habit.

The woman returned to picking up garbage. I gestured toward the tiny yard. "What happened, dogs get into the trash?"

The woman quickly straightened up. "No," she snapped. "After the Dickensons left for the funeral home, I saw two men in a van pull up. They got out, opened the trash can, and tore open the two bags that were in there. Then they quickly started picking things out of it."

"Like what kind of things? Did you see?"

The woman grimaced and glanced around the garbage-covered snow. "There's something missing now, isn't there? Holly did heroin, but she was also a pill junkie. What's not here?"

Plastic pill bottles and needles.

The woman didn't wait for me to answer. "I think those men were addicts. They probably thought that Holly's parents took the drugs she had stashed in her bedroom and threw them into the garbage. They were looking for Holly's drugs."

When I sighed, steam escaped my lips and drifted toward the sky.

The neighbor said one last thing before I turned and left. "Animals. They're goddamned animals."

—

The woman who met me at the door was about five nine and swimwear-model thin. Eva Preston wore a black silk long-sleeved top, gray slacks, understated gold hoop earrings and gold rope necklace. Her long, lustrous platinum hair cascaded over her shoulders and down her back. There were red rims around her blue eyes, her mascara was smudged, and her cheeks were flushed a bright pink. She was holding a tissue in her hand that was little more than a moist wad of ruined paper.

I immediately felt sorry for her and ashamed for thinking that because she'd married an older man, she might be a gold digger. She was obviously grieving. "Mrs. Preston, I'm Geneva Chase. I am so sorry about your husband."

She nodded. "Please come in."

I stepped into her expansive living room. The wainscoting was a dark brown balanced against the light blue color of the walls. Bright splashes of colorful Oriental area rugs dotted the parquet hardwood floors. The furniture was an eclectic combination of cloth and leather chairs and couches, accented by throw pillows with a Middle-Eastern flair.

A twelve-foot Christmas tree dominated the room, displayed in the wide bay window overlooking the snow-covered lawn. The holiday scent of pine filled the air. Tiny multicolored lights twinkled past dozens of ornaments and through silver strands of tinsel.

A small, ceramic nativity scene sat on the fireplace mantel.

"Thank you for seeing me, Mrs. Preston." That was when I spotted the drink in her hand.

"Please call me Eva. Can I get you something? Coffee? Tea? Cocktail?"

Cocktail.

She led the way into the kitchen, and along the way we passed a massive grandfather clock standing at attention against the wall. It told me that it was only slightly after one in the afternoon.

Too early for a cocktail?

"You have a lovely accent. Is it Eastern European?" I already knew the answer.

Eva looked back at me, smiled briefly, exposing perfect teeth. "I'm originally from Slovenia. May I take your coat?"

I stripped it off and draped it onto the back of a kitchen chair. "This is fine."

The brick walls of the room were painted white. Blue cabinets fronted with glass doors were mounted over gray granite counters. Framed, color photographs of Mediterranean seascapes hung on the walls. Gray light from a cold, cloudless sky came through floor-to-ceiling windows in the far wall.

Eva put the glass she'd been holding up to her lips and emptied it. Then she put it on the counter, took down another glass, and proceeded to pour vodka into both. She turned and fixed me with her slightly boozy gaze. "You'll join me, yes?"

She'd already poured the vodka. "Of course."

Eva went to the refrigerator, took out a container of cranberry juice, and tossed a splash into each glass. Then she picked up both tumblers and handed one to me.

"Thank you." I'm not much for adulterating vodka with anything other than tonic, but I took a healthy sip and felt the warmth slide down my throat. I thought the cranberry juice made it festive.

We sat on wooden stools at the kitchen's center island. Without asking for permission, I pulled my phone out of my bag, hit the recording app, and placed it on the wooden counter. "Once again, I can't tell you how very sorry I am about what happened to your husband."

She sipped at her own drink and gazed sadly out the window, staring at the snow-covered backyard. "I worried that something like this would happen to my husband."

"That he'd be murdered?"

Nodding. "He sends men to prison. Bad men. Eventually, they get out."

"Do you think that's what happened?"

She looked down at her left hand and absently felt her wedding ring with her thumb. "What else could it be? Everyone loved Niles. As far as I know, he had no enemies."

Except for those people he sent to jail.

For a moment I was distracted by the sheer size of the diamond in her wedding ring, a glittering rock surrounded by a lustrous family of smaller diamonds. The nosy Nora in me wanted to ask how much Judge Preston paid for that. The reporter in me wanted to ask where the judge got the money.

I tore my eyes away from the sparkler. "Can you tell me about the night your husband died?"

She shot me a suspicious look. "I told the police everything."

"Please?"

She stood up and steadied herself on the kitchen table.

How much has she had to drink?

Eva went to the counter and pulled a fresh tissue from a wooden container next to the coffeepot. She sat back down. "We were both in the den, he was reading, and I was watching *Longmire* on the TV. At about ten, the phone rang. I picked it up and it was a woman. She asked to speak to Niles."

I watched as her eyes glazed over with a shimmering film of tears.

"It was a landline? Not a cell phone?"

"Yes, the phone in the den."

I asked, "Do you know who it was?"

She bit her lip and slowly shook her head.

"When she asked to speak to your husband, is that what she called him, Niles? She didn't ask to speak to Judge Preston?"

"She specifically asked to speak to Niles."

"Your husband took the call?"

"Yes, it's a cordless phone. He took the receiver and left the den to talk with whoever it was privately. I couldn't hear his conversation."

"What happened next?"

She dropped her eyes. "He came back into the den and said that he needed to meet with a colleague about a very important case. Then he left. That was the last I saw him. He never came back home."

The sob escaping her lips almost sounded like a sneeze. It broke my heart. I know that kind of sadness, the sadness when someone you love dies before his time.

She held the tissue over her mouth and nose like a mask, her eyes squeezed shut, trying hard to stave off her emotions. Her head and shoulders shook uncontrollably.

It was one of those awkward moments when your instinct is to move to where she's crying and put your arms around her in a reassuring hug. But I'd just met the woman. There was nothing to do except wait until Eva regained her composure.

I sat in silence and sipped my vodka and cranberry.

Finally, she dabbed her eyes. "I'm sorry."

I decided to change the subject for a moment. "How did you and Niles meet?"

She blinked a few times, her eyes glazed with a thick film of tears. Eva cocked her head and attempted a tiny smile. "When we met, I was working as a model. Most of the time I did photo shoots in New York. But there was an assignment here in Connecticut that kept me here for a few days. On the first afternoon, we were shooting aboard a catamaran that was moored right next to Niles's sailboat." Her slight smile broadened a bit. "I was only wearing a little black bikini. I must have caught his eye because when we were done shooting, he asked if I would have dinner with him. The rest is history."

I took another hit on my drink and thought for a moment. "Where did your husband keep his boat?"

She took a deep sigh. "The marina out at Groward Bay."

Where he was killed. Wow.

"Eva, I'm sorry to ask you this, but do you have any idea who called your husband that night?"

She bobbed her head slightly, her eyes cast to the floor, smile gone. "I think my husband was having an affair."

I took another look at Eva Preston. Even torn by sorrow, she was one of the most beautiful women I'd ever seen. I could never understand how a man cheats on his wife.

Of course, not that long ago, I had been the "other" woman in a two-year-long affair with a married man, and *his* wife was gorgeous.

Forbidden fruit? The thrill of the hunt?

For a minute my mind flashed on an image of Frank Mancini. Dark hair, chocolate-brown eyes, dangerously handsome. Married.

I'd be willing to bet he and his wife were someplace in the Caribbean for the holiday.

I turned my attention back to Eva. "What makes you think your husband was having an affair?"

She stared at the black-and-white tiles at her feet, clearly embarrassed. "All the clichés. He was spending more and more time away from the house, sometimes late into the evening. I'd catch the occasional scent of perfume on him. I'd leave a room and when I'd come back in, I'd find him texting someone. When I'd ask who he was talking to, he'd tell me it was someone from work."

There wasn't any good way to ask my next question. "Were things good between you and your husband?"

Her nostrils flared and her jaw jutted out. "I'm a very good wife. I do all the cooking. I'm a very good cook. We have a lady who cleans for us once a week, but I keep the house tidy. I take good care of myself so that he would be proud of me. I work out at the gym and dress nice for him."

I nodded sympathetically.

"He wasn't always a good husband, though," Eva added. "He hadn't touched me in nearly six months."

That's not good.

I cleared my throat. "Was he physically capable of having sex?"

She smiled nervously. "He took pills...you know...to get hard."

"Did he ever talk about his cases? Say anything about the people he sent to jail?"

She nodded and played with the wadded ball of moist tissue in her hand. "Yes, drug dealers, thieves, wife beaters, child molesters, pimps. Bad people."

I thought for a moment, recalling the entry in the notebook. "Did he ever mention the name Jim Caviness?"

She shook her head.

"Did he ever mention the names of Valentin and Bogdan Tolbonov?"

Her brows furrowed as she thought. "No. I don't recognize those names. They sound Russian."

"Did he mention that one of the men he'd sentenced to prison had recently escaped from Lockport Correctional Facility?"

"Yes."

"What did your husband say?"

"That security at the courthouse would be increased and that the police told him they'd be doing extra patrols around our neighborhood. And they said that if he saw anything unusual at all, to call them immediately."

I glanced out the window into the backyard. A black cat was moving slowly across the snow, stalking something. "Did your husband seem concerned?"

Eva caught my line of sight. She stood up and went to the back door. Opening it, she shouted, "Scat, go home, you little shit."

I watched as the cat froze in place, its eyes buggy, then it vanished.

Eva closed the door and turned to me. "That cat is always hunting the birds that come to my feeder."

When she sat back down, I repeated, "Was your husband concerned?"

"He said that he wasn't. But Niles carried a handgun with him almost everywhere he went. And we have a shotgun hidden under our bed upstairs."

Handgun didn't do him any good out on that pier.

"Did your husband ever specifically say the name Merlin Finn?"

She nodded. "He said that Mr. Finn was a very bad man, capable of horrible things. He was big and mean. But Niles said that if he ever showed up, he'd get a bullet to the head. That would take care of things."

That only works if you get the drop on the bad guy before he gets the drop on you.

Chapter Eight

I left Eva Preston at the front door of her house and hustled quickly to the driveway to escape the biting gusts of wind. I slid into my Sebring and started the engine, silently swearing that the next car I owned would have heated seats.

I rubbed my hands together and waited until the engine warmed up enough that tepid air started blowing from the dash vent. A heatless sun had just poked through a moving curtain of dark gray clouds. I glanced up at the sky, wishing for spring.

That's when I noticed the glint, a brief nanosecond of bright reflection high above the Prestons' house.

A drone?

I reached into my bag and punched up Mike's number.

"Genie?"

"Do you have Eva Preston's home under surveillance?"

"Not me. But the FBI is crawling all over each other looking for Merlin Finn."

"When did this happen?" I couldn't see it anymore.

Had I seen it at all?

I glanced around me, expecting to see an unmarked van filled with listening devices and video equipment parked at the side of the road. But there weren't any vehicles parked at all.

Mike answered. "We had a few of them poking around right after Merlin Finn broke out of prison. It escalated geometrically when Judge Preston's body was discovered. What makes you think that Eva Preston is being surveilled?"

I scanned the sky again. All I saw was that the sun had once again been obliterated by snow clouds. "I thought I saw a drone."

"In spite of what you might see on television, the FBI knows their stuff. If they're watching you, chances are you aren't going to know about it."

"But it's possible they're watching Eva Preston, just in case Merlin Finn shows up."

"I'll tell you something I know and that's the Wilton cops are keeping a close eye on that neighborhood for that same reason. So watch yourself."

Meaning what? Don't be drinking and driving?

At that exact moment, I saw a black-and-white police utility vehicle pull into the cul-de-sac where I was parked. It was a Ford SUV with a massive black front bumper guard. "Got one headed toward me now."

"You're in Eva Preston's neighborhood?"

"I thought I mentioned that."

"Skipped that part."

The cruiser's red and whites came on.

I sighed. "Okay, I'm busted. Cop wants to talk."

"Good luck. If you need me, call."

The cop tapped on my window with his knuckles, and I slid it down, feeling the cold air rush in. "Hello, Officer."

I could see by the tag on his chest that this was Officer Lyle. "Do you live in this neighborhood?"

"No, sir. I'm a reporter for the *Sheffield Post* and I was here to get a statement from Mrs. Preston."

He leaned down, his face close enough to my own that I could smell cilantro on his breath. "A reporter. Look, this is a nice quiet neighborhood, and Mrs. Preston has been through a lot, what with her husband being murdered and all. Do you have any further business here?"

I shook my head.

He nodded and sneered. "Then I don't suppose I'll see you back here again."

I was going to make a smart-ass remark about how there was still a First Amendment, but then I recalled that my commuter coffee cup was filled with vodka. "Just leaving. Have a good day, Officer Lyle."

I slid my window up and pulled out of the driveway.

When I reached the bottom of the hill, I checked to see if I had any emails or messages. The only call in my voice mailbox was the one I'd gotten yesterday from Nathaniel Rubin about a possible job opportunity.

Braking for a stop sign, I punched in the number he'd given me.

He answered on the second ring. His voice was low, his words crisp. "Is this Geneva Chase?"

I smiled as I drove. "It is. Are you Nathaniel Rubin?"

"I am. Let me start by saying, I'm a fan of your work. Very impressive."

"Thank you."

"I read your story online this morning about the judge and an unknown woman being found underwater, chained to the prongs of a forklift. Graveyard Bay...is that a real place?"

I smiled. "It's really Groward Bay. The locals called it Graveyard Bay during the Revolutionary War."

"I see. Cops find out who killed them yet?"

"Not yet."

"Have you?" His question took me by surprise.

I chuckled and repeated my answer. "Not yet."

I could almost hear the man smiling over the phone. "You will. Are you familiar with Lodestar Analytics?"

"Only what I found on your website."

"What you didn't find on our website was a list of our clients. We're very discreet."

I stopped at the intersection to Route 7, watching for a break in the long line of traffic. "Discreet."

Nathaniel continued. "We have clients from all over the world, many of whom I'm sure you would recognize."

As I pulled onto the road, I recalled what the website had said. "Lodestar Analytics conducts open-source investigations and provides research and strategic advice for businesses, law firms, and investors as well as for political inquiries, such as opposition research."

They dig up dirt on people.

Funny how this job had sounded much better last night after I'd had a couple of hits of Absolut. "You said something about a job opportunity?"

"Yes, we're going through a growth spurt and could use someone in our company with your set of skills."

I glanced up into my rearview mirror to see a black Dodge Charger following much too closely.

A tail?

I asked, "My set of skills?"

"You're an excellent investigative journalist who has an outstanding body of work."

I smiled and momentarily forgot the dangerous driver behind me. Nathaniel's words reflected what Robert Vogel and Lorraine Moretti had told me, only without the bullshit about drinking myself out of almost every good job I've ever had. "You want me to be an investigative journalist for your company?"

"I want you to be an investigator for us. Written reports will be part of your job. I know you can write."

The black Charger braked and turned, pulling into the parking lot of Jordan's Pizza. "I don't want to sound crass, Mr. Rubin."

"Please, nobody calls me Mr. Rubin except my mother, and that's only when she's pissed off at me. Call me Nathaniel."

Nearly as formal as Mr. Rubin.

"Nathaniel, I don't want to sound crass but..."

"The salary is eighty thousand a year to start, with bonuses and a full set of benefits."

Suddenly, my heart started to race.

That was nearly twice what I would be making as a reporter.

"Where would I be working?"

"You'd be working remotely. On occasion you'd need to travel for us if the assignment required it. About once a month I'd like it if you come by headquarters to catch me up on whatever assignment you've been given."

"Where's headquarters?"

"Manhattan."

"I'm interested. What do we do next?"

I thought I could hear him rub his hands together. "I'd love it if you can come to my office to chat face-to-face and see where we work. It'll be very informal."

"Should I bring a résumé?"

"This is the twenty-first century, Genie. I already have all the intel on you I need."

What the hell does that mean? Does he know about the drinking?

"Just curious, how did my name come up?"

"Well, I know your newspaper was just gobbled up by Galley Media. They work their employees hard and are reluctant to pay them what they're worth. I think you'll get tired of them in short order. Plus, you came highly recommended by one of my other employees."

I flipped on my turn signal to pull into the *Post* parking lot. "Do you mind if I ask who that is?"

"John Stillwater."

John Stillwater?

I thought he worked for Shana Neese. I'd met John and Shana in October when they'd posted Betsy Caviness's million-dollar bail. They were both associated with the Friends of Lydia, a shadow organization dedicated to helping women and girls suffering from domestic abuse and violence, including forced prostitution and sex trafficking.

I'd been in their company when we'd tricked our way into the home of the nasty pimp named Lucifer and rescued four young girls.

Originally, Shana had told me she earned a living as a physical therapist, which was her own inside joke. When Shana Neese wasn't out saving the world, she was a professional dominatrix with a successful dungeon in New York.

Physical therapist, my ass.

I never knew how John Stillwater earned a living.

"Okay, Nathaniel. I'll come into the city. I'm going to have to try to figure something out so that I can get away without spooking our new owners."

"I understand completely. Call me when you think you can get here even if it's after hours. I'm looking forward to meeting you."

I grinned again. Then the reporter in me kicked in and I asked an inappropriate question. "Hey, you don't happen to know a woman named Shana Neese, do you?"

I honestly don't know if it's possible to feel a man blush over the phone, but at that awkward moment, I was certain Mr. Rubin's face was flushed a deep crimson. I heard him sigh, then he said, "John said you're very good at what you do. Let me know when you can come to town."

I struck a nerve.

Was Nathaniel Rubin a client of Shana's?

I was just pulling into the parking lot of the newspaper when my cell phone chirped. Driving through the alleyway to the employee lot in the back, I recognized the number on the screen. "Hey, Mike."

"Genie, we just got the autopsy report back from Foley."

I drove into my usual spot against the back of the building and parked. "How did they die?"

"Drowned. But that's not all."

I left the car running and the heater ramped up. "Tell me."

"They'd both been tortured—burned and beaten. Foley says they had burn marks that could have been caused by a blowtorch. They both exhibited dozens of marks that may have come from a whip or a metal cord."

"And the tall guy in the video was wearing, what, a bondage hood? Was this an S&M scene that went horribly wrong?"

I heard Mike exhale. "An S&M scene on steroids. One more thing. Foley thinks that the Jane Doe may have been raped."

"Is it possible that he's seeing evidence that the Jane Doe and the judge might have had sex earlier in the evening? Like you said, Eva Preston thought her husband was having an affair."

"Foley said there was evidence of tearing and abrasion. Whatever it was, he said it was rough."

I turned off the Sebring. "What's the latest on Merlin Finn?"

"When you do your follow-up piece, you can include that he's officially a person of interest and that the police are encouraging anyone with information about Mr. Finn to call us."

We said goodbye and I got out of the car. Then I glanced up at the employee entrance in the back of the newspaper building. As cold as it was outside, I didn't want to go inside.

Suck it up, Genie.

I trudged up the concrete steps and opened the door. Taking off my coat and hanging it on the department coat tree, I avoided looking into my old office. Instead, I went straight to my desk in the middle of the floor and started checking my emails.

"What do you have new on the marina homicides?"

Reluctantly, I slowly turned and looked up into Lorraine's face. She was staring back down at me through those silly glasses. "Cause of death. Medical Examiner says they were tortured before they were drowned. There's evidence that the woman was raped."

She balled up her fist and shook it in front of her chest as if she were celebrating a touchdown. "Nastier the death, the better the ink."

I considered myself to be a cynical, hard-bitten journalist always on the prowl to sell more newspapers. I was starting to think that Lorraine Moretti was beyond that. That she was as bloodless as Robert Vogel.

"What else do you have?"

I attempted a smile. "Cops say they have a person of interest. Merlin Finn, the white supremacist who busted out of Lockport Correctional two weeks ago. Preston was the presiding judge at his sentencing. Finn is still on the run."

"Oh my God, can this story get any better? Get at it, Genie. I want to see what you have in the next thirty minutes."

I watched as she slithered back to the editor's cube.

Thirty minutes, huh? You'll get it when I want you to have it.

Nathaniel Rubin's offer was looking better and better.

Chapter Nine

Before I started the follow-up piece on the homicides, I looked up as much as I could find on Merlin Finn. Other than the easy-to-find information on his arrest and conviction for killing two rival gang members and then his spectacular escape from prison, anything before that was almost nonexistent. He was born an only child in Grand Rapids, Michigan. His parents moved to Westchester County, New York, when he was seven. His mother cleaned other people's houses; his father worked in construction.

He graduated from high school but there was no record of going on to college. The only other bits of information I could find were a couple of arrests for minor infractions like possession of marijuana and petty theft.

I punched up the transcript from his trial. With Judge Niles Preston presiding, the trial had lasted three days. I read through the prosecuting attorney's presentation of the State's case offering evidence that Merlin Finn had been the head of a crime organization affiliated with the Russian Mafia.

Say what?

I scanned the rest of the document, but there wasn't any specific reference to Wolfline Contracting or the Tolbonov brothers.

It made sense, though, didn't it? White supremacists and Russians working together?

I continued to scan without really knowing what I was looking for. I read through the prosecution's case. It was open and shut. Someone had tipped the cops off that two men were buried in shallow graves on Finn's backwoods property. When the bodies were recovered, Finn's DNA was all over them. They found a torture chamber in his basement complete with the victims' DNA. The coroner concluded that the two men had been tortured and shot.

Open and shut.

Judge Niles Preston handed Merlin Finn two consecutive life sentences without hope of parole.

In one of the news stories, there was a photograph of a woman identified as Bristol Finn, wife of the man on trial for murder. The image was black and white, and the resolution was grainy. She appeared to be in her late thirties, had hair down to the back of her neck, and a hard look on her face.

Pissed off at being photographed? At being married to a killer?

I wrote down the woman's name and then looked up her address. Was there a chance that she knew where Finn was?

I plugged my thumb drive into the computer and brought up the notebook Betsy Caviness had sent me. Among the entries that made no sense to me was one that referred to a town called Brockton, where the bodies had been found. I clicked through the pages until I found what I was looking for.

April 9, noon, drop pkg, MF, #1 Oak Hill Rd, Brockton

I looked up ownership of the property in Brockton. It was in Bristol's name but there was an addendum that said there was a sale pending.

Merlin must have made certain that the property was in his wife's name in case he was ever arrested. He knew that he would most certainly have lost the property if he ever went to prison.

Always plan ahead.

The address was easy to find, but I couldn't find a phone number, email address, or any kind of social media presence. The only item on the internet pertaining to Bristol Finn was that she attended her husband's trial.

That entry about dropping a package off for MF appeared nearly every week, for three months, until early June, when Merlin Finn was arrested for a double murder. Then the entries stopped.

Before I got around to hammering out the follow-up piece about the Groward Bay homicides, I wandered over to the circulation department where I knew there was most likely a fresh pot of coffee brewing, mulling over what my next move should be. I made sure that Lorraine saw me as I left the newsroom.

Taking my time, I got back to my desk with my cup of steaming caffeine and put the story together, sending it to Lorraine's queue. Taking a last gulp of coffee, I stood up and stretched. Without looking at my new editor, I put on my coat and started toward the back door of the building.

"Genie."

Christ, now what?

I turned. "Lorraine?"

"Where you headed?"

I bit my lip and answered. "I found the address of Merlin Finn's wife. I thought I'd pay her a visit."

She nodded slightly. "I need for you to get into the habit of letting me know where you are at all times."

I felt my face flush with anger. Taking a deep breath, I offered, "Sure. Just so you know, she lives in Brockton. That's about forty-five minutes from here."

Lorraine frowned. "This isn't something you can do over the phone?"

I wasn't used to being second-guessed. "I can't find a number for her."

I watched as the gears in her head spun, processing, thinking about how far she wanted to push me. "See you when you get back."

My anger burned even out in the biting cold of the parking lot. Lorraine Moretti and I were not going to be a good fit.

—

Ten minutes into the trip, driving past stores and shops decorated with Christmas lights and wreaths and houses with inflatable snowmen and reindeer on their front lawns, I got a call from Mike Dillon. "Mike, what's up?"

"We caught a break on the Jane Doe."

"Oh yeah?"

"Her name's Abigail Tillis, thirty-nine years old, lives in Manhattan. She's a private detective."

I was just getting ready to hop on the Merritt Parkway and then onto Route 7 North. "How did you find out who she is?"

"One of her associates in New York read your story online about the double homicide at Groward Bay. He told us that he drove up to Sheffield to identify the body. He said he knew Miss Tillis had come to Connecticut to meet with Niles Preston. He put two and two together. It looks like she was in the wrong place at the worst possible time."

"Did this guy say why she'd come to Sheffield to talk with Preston?"

Mike hesitated, as if he were thinking about something. "He claims he didn't know. But he did tell me who she was working for."

"Who?"

"The Friends of Lydia."

I felt like I'd just gotten a tiny electrical shock. "What's this guy's name?"

"John Stillwater."

It was the second time I'd heard his name in less than three hours.

I pictured him in my mind. He was in his early forties, tall, about six feet and he weighed in at about two ten. John Stillwater was clean-shaven, had a strong jaw, and a pleasant smile. The lines at the corners of his blue eyes and the sides of his mouth gave him character. The last time I saw him, his full head of brown hair fell boyishly over his ears and the back of his collar. I guessed that he'd been about two weeks overdue for a trim. The square black-rimmed glasses he wore gave me the impression that he was both intelligent and vulnerable.

The despicable Valentin Tolbonov had hinted that John had once been a New York cop but was kicked off the force. I never had a chance to ask John about that.

How are the Friends of Lydia associated with Judge Niles Preston? Did they suspect that he was dirty?

"Did he say if he was heading back to New York?"

"He told me that he'd contact next of kin for Miss Tillis. He also said he'd be in town for another day or so before he went back to the city."

"But he didn't say why Abigail Tillis was with Judge Preston?"

Mike repeated, "He claimed that he didn't know."

I'll bet that's a big fat lie.

—

Brockton is about halfway between the Long Island coastline and the Massachusetts border. The town's not much more than a few stoplights, a Baptist church, a Stop-n-Shop grocery store, a few retailers along the single main street, and a couple of restaurants. The farther away from the coast, the more the terrain became rolling, wooded hills. Much farther north and I would have been driving through the foothills of the Berkshires.

I used the GPS in my phone to find Oak Hill Road. Exiting on Route 7, it took me another ten minutes to find the turnoff I was looking for. The address wouldn't be difficult to find. The road was rutted dirt and gravel up the side of a steep hill, thick forest on either side.

The only house on Oak Hill Road was Bristol's. I figured I'd come to the end of the line when I approached an old entrance gate with a metal sign that shouted in red letters against a field of white: NO TRESPASSING.

I stopped the car, turned off the engine, and got out. Zipping up the front of my parka, I stepped up to the gate. Glancing left and right, I saw fencing with multiple warning signs saying, "Danger. Electrified."

So climbing over is out of the question.

Then I noticed a metal post, painted yellow, planted off to one side of the gate. It was topped with a closed-circuit camera, and attached were a keypad and a call box. I pressed the red button on a metal box about the size of a cellphone.

After a few moments, a male, disembodied voice crackled to life. "What is it?"

"I'd like to meet with Bristol Finn, please."

"Who are you?"

"Geneva Chase. I'm with the *Sheffield Post.*"

I heard the man snort. "No reporters."

"I told you who I am. Who are you?"

"None of your damned business, that's who I am."

I took another look at the electrified fence. I was starting to think I'd just wasted forty-five minutes of my time driving up there. "Look, I'm working on a story about Merlin Finn. Do you know where he is?"

The call box was silent.

I tried again. "I'm going to be writing a piece whether you talk to me or not. I'd much rather get it right rather than wrong."

Or not at all.

The man's voice was replaced by a woman's. "Have they found Merlin yet?"

"Not yet," I answered.

There were a few moments of silence. "Can you do the story without using our names?"

"If that's what you want."

Without another word, I heard a loud click and the gate started to slide to the side with a humming noise.

I guess this is my invitation.

Chapter Ten

The road to the house was another hardscrabble half mile up the hill. The woods on either side of the dirt path were thick and dark. The clouds overhead were the color of painful bruises, and I had no doubt they were pregnant with snow. I dearly didn't want to get caught on this road during a snowstorm.

At the very end of Oak Hill Road, the imposing, two-story, fieldstone house came into view. The shingled roof was as gray as the sky; the shutters and the doors were painted red. The building was fronted by a rustic wooden porch and railing.

This huge house in the woods should have struck me as serene and peaceful.

But the man standing on the porch, glaring at me as I drove up, was jarringly out of place. He cradled an AR-15 in his arms.

Parking my car behind a mud-covered Jeep Cherokee, I got out, zipped up my coat again, hung my bag over my shoulder, and closed the car door. Standing next to the Sebring, I wondered what I should do next. Should I wait for a signal to advance? Should I go ahead and climb the steps to the porch?

There was a third choice. I simply stood there and waved my hand at the man.

He was dressed in a camouflage coat, blue jeans, and black

work boots. The hands holding the semiautomatic weapon were protected from the cold by black leather gloves. He stared at me from behind mirrored sunglasses. He was somewhere in his thirties, his black hair was buzzed military short against his scalp, his face was clean-shaven, and his lips were compressed into a near snarl.

He motioned me to climb the steps. Once I'd ascended to the porch, he slung the gun on his shoulder. His voice was low and steady as he reached out. "I need to see your bag."

I stepped back.

"If I don't check your bag, you'll have to leave."

I took it from my shoulder and handed it to him. He opened it and poked around with his gloved hand. The man gave it back and said, "I need to pat you down."

"Seriously?"

He nodded.

I placed my bag on the wooden floor of the porch, spread my stance, and lifted my arms. I was pleasantly surprised by the professional manner with which he checked to see if I was carrying a weapon. I would have bet money that he'd take the opportunity to grope something, but he didn't. When he was finished, he stepped to the edge of the railing and looked up at the sky. Shaking his head, he said, "Okay, let's go inside."

The interior of the house was a glorified log cabin—wood grain walls, thick beams in the vaulted ceiling, hardwood floor. There was a fire flickering in the stone fireplace. Deer antlers hung over the mantel. Two fabric-covered couches and two easy chairs populated the living room. An Oriental throw rug lay in the middle of the floor, and in front of one of the couches stood an oak coffee table laden with magazines. I noted that one of them was *Guns & Ammo.*

I was mildly surprised to see an artificial Christmas tree, decorated and gaily lit, off to one side of the room. There were already some presents tucked away underneath.

A woman in her late thirties emerged from the doorway to the kitchen. She had long brown hair pulled back into a ponytail. She might have been pretty once. But that was many years ago. Her face was an unsmiling mask of resolution, and she had the air of toughness about her, made even more harsh by the lack of any makeup. Her green eyes were wary, suspicious, her mouth compressed, expressionless. She wore a turtleneck sweater and black jeans and came toward me carrying a steaming cup of coffee. She extended her hand. "I'm Bristol Finn."

I took her hand in my own. "I'm Genie Chase."

Bristol nodded to the man standing behind me, AR-15 still slung from his shoulder. "This is Karl."

No last name. That worked for me. I learned later that his full name was Karl Lerner, formerly an Army Ranger who had managed to become Merlin Finn's right-hand man.

I gave him a curt bob of the head while he took off his sunglasses, placed them on the top of his head, and studied me one more time. I tossed him a hello. "Hey, Karl."

Bristol's eyes formed narrow slits as she appraised me. "What are you here for?" She had a slight Southern lilt to her words.

I glanced back at Karl again, then answered, "I've been covering the death of Judge Niles Preston. The police tell me that Merlin Finn is a person of interest. I'd like to get some background information about him."

She put the cup of coffee to her lips and sipped. "What makes you think I can tell you anything about Merlin Finn?"

"You're his wife."

"He never told me much about what he was up to." She attempted a tiny grin.

"So you didn't know that he headed up a criminal organization."

She shot a glance at Karl. "I had my suspicions. He wasn't up here much, and that was okay by me." Bristol glided away from me and sat down in one of the chairs, coffee mug still clutched in her hand. "You want to sit down?"

I stole one more look at Karl, who had apparently lost interest in me and was staring out the window. I sat on the couch closest to Bristol. "Do you know where Mr. Finn is?"

Karl might have been focused on the driveway, but he was listening. His words came out loud. "We do not. And if we did, we sure as hell wouldn't tell a reporter."

"Of course. Does Mr. Finn have any family?"

Bristol nodded. "I told this to the FBI when they came to talk to us. He doesn't have any brothers and sisters, and his mother passed away when he was only eleven. But his father is still alive, and Merlin was always close with him. If anyone knows where Merlin is hiding, it would be his dad. I think he still lives in White Plains."

"Did you ever visit Mr. Finn while he was in prison?"

Karl answered. His reply was simple but emphatic. "No."

"So you had no way of knowing that he was planning to break out of Lockport?"

He studied me. "I hear things. Word was he was organizing with the Brotherhood on the inside and some of his old crew on the outside. There was an investigation that said the Brotherhood was behind his escape. I saw it on the news."

I had my phone out, hit the record app, and placed it on the seat next to me. It was less intimidating than my recorder. I focused on Bristol again. "Do you know a man by the name of Jim Caviness?"

She jerked slightly as if hit with a tiny static electrical shock. Bristol cleared her throat. "He's that man that got burned up by his wife."

I leaned forward. "Did he come by here every so often?"

Like nearly every week?

I heard Karl's steps across the hardwood floor until he got to the throw rug, where he stopped, looking down at me. "Jim Caviness was one of Wolfline's crew."

Sometimes it's best to act dumb. "Wolfline, what's that?"

He took a breath, pondering how much to share with me.

Finally, he took the weapon off his shoulder, and sat down on the couch facing me, placing the AR-15 on the seat next to him, barrel aimed at the doorway. He pointed to my phone, recording our conversation. "Turn that off. This is all off the record."

I reluctantly reached over and made a show of turning it off and putting back in my bag. "Okay."

"Wolfline Contracting, it's a front for the Russian Mafia."

"Russian Mafia?" I repeated.

Karl scratched the back of his neck. "This better be off the record, Reporter. I don't want this showin' up in any newspaper, understand?"

I nodded. "Guaranteed."

"Up until Merlin killed two of their dope dealers, we did contract work for Wolfline."

"How many of you are there?"

"Our chapter of the Brotherhood?" He silently counted in his head. "Twenty when Merlin was still running the show. Maybe there's half that now."

"What happened?"

"When Merlin went to prison, some of the Brotherhood decided it was better to go to work directly for the Russians."

Bristol spoke up. "Up until Merlin busted out of prison. That's a game-changer. If he finds the men who turned on him, he'll kill them."

I wanted to move the conversation back to Wolfline. "So before Merlin killed those two men, Jim Caviness would stop here every week?"

She frowned. "How do you know how often he came here?"

Crap.

I shrugged. "I have my sources, same as the cops."

Bristol studied me. "Our cut. Jim would bring by the Brotherhood's cut for the week."

"Cut of what?"

Karl growled again. "This better not see the light of day, Reporter."

I held up my hand and shook my head. "All off the record."

Bristol explained. "Drug sales, mostly. Prostitution, gambling. We're out of that now. Laying low."

"How are you paying for your groceries?"

Karl raised his chin and gave me a cocky look. "We have money set aside, investments and such."

Bristol offered, "And I own this house outright. When Merlin bought it, he put it in my name. Said if he ever got busted for something, we'd keep possession of the house."

"Tell me a little bit about Merlin Finn."

Karl and Bristol glanced at each other. She took a breath. "We met when I was dancing at Ivan's."

"The club in Bridgeport?" I purposely didn't call it a strip club. As I studied her, I wasn't sure I could visualize her as a stripper in a seedy bar.

She nodded. "Merlin's boys worked security there. Merlin and me started going out. I think I was attracted to him because he had everyone's respect. When he gave an order, men did what he told them to do. There's no question that Merlin's an alpha dog."

"Alpha dog?"

"Alpha dog, top dog. He likes being in charge. But he has a sweet side too."

At that, Karl coughed in derision.

"He does?"

"Back when we were dating, he was always bringing me presents. Clothes, jewelry, once he surprised me with a trip to Nashville. I always wanted to go to Nashville. Back in the day, he could be a big, old teddy bear."

"Does he have a dark side?" *In relationships, there's almost always a yin to the yang.*

She looked down at the floor. "Being an alpha dog means he's very controlling and domineering."

"Domineering?"

Karl leaned forward. "Bristol's being nice. He's a sadistic son of a bitch."

"How so?"

He stood up. "I'll show you." He turned and headed for the kitchen.

An invitation?

I got up from the couch, threw my bag over my shoulder, and followed. Passing through the doorway, I noticed that the cramped kitchen had all the amenities, refrigerator, stove, microwave, dishwasher. There wasn't a lot of counter space, and what there was had been crammed with plastic storage dishes, boxes of rice and instant potatoes, canned vegetables, fruits, and cooked chicken.

Karl was moving fast, and he was already at a doorway on the other side of the room. Along the way, he'd shaken off his camouflage winter coat and tossed it on the back of a kitchen chair. I could see how broad his shoulders and slim his hips were. This was a guy who was in very good shape.

He disappeared through the doorway, and when I caught up, it was to see Karl descending a set of wooden steps. At the bottom, he flipped on a light, and I came down to where he was standing.

Descending, I felt the cold. There wasn't any heat in this part of the house. I was glad I'd kept my coat on.

Getting to the basement, I saw we were in a large storeroom of aisles of metal racks and shelves filled with canned goods, bottles of water, medical supplies, and guns. Lots and lots of guns. Karl stopped and stared at me. "We got everything down here. Merlin even put in an escape tunnel, just in case."

I walked out into the middle of the room, amazed. "Wow. I guess you guys are ready for the zombie apocalypse."

It was the first time I saw Karl grin. He showed me a set of uneven teeth. Once you got by his badass routine, he looked like he could be a big, old-fashioned country boy. He drawled, "Won't be zombies, Reporter. But it's comin'."

Doomsday preppers?

"What's coming?"

Karl nodded slightly. "Race war." He walked by me toward another doorway. "C'mon."

As I followed, I glanced back and saw Bristol slowly coming down the steps. She stopped at the bottom, arms folded, staring wide-eyed at the door where Karl stood waiting. He opened the door and motioned me in.

If I had a concept of hell, that's what I'd call that room.

It was the size of a very large master bedroom. Fluorescent lights showed me cold stone walls and a concrete floor with a drain in the center of the room. There was a toilet and a shower stall in the far corner.

Metal hooks and eyebolts were screwed into the thick beams in the ceiling. Along the walls hung dozens of whips, canes, crops, ropes, chains, and leather restraints. A shelf on the wall to my left contained gas masks and leather hoods.

Just like the hood the killer at the marina wore the night Judge Preston and Abigail Tillis were murdered.

Manacles were attached to a low wooden bench off to my right. Across the room was a wooden structure in the form of an X that I knew was called a St. Andrew's Cross.

The display that chilled me the most was on the wall facing us. Hung by leather straps on metal hooks was an array of metal saws, picks, serrated knives, hooks, and clamps. A simple shelf held several small blowtorches.

I tried to speak but all I could manage was a whisper. "What is this place?"

Bristol came up behind me and stood close, her voice low as well. "This is where he would take me if he felt I needed discipline."

Without thought, I reached out and put my arm around her. She was shivering like a frightened dog. "Did he bring you down here a lot?"

She nodded, sadly staring at the St. Andrew's Cross. "Yes, ma'am, he did."

Karl spoke up. "Show her your back."

I took my arm away from her shoulder, and she turned around, hitching up her sweater so I could see a portion of her skin. It was crisscrossed with dozens of angry, red scars.

"How long were you with him?"

She lowered her sweater and faced me. "Three years."

"She's with me now, we love each other," Karl stated defiantly. "He'll never touch Bristol again."

"Aren't you afraid he'll come here?"

He slowly shook his head. "If he does, I'm ready for him. Trip wires and traps all over these woods."

Bristol touched my arm. "He won't come here, anyway. The cops have the property under surveillance. They want him bad. Anyway, we're movin' soon. I can't stay here anymore."

I took a breath and looked at the cutting tools on the back wall. The bone saws and scalpels made me shudder. "I'm surprised you've stayed here as long as you have."

Karl glanced around him, not answering me. "This house has seen a lot of pain."

"You said you're going to be moving?"

"Right after Merlin went to prison, we put this place on the market. Took a while to find a buyer." She leaned over to whisper to me. "Got a bad reputation, ya know."

"Did you sell it?"

"We did."

"Really?" Who in their right mind would want to live in this house of horrors?

Bristol nodded slightly. "The buyer's attorney is handling the closing. The buyer is a property management company insisting on anonymity. Attorney says the buyer likes the location but is concerned with the notoriety, what with the dungeon and the two men killed up here and all. He says they're planning on turning this place into a hunting resort."

I shivered again.

Buyer must have a strong affection for the macabre.

I chucked my chin at Karl. "You said this place is under surveillance?"

He chuckled. "You didn't notice the repair truck at the bottom of the hill before you turned onto our road? It's been there since Merlin escaped."

No, I hadn't noticed.

"And I'll bet you didn't see the drones?" He pointed toward the ceiling. "There're about a two or three of 'em buzzing around at any one time."

I shook my head. What was it that Mike had told me?

If the FBI has you under surveillance, you'll never know.

But Karl knew.

He frowned. "For a reporter, you're not very observant."

I dismissed his insult. "Did Merlin ever bring anyone else down here?"

The smile on Karl's face vanished, and the color drained from Bristol's face. She nodded. "Those two drug dealers who worked for Wolfline. Merlin claimed they were assassins that the Russians sent to kill him. He brought 'em down here and tortured them. Took him most of the night. There was so much screaming. When he was done playing with them, he killed them and buried the bodies out in the woods."

"Cops find the bodies?"

Bristol nodded and glanced briefly at Karl. "Someone tipped 'em off."

Karl chewed on his lower lip. "They brought in cadaver dogs."

Bristol said something I couldn't quite make out.

"I'm sorry, what did you say?"

She cleared her throat and repeated, more loudly, "He made me come down here the next day to clean up the blood."

Karl spit on the floor. "That son of a bitch will never lay a hand on Bristol again. Not as long as I'm alive."

Chapter Eleven

Leaving the house and stepping out onto the porch, I took a deep breath of the icy air and went to the railing. I gazed up into the ashen sky. My eyes strained as I scanned the expanse above the trees for any evidence of a drone, a mote, a flying speck against the iron-colored clouds.

Seeing nothing, I went down the steps and got into my Sebring. I grabbed my phone out of my bag and saw that Caroline had texted me.

> Condo here in Aspen is fabulous. Right on the side of the mountain. Skiing out the front door. Jess can't stop grinning. Aunt R must have spent a fortune. Wish u were here. Hugs.

I surrendered up a tiny smile. She had gotten there safely. I was sure that Caroline and Jessica were going to have the time of their lives.

And I'm spending Christmas alone.

Glancing up at the stone house, I shuddered at the thought of the torture chamber in the basement. Up there on that hill, tucked back in the woods, no one would ever hear you scream.

I turned up the heat.

When I got to the bottom of that long, dirt road, I looked for the surveillance truck that Karl had mentioned.

Nothing. The road is empty.

I pondered the possibilities. Either the FBI had found Merlin Finn and no longer needed to keep an eye on this place, or Karl and Bristol were paranoid, and the repair truck was just that…a repair truck.

And where were the drones he talked about?

I hoped it was that Finn was under lock and key. Because if the law wasn't watching this property, it made Karl and Bristol vulnerable as hell. And in spite of Karl's bravado, the more I learned about Merlin Finn, the less I wanted to meet him.

Unbidden, my mind flashed onto the video from the marina. Four men in black, Finn wearing the bondage hood.

Would Karl and his AR-15 be any match for Finn and his crew?

I drove back to Sheffield and spent the rest of my workday in the newsroom reading through police reports that outlined the investigation of the murders by Finn of the two dope dealers who allegedly worked for Wolfline. What I read had been sanitized. All it told me was that the two men, Parker Graff and Jason Starnes, both in their twenties, had been tortured, shot to death, then buried in the woods up on Oak Hill.

What it didn't tell me was why. Finn was supposed to have been working for Wolfline. Why did he go rogue? Why kill two of the Russians' men?

What did Bristol say about them? That Merlin claimed they were sent to assassinate him?

I glanced at the clock and then peeked at Lorraine, her eyes plastered to her computer screen. For me, it was quitting time. I had a hunch that for Ms. Moretti, there was no real end to the day. She was corporate through and through.

When I'd been in her office, I noticed that she wasn't wearing a wedding ring.

She's the kind of woman that, if you ask her if she has a husband, she'd say she was married to her job.

I needed a drink.

—

I toyed with the thought of stopping by Brick's for a vodka tonic. Caroline wouldn't be waiting for me and I wasn't anxious to face my empty house alone.

But Tucker was overdue for a walk and I couldn't let the little guy down. Plus, with the new regime running the newspaper, I sure as hell didn't want to get caught boozing alone in a dark bar.

So I parked the car in my driveway, collected my mail from the streetside box, and took a quick peek at a handful of nothing but bills.

Doesn't anyone send Christmas cards anymore?

Unlocking the front door, I was mildly surprised that Tucker wasn't waiting for me. I took off my parka and hung it in the closet, dropped the unopened envelopes on the table in the hallway, and called out. "Tucker. Where are you, buddy?"

Quiet.

Once, while I'd been at work and Caroline had been at school, there'd been a horrible thunderstorm that had swept through off Long Island Sound and across western Connecticut. The lightning and thunder display had been magnificently terrifying. When I got home that evening, I found Tucker hiding under my bed.

Is that where you are? Under my bed?

But there had been no storm, nothing to have frightened my terrier.

"Tucker. Where are you, little guy?"

I took a half-empty pint bottle of Absolut out of my bag and trudged up the carpeted steps to the second floor, flipping on the hall light when I got to the top step.

Silence.

I stopped at Caroline's room, turned on the light, peered in.

I miss her.

Bed neatly made, laptop closed, stuffed toys on the dresser. As a rule, she wasn't this tidy. I went to the closet and opened it. I was greeted with a pile of dirty clothes as high as my hips.

Ugh. That's my girl.

Turning off the light, I went back out into the hallway.

"Tucker, c'mon, buddy. Want to go for a walk?"

Silence.

I got to my bedroom and flipped on the light. "Tucker?"

Almost before I stepped into the room, I saw the little dog squirming out from under my bed, tail wagging cautiously, ears pinned back. Stooping down, I swept his tiny body up into my arms. I felt Tucker shivering, vibrating, as I held him.

"What's the matter, buddy? You okay?" I looked him over, felt his fur to make sure he hadn't hurt himself. I didn't find anything out of place. "What's got you spooked?" I placed him on the top of my bed, sat down next to him, and pulled off my leather boots. Tucker pressed against me, climbing onto my lap, still shuddering uncontrollably. "Poor baby."

I scratched him behind his ears and petted him until his waves of shivering slowed and finally ceased. "I'll be right back." I picked up the pint bottle of vodka I'd brought upstairs with me and saw that it had enough left for another drink or two. With Caroline out of the house, I could have gone downstairs to the kitchen for ice, but I wanted that drink right then. Using the glass on the headboard of the bed, I poured two fingers and took a healthy swallow.

The familiar feeling of heat sliding down my stomach, warming my tummy, spreading through my core like the embrace of an old lover. I was at peace.

Until I saw it.

The pile of books on my nightstand was wrong. The book on top should have been a book of short stories, *Allegiance and*

Betrayal by Peter Makuck. I'd been reading it last night before I turned off the light to go to sleep. Instead, the book on the top of the stack was *The Bully Pulpit* by Doris Kearns Goodwin.

My heart started slamming against my rib cage.

I put the glass down and peered around the room.

Is there anything else out of place?

The bookshelf next to the closet. The books were wrong, not where they were this morning.

I took in every detail of the room. Nothing obvious seemed amiss. I went to the closet and slid open the door. Everything was hung where I'd put it.

Or is it? Shouldn't my blue floral dress be next to that pink top?

I went quickly to my bathroom and studied the countertop. Vitamins, mouthwash, tweezers, makeup, toothbrush, toothpaste, deodorant—all where they were supposed to be.

My reflection stared back at me from the mirror on my cabinet. My eyes were wide, I looked scared. Swinging open the door, I looked inside at the lipsticks, eyeliner, box of Band-Aids, ointments, and creams.

Where's the Vicodin?

Just before I moved to Sheffield, I was supplanting my doses of vodka and wine with a few pills every day. Then I woke up one morning in a pool of my own vomit.

That was even too much for me. I swore off the pills but kept the half a bottle of Vicodin thinking that I might need it one day. It was woefully out of date.

But now it's gone.

I turned and looked at Tucker, sitting, staring at me from the top of my bed. My heart was pounding.

Was someone here? Is that why you were hiding under the bed?

I stepped back into the bedroom, and my eyes went automatically to my black wooden jewelry box. Flipping it open, I saw that everything appeared to be there. Not that I owned anything expensive.

Then my stomach dropped.

The goddamn notebook hidden in the freezer!

I picked the dog up, tucked him under my arm like a football, fled down the hallway, flew to the ground floor. Stepping into the kitchen in my stocking feet, I felt the water before I saw it.

Puddles all over the floor.

Holy shit.

A set of silver handcuffs dangled from the door handle.

S&M jewelry.

My heart did a slow roll.

Fucking Merlin Finn.

I carefully placed Tucker on the floor and went to the refrigerator.

I thought my hiding place for Jim Caviness's notebook was brilliant. Tucked into a ziplock plastic bag and hidden under the cache of ice cubes in the container under the icemaker.

I opened the freezer. Air caught in my throat when I saw there was nothing in the box. He'd emptied all the ice onto the floor.

Merlin Finn's got the notebook.

Chapter Twelve

"Any idea why Merlin Finn would break into your house?" Mike Dillon and I sat in my living room on my couch, next to each other, while his people dusted for prints and photographed the interior of my home. A B&E like this, with nothing of value taken, wouldn't have warranted such scrutiny, but this was Merlin Finn, and the cops wanted him badly.

I did, of course, know why he broke into my house. Somehow, while he was in prison, he'd heard that Jim Caviness had been killed by his wife. Before going rogue, Finn worked for Wolfline. Indeed, Caviness brought him the Brotherhood's cut of Wolfline's action on a regular basis. He must have known that Caviness kept a notebook and it was the key to bringing down the Russians.

But how did he know that I had it?

I shook my head and lied. "No clue."

Mike frowned. "Other than the story you wrote about the murders at the marina, do you have any other connection with him?"

Tucker had long ceased shaking with fear and he was comfortably curled up on my lap while I stroked his fur. "I don't know. I visited his wife today."

Mike's eyebrows knitted together as he thought. "Do you think she threw you under the bus?"

I shrugged. "It appears that she has a new boyfriend now, and from what the two of them told me, they don't have a whole lot of love for Merlin Finn. They told me that they thought the property they're on was being watched by the FBI. Maybe they're not the only ones watching who comes and goes up there."

Mike reached over and gave Tucker an affectionate scratch behind the ears. "Maybe. What do you think Finn was looking for?"

Visualizing how Tucker had been alone in the house with Merlin Finn made the hair on the back of my neck stand up. "Don't know," I lied. "I'm missing a bottle of Vicodin. Maybe he was looking for drugs."

He chuckled. "I doubt that was his primary goal. He can lay his hands on all the drugs he wants. Maybe he just wanted to spook you."

I glanced into the kitchen where I could see the refrigerator through the doorway. The cops hadn't unlocked the handcuffs and taken them down yet. They glimmered in the bright kitchen lights. "It worked."

We both turned as Officer Christine Fuller opened the front door and came in, still in her SPD winter coat. She glanced at me but quickly directed her attention to Mike. "We talked with the neighbors."

He stood up. "Anything?"

She took a tiny notebook out of her pocket and consulted it. "Only one was home when the break-in occurred. Mrs. Pohoresky, 1203 Random Road, right next door, saw a van pull up at about three p.m. She told me that the logo on the side of the van said it was Gold Coast Exterminating Service. Mrs. Pohoresky says she saw two men get out. Didn't see them clearly enough to give me a description other than they were both Caucasian and the one getting out of the driver's side was, in her words, a really big guy."

Still holding Tucker, I stood up. "Could she see any tattoos on the big guy's face?"

Officer Fuller shook her head slightly. "She just couldn't get a good look. But then again, she didn't give them much thought." The cop smiled sheepishly at me. "She said she wasn't really surprised that a pest control company was coming to your house. I'm afraid Mrs. Pohoresky doesn't think much of your housekeeping skills."

Involuntarily, I glanced around the living room. There was a stack of newspapers next to the couch, a little dust on the end tables, but that was it. No used pizza boxes or half-empty Chinese food takeout containers or cockroaches. Mrs. Pohoresky was just being a bitch.

Mike grinned. "Did she say anything about how long they were here?"

"She wasn't sure. Thought they might have been here an hour, maybe longer."

Dear God, what if Caroline had been here?

He focused on me again. "Are you sure that the only thing they took was a bottle of pills?"

"You and I went through the house, top to bottom and I didn't see anything obvious that might be missing." Mike had accompanied me while I searched the house. The one place I didn't poke into was my underwear drawer in the bedroom dresser. It was where I hid my vodka. That bottle was from last night and nearly full.

Didn't want Mike to see my stash.

I glanced nervously around the living room. "Have you figured how they got in?"

Mike nodded. "Scratches around the lock on your back door indicate they probably picked their way in. Look, how about if I have an officer park out in front of your house tonight?"

I noticed that he didn't offer to spend the night like he had when someone shot through my front window back in October. I smiled and answered, "I think I'm going to pack a bag and stay in a pet-friendly hotel for the night."

Mike reached out and gave Tucker another scratch. "Sheffield Inn takes dogs."

I gently touched the top of his hand. "Thanks."

—

After the police left, I went upstairs and packed an overnight bag. When I was done, I pulled open my panty drawer to pour myself a quick drink.

A scrap of paper was on top of my underwear.

Sitting on top of the Absolut, nestled in my silk panties.

For the second time that afternoon, my heart nearly stopped. A handwritten note:

I'm going to make you model these for me.

My heart thumped against my rib cage. I nervously glanced around the bedroom, even though Mike and I had searched through it only minutes ago.

Icy fingers of fear tickled the back of my neck.

I skipped the drink and tossed the bottle and a random jumble of clothes into an overnight bag. Then I pulled on my boots and hurried downstairs with alternating waves of terror and rage. The man had touched my things, my most *intimate goddamned* things.

I'm going to have to throw all of that away.

I threw on my parka, and meaning to put my suitcase in the car and then come back for Tucker, I opened the front door.

John Stillwater stood on my front porch.

His hand out, ready to push the doorbell.

I was too stunned to speak.

John took up the slack. "Hey, Genie." He glanced down at the bag in my hand. "Going somewhere?"

I could hear the stress in my own voice when I answered,

"Merlin Finn broke into my house. I can't stay here tonight. I'm going to a hotel."

"Did he get the notebook?"

The shock made me jerk backward.

Up until tonight, nobody knew I had that notebook except for Betsy Caviness. Somehow Merlin Finn figured it out.

And now John Stillwater.

How?

He managed a small, boyish smile and turned up his collar. "Can I come in? It's awfully cold out here."

I waved him in through the door. He spent the first few seconds glancing around, studying the living room. "No Christmas tree?"

I eyeballed the room, bereft of decorations. "Not yet," I whispered.

John was dressed in an insulated black leather coat, fur collar up, black leather gloves on his hands. He was hatless, and his dark-brown hair was disheveled and tousled by the wind. He slipped off his gloves, pushed them into the pockets of his coat, and raked one hand through his hair.

I was still stunned that he was there.

He focused his eyes on me. "So?"

I blinked in confusion. "So, what?"

He cocked his head. "Did Merlin Finn get the notebook?"

"What notebook?"

John shook his head and frowned. "Betsy Caviness doesn't have any family or friends. Not wanting to be a target of the Tolbonovs, Betsy's attorney was very vocal about not having it. The logical conclusion is Betsy sent it to you. It appears that Merlin Finn figured that out as well. So the big question is, did he get it?"

I bit my lip. "Yes."

He sighed, and his expression fell in disappointment.

"But I have a photographic copy on a thumb drive."

His face brightened, and he grinned. "You are a brilliant woman."

"He found my hiding place. I don't feel particularly brilliant."

I glanced down and saw Tucker seated next to my left foot. After the home invasion, I didn't think he wanted to be very far away from me. "Look, John, any other time, I'd ask you in for a drink and to catch up. But I'm kind of rattled. I think I'm going to check into a hotel and crawl under the covers for the night."

He glanced at his watch, then looked at me through his black-rimmed glasses. "How about this? We drive into the city, and you stay with Shana. I know she'd love to see you. Then in the morning, bright and early, we drive back here."

I knew that unless there was an accident on I-95, it was a forty-five-minute trip to New York, but it wasn't rush hour, and we were doing a reverse commute. And perhaps I could stall John's return and see Nathaniel Rubin from Lodestar Analytics in the morning.

And maybe Merlin Finn's father in Westchester?

Chapter Thirteen

As we drove, wet snowflakes the size of dimes fell in front of our headlights and slapped against the windshield only to be pushed aside by the wiper blades. I noticed that John was checking his rearview mirror more often than normal. I turned and looked out the back window of his all-black Mustang, staring at anonymous sets of headlights behind us. "Is there anything back there I should know about?"

He smiled slightly, his face faintly illuminated by the dash lights. "Not sure."

"Perfect." My voice was a little more sarcastic than I thought it would be. In my defense, it had been a stressful day, and the thought of someone tailing us wasn't helpful. I glanced around the interior of the car. Everything looked and smelled brand new. Plus, heaven, the seats were heated. "Nice ride."

His grin grew larger. "Less than a month off the showroom floor. It's got a five-liter V-8 engine with a manual six-speed transmission. They say she'll do zero to sixty in under four seconds. I haven't tried it."

I gently felt the soft leather of my bucket seat. "Yeah, this car fits you."

I heard him chuckle. "This car isn't mine. It belongs to Shana.

I own a Lexus hybrid. Gets over fifty miles a gallon. This car is a little too conspicuous for my taste."

"Then why are we driving it?"

John glanced up at the mirror again. "When I came up here to see if the Jane Doe was Abby, she said that it might be a good idea to have something with a little horsepower."

I needed to make myself feel more in control of my environment, more like myself. "Hey, I want to talk to you about Abby Tillis. But first, I've got to call my boss and tell him I'm going to be late tomorrow."

He looked confused. "I can easily have you back to your office by nine."

I rolled my eyes. "Before we go back to Connecticut, I'm going to need to make a pit stop." I rambled around in my bag until I found my phone. Then I punched up Ben's personal number. After the fourth ring, he picked up.

"Genie? What's up?"

"I'm going to be late tomorrow morning. I need for you to let Lorraine Moretti know."

"Oh, she's not going to be happy about that."

I know.

"Grow a pair, Ben. You're still in charge of the newspaper until January first."

He was silent for a moment. "Okay. Why are you going to be late? Do you have a real reason or are you just trying to see how far you can push the new regime?"

I glanced over at John, his eyes still on a busy I-95. I knew he could hear both sides of the conversation.

I answered, "The guy who the cops think killed Judge Preston and Abby Tillis out at Groward Bay? He broke into my house this afternoon. I'm spending the night with friends in the city."

"Are you okay? Is Caroline all right?"

"She's in Aspen. Nobody was home except for Tucker." I glanced back at the puppy quietly snoozing in his carrier.

Holy crap, I still need to call Caroline.

I continued. "I don't feel safe in my house. And tomorrow, on the way back, I want to get a statement from Merlin Finn's father."

John's eyebrows shot up when he heard that.

Ben was silent for a moment. "Okay, Genie. Do you think that's a good idea? This Finn guy sounds bad. No story is worth getting hurt over."

"Thanks, boss. I'll watch my back."

I hit the End Call button and then considered calling Caroline. Glancing at the time on the smartphone screen, it told me that it was only six fifteen. Still plenty of time to call her once I got to New York.

John glanced at me. "Tell me what you know about Merlin Finn."

I spent the next fifteen minutes telling him what I saw in the video from the night of the murders. I described the transcriptions from the trial that sent Finn to prison and what I knew about the escape. Then I talked about my trip to Brockton, up on Oak Hill, my discussion with Bristol and Karl, and the torture chamber Finn had in the basement.

John asked the occasional question but was silent the entire time I talked about Oak Hill. He cleared his throat. "You said they sold the place?"

"Yes."

"Seems to me it would have been easier to sell if they'd emptied the dungeon and turned it into a family room or something."

I shrugged. "I got the feeling that Bristol Finn didn't want to get anywhere near that room again." I changed the subject. "What was Abby Tillis doing in Connecticut?"

He gave me a quick look and then turned his attention back to the traffic ahead of him. "After Finn escaped from prison, Judge Preston got spooked. He knew that Finn would be coming for him. He called the Friends of Lydia."

I frowned. "Why did he call the Friends?"

"He needed someone motivated enough to keep him safe. Someone who wasn't afraid to break the law if it was needed. Shana was the first to hear from him. He knew her from when she bailed Betsy Caviness out of jail."

The Friends of Lydia had posted the million-dollar bond after her arrest for torching her husband. There was no way she could have done it on her own. Betsy Caviness literally did not have a pot to piss in.

"Preston was dirty, wasn't he? He was working for the Tolbonovs. Didn't Preston think the Russians could keep him safe from Merlin Finn?"

John's attention was drawn by something he noticed in the rear-view mirror. He accelerated. "Is Preston's name in the notebook?"

"The notebook was in some weird Jim Caviness code. It was hard to decipher. There were a few notations with Judge P in them. After the homicides in the marina, I put two and two together and figured out that the judge was taking payoffs."

He continued to split his time studying the road in front of the car and glancing up at the mirror. Jerking into the passing lane and stepping on the gas, he answered, "The Tolbonovs are very, very smart. They didn't use the judge very often. Just when they thought he could quash a case without giving himself away."

I turned and glanced out the back window. Not seeing what was spooking John, I glanced down at the plastic critter carrier in the back seat. Tucker was oblivious, obviously weary from the home invasion earlier that day. I turned back and faced John. "That's what happened at the Del Randall trial. Preston ruled there was insufficient evidence."

"That's right." John picked up speed.

"What's back there?" I twisted around and stared hard, looking for what had John concerned.

He slowly shook his head. "Don't know. There's a beamer a few cars back, pacing us."

"So if Preston's tight with the Tolbonovs, why wouldn't they keep him safe?"

He gave me a quick glance. "Word on the street was that the Tolbonovs are restructuring Wolfline, changing up the chess pieces. They're worried that someone has Caviness's notebook and is using it against them."

I felt tiny tendrils of guilt and anxiety twist around my gut. "What made them think someone was using the notebook against them?"

John knows I had the notebook. He knows it's me.

"Their drug dealers work in pairs. One is the front, selling and dispensing merchandise. The other acts as a lookout. One night, someone with a camera staked out one of Wolfline's dealers. The lookout was posing as a homeless man and spotted the surveillance."

Damn it.

That night on Edison Avenue, I'd staked out Travis Monk in his shiny black Escalade and taken photos right up until a smelly, old street creep came up to my car begging for money.

He was the lookout.

John gave me the eye. "That was you, wasn't it?"

I changed the subject. "Because of that, the Tolbonovs cut the judge loose?"

"Actually, I think they were using him as bait. Give me a minute. We're going to take a short detour."

When he accelerated, I sank back in my bucket seat like I'd been pushed back by an invisible hand. John pulled up close to the rear end of a Volvo SUV directly ahead of us and then cut fast to the right, sliding quickly across the middle lane into the right-hand lane, cutting off traffic, nearly hitting the front end of a Jeep Wrangler.

The Jeep's horn blared.

John continued his fast drift to the right as we fell into the exit lane for Mamaroneck Avenue, and we were off the highway, travelling at sixty miles per hour. He braked hard to slow for the sharp curve, eyeballing his mirror. "Whoever was tailing us never got out of the passing lane."

I stared at him with wide eyes, adrenaline pumping through my veins. "That's where I left my heart."

"Sorry. I saw the opening and took it. Better to be safe than sorry."

My heart *was* still in my chest, beating a samba against my rib cage. "Safe, that's the word, John. Safe."

We stopped at the bottom of the ramp, waiting for the red light. John kept his eye on the mirror, watching to see who came up behind us. "We'll get right back on the highway."

"Who do you think might be tailing us?"

John shrugged. "The Russians, the Brotherhood, the feds. Between the two of us, we have a lot of people interested in what we're doing."

My blood pressure was nearing normal again. "You said that the Tolbonovs were using Preston as bait?"

"That's what he told Shana. He thought the Tolbonovs were letting him dangle, trying to smoke Merlin Finn out of his hiding place. And worst-case scenario, Finn takes care of the judge and ties up a Tolbonov loose end."

The light turned green, and John rolled through the intersection and got right back onto the on-ramp to I-95 South. "Shana sent Abby Tillis to protect him?"

He accelerated into traffic. "Abby was going to take him to Hartford. We have a safe house there. In return, he was going to give us evidence against the Tolbonovs."

"But it all went south."

He nodded in silence.

"Did Preston's wife know about any of this?"

He glanced over at me. "He was going to bring her to Hartford with him. The night it was all supposed to go down, Eva Preston got cold feet."

"Wait a minute. She told me that Preston was having an affair and she thought he was going out that night to meet with his mistress."

John nodded slowly. "All bullshit. That's her line to the cops. I'll let Shana fill you in on all that."

"Eva Preston lied to me? She lied to the police?"

Did Eva Preston betray her husband to Merlin Finn?

I exhaled while mulling that over. "Sorry. How well did you know her? You know, Abby Tillis."

He was very quiet for a moment. Then he cleared his throat as if he had something caught there. When he answered, his voice was low and steady. "Abby Tillis was my ex-wife."

Chapter Fourteen

John made his call on the car's hands-free system. "Shana?"

"Hi, John, where are you?" Her voice was low, parsing every word like it was something of value, accented by the slightest hint of a sophisticated Southern lilt.

"We're on the FDR. I'm maybe ten minutes out, depending on traffic."

"Gerald will be waiting for you in the lobby."

"See you soon."

When they disconnected, I asked, "Who's Gerald?"

John grinned. "Shana's manservant."

My laugh burst out as an explosive guffaw. "What?"

"I know, right?" He eased us off the highway onto I-495 Midtown.

As he turned right on East Thirty-Fourth Street, I watched the lights and the buildings go by until we got to Sixth Avenue. Finding our destination, he slowed and stopped in front of a four-story brick walk-up. The building was fronted by the Golden Dragon Chinese Restaurant and Arthur's Fine Liquors. Looking up and down the block, I could easily see there was no place to park.

Still in the street, John put the Mustang in park, letting the car idle. He opened his door and said, "We're here."

I opened my door, got out, and pulled my overnight bag out of the back seat. John lifted Tucker's carrier out and hustled to the curb, which was covered in gray city slush that was once snow.

As we moved across the sidewalk, a tall man in his thirties, clean-shaven, wearing a blue stocking cap and black ankle-length overcoat, burst out of a doorway nestled discreetly between the restaurant and the liquor store.

Walking past him but not stopping, John nodded and mumbled, "Hey, Gerald."

The man nodded back but never slowed down. "Mr. Stillwater."

I turned and glanced behind me. Gerald hopped into the driver's side of the Mustang and smoothly glided off. "Where's he going?"

John opened the metal door for me. "Shana rents space in a garage where she keeps her other vehicles. It's about four blocks from here."

"How's Gerald getting back?"

John shrugged. "He usually hoofs it unless the weather is really nasty. Then he'll catch a cab or take an Uber."

We went through a narrow corridor until we got to the elevator. John pressed a code into a keypad mounted on the wall. The door slid open, and we got in. The elevator had an Up-and-Down button and another keypad. He tapped in another code, and the door closed.

"The only way to get to the fourth floor is with the code," he explained.

"What happens if you push the Up button?"

"It takes you to the second floor where you're greeted by a receptionist." He glanced at his watch. "But I think the place is closed for the night."

"The place?"

"This place, the Tower."

I frowned and was about to ask him what the hell he was talking about, but the short elevator ride ended, the door slid open, and we stepped out into a spacious living room. The floor was polished hardwood, and the walls were red brick. Dark-brown timbers served as ceiling beams. A black leather sofa and two tan cloth chairs faced a blazing, cast-iron fireplace embedded in the wall. Off to one side of the large room was a bank of tall windows that overlooked the street below.

A ten-foot, gaily decorated, festively illuminated Christmas tree stood in a corner of the large room.

Am I the only one who hasn't decorated at all this year?

Shana was seated in one of the chairs, leaning forward, tapping away at her laptop that sat on a small table in front of her. She looked up at us and smiled. A man I didn't recognize sat on the couch, nursing a glass of red wine.

Shana Neese was nearly as tall as I am. She was five nine, athletically trim, African American, with layered raven hair that framed her sculpted cheekbones, perfect lips, and classically beautiful face. Wide brown eyes fixed on my face, and she stood up. "Genie Chase, it's so nice to see you again."

She wore a white long-sleeved top and black, fitted jeans. Shana came close and gave me a hug. I could feel the strength in her muscular arms and shoulders.

"Thank you for letting me stay here tonight."

Her grin widened. "I have more than enough space."

I glanced at the stranger, who by then was also standing. He was about six three and very thin. He boasted a full head of hair gone silver, though I guessed his age to be in his early forties. He blinked at me through wire-frame glasses. The man wore a dark-blue button-down shirt, red bow tie, black slacks, and black dress shoes.

Shana noticed my line of sight. "I took the liberty of inviting a friend of mine to have dinner with us tonight. Geneva Chase, meet Nathaniel Rubin."

He held out his right hand for me to shake. As I did so, I noted the watch on his left wrist. It was a Breitling easily worth several thousand dollars. "Nice to meet you, Mr. Rubin."

Digging up dirt must pay well.

"Please, call me Nathaniel." His words tumbled out in a blur.

I glanced back at Shana.

She shrugged. "John told me that you're thinking about taking a position with Nathaniel's company, and since you were going to be here tonight, I thought this would at least give you two a chance to get to know each other in a social setting." Then she looked at John and the critter carrier he was still holding. "Is that Tucker?"

I grinned. "That's Tucker."

She went over and opened the door to the container. While cooing at him, she took my terrier out of his box and held him to her cheek. All the while, his tail flapped happily back and forth.

"He loves being the center of attention."

Shana gave me a sideways look. "So do I."

I snuck another glance at Nathaniel.

This isn't awkward at all.

The elevator door opened again, and Gerald entered the room, taking off his knit cap as he did.

Shana remarked. "That was fast."

I took the opportunity to get a better look at Shana Neese's manservant. Attractive, blue eyes, brown hair cut tight to his scalp, rugged features, full lips, wide shoulders. He answered, "I took an Uber back. I thought you'd be ready for me to serve dinner."

She flashed him a smile. "Yes, tell us what you've prepared for us, Gerald."

"Prosciutto-wrapped asparagus as a starter. The entrée is lemon red snapper in herbed butter on a bed of brown rice. If you have room for dessert, I picked up a raspberry chocolate cheesecake at Bouchard's while I was out shopping this afternoon."

"Nicely done, Gerald. Before you serve dinner, be a dear and take John's and Geneva's coats."

Before he took off his own coat, he helped us out of ours, draping them over his arm and hanging them in the closet.

Shana stepped up to me. "Would you like a glass of wine before dinner? I just opened a lovely pinot grigio."

You bet.

My nerves were still jangling from discovering a killer had gone through my dainties in my house, so my preference would have been a strong glass of Absolut. But I responded enthusiastically. "I'd kill for a glass of wine right now."

Shana glanced at Gerald, who was just returning from the closet. "Get Miss Geneva a glass of wine and Mr. Stillwater a Dewar's over ice."

"Of course."

I watched Gerald disappear into the kitchen.

I want one of those.

—

As I cut into my snapper, I glanced back at the living room. Pointing with my fork, I asked, "There's a single photograph in a silver frame on your mantel. There are two little girls hugging each other. Are you one of them?"

Her usually fiercely bright eyes faded for a moment. "My sister and me."

"Lydia?" I wished I hadn't brought it up.

"Yes." It was simply said before she took a sip of her pinot.

I knew that Shana Neese was the driving force behind the organization called the Friends of Lydia. Their alcoholic father had sold Lydia when she was only sixteen to a pimp who eventually beat her to death with a broomstick. The FOL was an underground vigilante group of volunteers dedicated to helping women, particularly minors, who were enslaved by sex traffickers as well as women who were victims of domestic abuse.

Changing the subject, Nathaniel offered, "Shana told me that you had a visit from the infamous Merlin Finn."

I nodded. "He even left me a token of affection, a nice, shiny pair of handcuffs dangling from my freezer door." I sipped my wine, then quickly added, "Oh, and a handwritten note in my underwear drawer that said he wanted to make me model my panties for him."

Shana nearly spit her words. "Bastard."

John finished chewing. "The handcuffs on the freezer were a nice touch. It was where Genie had hidden the notebook."

Shana leaned in. "Finn has it?"

I sighed. "Guess I wasn't as clever as I thought. I should have put it into a safe deposit box at my bank."

John smiled. "But you are very clever, Geneva Chase. You made a copy."

Nathaniel had been silent, following the conversation. I guessed that at some point before we'd arrived, he'd been informed about the mysterious notebook and what it might contain. He said, "It may not do Merlin Finn's organization any good anyway. From what I hear, over the last month, the Tolbonovs have been shutting down most of their illegal operations and going legit."

Shana sat back, gazing at Nathaniel with skepticism. "I'll believe that when I see it."

I was curious. "Why are they shifting gears?"

Nathaniel cut into his fish and speared a piece. "Two reasons. One, the feds have them so bottled up, they can't breathe. And they were always concerned about the notebook falling into the wrong hands. It appears as if those concerns were warranted."

I studied him carefully. He had an awful lot of information about the Russians. "How do you know all this?"

Nathaniel gestured toward John.

He answered, "Just like anyone else, they leave digital footprints."

"You've been hacking into their computers?"

"I've been tapping into their emails."

"They aren't encrypting them?"

John took a sip of his scotch. "If they're seriously going legit, they're not worried about someone looking over their shoulder."

I wasn't convinced the Tolbonovs would ever go straight. "Is it possible that's what they want you to think?"

John answered. "It's possible. But I'm also seeing an increase in Aryan Brotherhood activity. They're filling the void that the Russians are leaving behind."

"Do you think the Tolbonovs already know that Finn has the notebook?"

Nathaniel popped a forkful of fish into his mouth, chewed quickly, and swallowed. "Bad news travels fast, Genie."

I was gripped by an immediate attack of fear. "Is Betsy Caviness safe?"

Shana looked serious. "I hope so. I hope the Tolbonovs understand that it wasn't her fault that the notebook fell into Finn's hands."

Then I realized that I might be their target. "How about me?"

John reached over and put his hand on mine. I liked the feel of his skin on mine. He said, "With your permission, I'd like to be your insurance policy."

"What's that mean?" The feel of his warm hand was soothing.

"For the next week or two, I'm going to be your personal bodyguard."

Nathaniel frowned at John. "And the project you're working on for me?"

John grinned at him. "I'll have my laptop and my phone with me. Have I ever let you down?"

Nathaniel focused on me. "There's a very large corporation that, for tonight, will remain nameless. They want to hire a well-known businessman for their CEO, but there have been rumors that he might have a history of sexual impropriety. They'd like us to find out one way or another if those rumors are true."

I took another sip of wine. "Is that what Lodestar is all about? Finding out if old rich guys are groping the help?"

He didn't appear to take offense. "It's about saving this company millions of dollars in potential litigation as well as saving its employees pain and humiliation. And that's not all that we do, Genie. We don't just do work for corporations, governments, and political parties. We do plenty of pro bono work." He pointed a fork toward Shana. "Such as the Friends of Lydia."

She smiled and nodded. "Thank you, Nathaniel."

He continued, now singling out John. "I'll tell you what. I'll not worry about the project if you persuade Genie to come work for me."

My heart began to race.

Did I just get a job offer?

I stammered. "I'm sorry? What did you say?"

He grinned. "Come work for me, Geneva Chase. It'll be the best move you'll ever make."

"When?"

"As soon as possible. I'm sure you'll want to give your ungrateful new employers some time to replace you. Although replacing you will be next to impossible. How about for the sake of propriety, we give Galley Media three weeks? Is it a deal?"

Wow, moving fast.

"Why, yes. Three weeks sounds right."

Slow it down, Genie.

I added, "I'd like to talk with my ward before I give my notice. I'll be talking with her tonight."

He sat back in his chair and held up his wineglass. "Of course. Welcome to Lodestar Analytics."

Chapter Fifteen

After dinner and a small portion of the sinfully delicious cheesecake, John and Nathaniel left for their own apartments. "I'm your bodyguard tonight, Genie," Shana had whispered. "Nobody will hurt you while you're staying here at the Tower."

When she said it, her shoulder grazed mine.

I suddenly felt a weird vibe. Once, when I was in college, I had a bedtime romp with another woman, more as a drunken experiment than a conscious lifestyle decision. It was fun, strange, and deliciously taboo all at the same time. Even so, it wasn't something I'd considered doing again.

But I just got a quiver of sexual adrenaline.

I know that if I'd been a guy, I would be incredibly attracted to Shana Neese. She was a cocktail of poised sophistication, classic beauty, and raw power.

I'd watched carefully through dinner as her manservant Gerald had efficiently served us plates of food and kept our glasses filled with wine. As soon as we were done with one course, he'd whisk the dishes off the table and disappear into the kitchen, only to reappear with another course.

I'd wondered about him.

Is he eating dinner by himself in the kitchen?

After the boys left, Shana and I sat in the overstuffed chairs in front of the fire, sipping white wine. It was so pleasant that if I'd been a cat, I would have been purring. "So tell me about Gerald. Is he live-in help? Does he do windows? Can you clone him for me?"

She smiled slightly. "Gerald was a client of mine for years. He used to be an investment banker and a very successful one at that. Then about six months ago, he tossed it all and begged me for a position here at the Tower."

"Begged you?"

"Literally on his knees. It was adorable."

I gazed at the crackling fire. "So you pay him. He's not like a slave or something?"

Shana laughed. "Oh, he's exactly like a slave, although I do give him an allowance and time off for good behavior."

I couldn't help but smile. "And do you punish him for bad behavior?"

"Bet your ass, I do." She leaned forward. "Sometimes I punish him just because I feel like it. Are you ready to see what I do for a living?"

I put my glass on the coaster on the end table next to my chair. "Please."

She stood up. "Bring your wine."

I smiled. "Yes, ma'am."

Oh, yeah, she likes to be in charge.

—

Inside one of her dungeons, I couldn't help but draw parallels and differences between where I stood and the chamber of horrors that belonged to Merlin Finn. His was dimly lit and dirty.

This was well illuminated and spotless.

Finn had an entire wall devoted to cutting instruments and drilling tools. His torture chamber featured a blowtorch.

Shana had nothing like that. She did, however, have an enormous collection of S&M equipment.

Finn had a drain in the center of the concrete floor.

For a place for the body fluids and the blood to go.

There was no such drain in Shana's dungeon.

Shana told me about the Tower. "We have nine different playrooms. Three of them are dungeons like this one. We have a cross-dressing room complete with wardrobe, wigs, shoes, stockings, maid uniforms, lingerie, outerwear, and, of course, a lot of cosmetics." She smiled. "Does that shock you?"

"The only contact I've ever had with this sort of thing was when someone had a fatal heart attack in the dungeon of a professional dominatrix in Boston about five years ago. Up until then, I had no clue that cross-dressing might be part of your world."

She nodded. "We also have two medical rooms for clients with nurse or doctor fetishes. We have one school room and one prison room. Each space has a bathroom with a floor large enough for a submissive to lie down on just in case that's part of the scene."

What?

Shana continued, "After a session, a client can wash up in a thermostatic jet shower with six multifaceted jet nozzles. The bathrooms are stocked with all the amenities like mouthwash, sterilized combs, prepasted toothbrushes, hand sanitizer, and extra towels. All the playrooms have a fully stocked mini fridge with sodas and water. There is no alcohol allowed in the Tower."

I glanced down at the wine in my hand. "Except after hours?"

She took a sip of hers. "Exactly, but then again, I'm the boss. I have a dozen women who work for me and two men who act as dominants, if that's what's required."

"How much do you charge?"

"Five hundred dollars an hour. But as you can see, we have absolutely everything." She gestured toward the padded leather furniture and BDSM appliances hanging on the walls. "We have bondage tables, spanking horses, vertical bondage racks, cages, floggers, whips, canes, paddles, shackles, spreader bars, blindfolds, gags, nipple clamps, electro, and hoods."

I stopped her. "Hoods, tell me about hoods. Merlin Finn was wearing one the night he killed the judge and Abby Tillis."

"They can be worn by either the submissive or the dominant or both. When it's worn by the dominant, it's reminiscent of the torturers during the Inquisition. If Finn wore one, he did it to terrorize his victims."

Scared the hell out of me.

"How well did you know Abby Tillis? John told me she was his ex-wife. He didn't say anything more than that."

Her eyes gazed at something on the wall as if visualizing her face. "Abby and John met while they were on the NYPD together. When she quit, she went on to create her own private investigation company. When John left the force, he went to work for Lodestar. They're both Friends of Lydia. Or Abby was when she was alive."

"How long were they married?" It was a question I liked using rather than the obvious one about why they split up.

"Seven years." She frowned. "She must have gotten the seven-year itch, because she met someone else. It broke John's heart."

"Sorry to hear that. I like John."

She glanced at me, trying to discern just what I felt about John Stillwater. Shana smiled. "They were able to put it all behind them and occasionally worked on projects together for the Friends. Abby was a big believer in the cause."

"The man Abby left John for, did it work out for her?"

Shana slowly shook her head. "No, and privately, she told me that she knew she'd made a mistake with John. She wished she could go back in time and make it right."

"John wasn't interested in reconciling?"

"He'd already moved on."

"Is he married? He doesn't wear a ring."

Her grin grew, and she cocked her head as she studied me. "He is currently unburdened with a partner. As far as I know. But he doesn't tell me everything."

"So tell me about what Abby was doing in Connecticut."

Shana sipped her wine. "We had high hopes for Judge Niles Preston. We'd always suspected that he was on the Wolfline payroll. Getting him to flip on the Tolbonovs would have been huge."

I said, "When I talked with Eva Preston, the judge's wife, she told me she suspected that the judge was going out that night to meet his lover. She thought her husband was having an affair. John said that Eva Preston was lying."

Shana shook her head angrily. "The deal was that Preston and his wife would meet up with Abby and she'd escort them to Hartford. They'd vanish off the face of the earth, live happily ever after with different identities."

"Eva Preston flipped on her husband?"

"Somehow, Merlin Finn got to her. I don't know how. But she betrayed her husband." She was silent for a moment, then continued in a bitter voice. "She killed him, and she killed an associate of the Friends, someone I liked very much."

Did she and Abby have a relationship?

I didn't know what to say, so I stayed silent.

Her next statement was no more than a bitter whisper. "Abby was in the wrong place at the wrong fucking time."

"Eva Preston is a looker. How did she end up with the judge? Granted, he wasn't bad looking, and he had some money, but let's face it, he was old." I already knew this story but wanted to hear it from her.

Shana looked at me like I was an idiot. "She was payment for services rendered. Before she married the judge, she was working the hotel and convention circuit for the Wolfline crew."

"A hooker? Not a model?"

"She did some modeling, mostly for a swimsuit line. But her real money came from the Russians."

"So you're telling me the Tolbonovs gave Eva to Preston?"

"To them, humans are something to be owned, nothing more than property."

A horrible realization washed over me as I stood in that dungeon. "You don't think that she got cold feet about going to Hartford and she told the Tolbonovs about what the judge was up to? Then they handed it all off to Merlin Finn?"

Her eyes narrowed. "It's crossed my mind. The judge was a loose end that needed to be tied up. By handing him to Finn, they could have it taken care of without dirtying their own hands."

I shook my head. "Eva Preston had me completely convinced that she was heartbroken with grief. She had me completely convinced that she was totally in love with her husband."

She frowned. "She's had a lot of practice at pretending."

I drained my wineglass. "Any thoughts on how Finn broke out of prison?"

Shana shrugged. "There was an investigation that concluded the Brotherhood somehow managed to get him the tools he needed. He had help, that's obvious. We don't know for sure who that was. Not yet."

—

When we got back to Shana's apartment, Gerald was waiting patiently, standing next to the kitchen door, ready for any command that Shana might utter. He was striking in appearance, with his military bearing, wide shoulders, and trim waist. He wore black slacks and a black, long-sleeved shirt, buttoned at the wrist. He stood at parade rest, eyes ahead, hands behind his back.

We sat down in front of the fire again, and I'd had enough wine and was relaxed enough to ask a sex question or two. I leaned over and whispered into Shana's ear. "What does Gerald get out of this relationship?"

"You don't have to whisper, Genie. Feel free to say or ask anything you like. Gerald doesn't mind, do you?" She'd turned toward him.

His face was expressionless. "No, ma'am."

Shana tapped her chin with her finger in contemplation. "So, Gerald, what do you get out of our relationship?"

Clearly flustered, his face colored scarlet. He wrestled with a tiny smile until it turned into a full-on grin. His eyes turned to me. "I'm not sure I can explain it, Miss Chase. I guess the closest way to describe it is that I have a need, and the only way to fulfill that need is to be Miss Shana's submissive. Serving her brings me great joy."

I cocked my head and studied his face. He was pretty in a manly way. "Have you always been a submissive?"

He thought for a moment. "I think I have. For as long as I can remember, I've felt the need to submit to women somehow. I've felt the need to do anything and everything to please them."

I wanted to ask what kind of relationship he had with his mother but resisted. Instead, I turned to Shana. "If you ever decide you don't want him anymore, I'll take him. Are all your clients like Gerald?"

"To one degree or another. Trying to explain why one person is submissive and another is dominant is exhausting. It's how some people are wired. I'm just happy it is what it is."

Self-destructive.

I'm not sure why that word popped into my head right at that time, but it did.

Is that how I'm wired?

Alcoholic? Married three times? Making bad life decisions?

Dear God, I'm raising a fifteen-year-old daughter now. I need to get my life on track. Taking the job with Lodestar certainly seemed to me to be the right direction to take.

I glanced at my watch.

I've still got to call Caroline.

Shana continued. "I didn't even know I was a dominant until I was in my early twenties and I was sitting in a restaurant with a boy I was seeing at the time. Seated at a table next to us was a middle-aged couple. I listened in on their conversation. The woman spent the evening telling the man what to do. Pour her more water, order another glass of wine, telling him what *he* was going to have for dinner. Then when I heard her clearly say that once they got home, she was going to punish him, that's when I felt it kick in. I wanted to be her, the one with the power. Always be the one in control."

Her eyes were gleaming as she gazed at Gerald. "I dumped the boyfriend, moved to New York, and got my first job with a pro domme until I learned the ropes."

I smiled. "So to speak."

"Pun intended. The rest is history."

"And your work with the Friends of Lydia?"

Her eyes narrowed. "Part of that is to honor my sister, of course. But part of it is that it's empowering, almost as much as what I do here at the Tower. Something you should know about me, Genie…" She gave me an appraising look. "I don't do anything unless I enjoy it."

Whoa, there's that sexual tension again.

—

Gerald had already deposited my overnight bag in the small guest room that was nearly overwhelmed by a queen-size four-poster bed that, knowing Shana, would have been perfect for tying someone to. It was covered with a thick, down comforter that had already been pulled down for me. Clean towels and a fluffy bathrobe were neatly folded at the foot of the bed.

I squeezed by the bed and gazed out my window onto Sixth Avenue four stories below. I missed living in New York. The lights, the skyscrapers, the constant movement twenty-four hours a day—it was hard not to be swept away by the thrumming energy.

I unpacked my toothbrush and cosmetics and put them in the guest bathroom, studying myself in the mirror. I didn't look as spooked as I did that afternoon at my own house when I'd discovered that Merlin Finn had violated my house, my space, and my panty drawer.

I'm going to make you model these for me.

Stomach queasy with the thought, I reached for the bottle of vodka in my overnight bag. Then I checked the time. It was ten o'clock there in New York, making it eight in Aspen.

You've already got a little buzz on from the wine. Call Caroline before you have any Absolut.

I punched her up on my phone.

She answered on the first ring. She practically shouted, "Hi, Genie."

"Having fun?"

"We skied so much this afternoon, my legs are sore."

Then in the background, I heard Jessica Oberon laughing. "We fell down so much, our butts are sore."

"I've got you on speaker, Genie."

"Is Ruth there?"

Aunt Ruth piped in. "Hi, Genie. These girls ran me ragged today."

Sadness gripped my chest. I missed Caroline. "They've got the energy, don't they, Ruth?"

Jessica sang out. "Tell her about dinner."

"We had dinner at the White House Tavern in downtown Aspen. Jess and I split a French dip because the portions are huge." Her voice went up when she said the word *huge*. "One of the waiters must have thought we're older than we are 'cause he asked if us ladies wanted cocktails."

"He was cute, Genie," Jessica added.

"Of course he was," I chuckled.

Ruth nearly shouted, "I kept them straight, Genie. No boozing for these girls on my watch."

Anytime Ruth said something about liquor, I took it personally. She knew I used to drink too much.

Still do.

"Good for you, Ruth."

I eyed the vodka bottle sitting on the bed next to where Tucker was sleeping. "Hey, Caroline, I got a job offer today."

There was a moment of silence as she processed the possibilities. She said, "Is it more money?"

"A lot more."

Her next words were tentative, frightened. "Will we have to move out of Sheffield?"

"Nope, mostly working from home. You'll still be at West High."

Her voice got high and happy again. "Yippee. Good for you, Genie. I want to hear all about it when I get back."

"I'll fill you in when you get home. I don't want to keep you. I just wanted to give you a quick call to see how you're doing."

I heard Ruth say, "I want to talk to Genie for a minute."

Caroline remarked, "Ruth wants to say hi. Thanks for calling, Genie. Talk tomorrow?"

"Sure, baby."

We said our good nights, and then Ruth came on the line, taking me off speakerphone. "Genie."

"What's up, Ruth? Everything okay?"

"Do you remember that business last October when you had those people following you?"

Bogdan Tolbonov tailed me in his black Ford F-150 pickup truck, not so much to keep an eye on me but to intimidate me. It had worked. "Of course."

"I don't want to upset you, because I can't be sure. But I got a weird feeling while we were at the restaurant, someone was watching us."

Fear gripped the pit of my stomach.

Ruth added, "Then driving back to our rental cabin, I thought I saw a car following us."

Jesus Christ, they're too far from me to help them if Ruth's right.

Ruth was deadly serious when she posed her question. "Are you working on something dangerous, Genie?"

Yes.

"Look, I'm going to have Mike Dillon call the Aspen cops and see if they can do some extra drive-bys to keep an eye on you."

That seemed to take the nerves out of her voice. "Okay, I'm probably just being paranoid."

You can't be too paranoid.

We said goodbye, and I called Mike and talked to him for a few minutes, wondering if Vicki Smith was lying naked in his bed next to him. Mike promised that once he hung up, he'd call the Aspen Police Department. "Most likely nothing," he said. "But better to be safe, right?"

"Thanks, Mike."

Say hey to Vicki for me.

I shook my head at how petty I can be. I liked Mike. I only wanted the best for him. And God knows, that ain't me.

Chapter Sixteen

"What's the address?"

I told John, and he deftly punched it into the GPS with one hand while with the other he negotiated traffic going north on I-95. We were back in the Mustang GT, and Tucker was in the critter carrier sitting on the back seat. Whatever snow had fallen overnight had turned into gray slurry.

"What are you hoping to accomplish?"

I answered honestly. "I don't know."

"You're already on Merlin Finn's radar. Are you sure you want to make yourself a more obvious target?"

I took a breath. "He broke into my house and violated my space. I want to see him back behind bars." The words on the note he left behind in my underwear drawer kept going through my mind.

I'm going to make you model these for me.

I recalled his mug shot. Shaved head, dark eyes, heavy brows, pronounced earlobes, thick-lipped snarl, a supremacist tattoo on each cheekbone. I remembered seeing the scars on Bristol Finn's back from the beatings she'd taken from him.

The difference between the S&M Shana practiced and the abuse that Finn handed out? Shana's was about pain for mutual pleasure. Merlin Finn was about pain for only his pleasure.

I could tell from John's voice that he wasn't convinced seeing Finn's father was a good idea. "Maybe you're trying too hard, Genie. Every cop in the tristate area is looking for him. He killed a judge. It's only a matter of time before they find him."

I didn't argue with him but changed the subject. "I noticed that the palms of Shana's hands have a lot of callous tissue. That's typical for someone who works with their hands, like a farmer or maybe a gravedigger. I wouldn't imagine that it's typical of a dominatrix. Is it from cracking the whip?"

He slowly shook his head. "Before Shana left Louisiana, when she was around sixteen, she was beaten and raped. She's carried the physical and psychological scars around with her ever since. When she bought the Tower, she put in an exercise room where she practices Krav Maga. It's a martial art developed by the Israelis for Shin Bet and Mossad. It combines wrestling, karate, and boxing. It's really just about fighting dirty."

"I know what it is."

"She also practices tae kwon do, karate, and kickboxing. Spends a couple of hours a day working at it. She's got a punching bag that takes a lot of punishment. It toughens up her hands. She says that if anyone attacks her again, she's going to either kill him or die trying."

I thought about Shana as we took the exit to White Plains and I watched the houses whiz by, nearly all of them with Christmas decorations in their windows, wreaths on their doors, or plastic reindeer on their lawns. The more I found out about her, the more impressed I was.

Taking advantage of the silence, John spoke. "Did Shana take you for a tour of the Tower?"

I grinned. "Yes, she did. It makes quite an impression." I eyed him playfully. "Are you a client?"

John chuckled. "Not my thing. Nothing wrong with it if that's what you're into. It's all legal, by the way. Did you know that? As long as there's no sexual contact."

I rolled my eyes. "It's all sexual, John. C'mon."

"It clearly states on her website that if you even ask for anything sexual, you'll be banned."

I repeated. "It's all sexual. It's hardcore foreplay."

John stayed silent, but I could see a tiny smile on his lips.

"If you're not a client, how did the two of you meet?"

"I went to work at Lodestar after I left the NYPD. Nathaniel takes on occasional pro bono jobs for the Friends of Lydia, so he made the introduction. I like working with Shana. She's a genuine badass."

She's a sexy badass.

"Is Nathaniel one of her clients?"

John frowned. "Ask Nathaniel."

"What made you want to be a cop?" Gerald's coffee must have kick-started the nosy reporter in me that morning.

John was silent for a few moments, obviously wrestling with what he should say. When he answered, it was with the voice of a cop. "My mother was the victim of a homicide. She and my father had divorced when I was eleven, and Mom had to work two jobs to make ends meet. One of them was as a bartender. We were living with my grandparents in upstate New York at the time. One night, after the bar closed, she got into her car but never arrived home. Her car was found torched, and her body was found in a ditch."

Our histories make us who we are.

I reached over and put my hand on his shoulder.

He continued. "They never found who did it. It made me want to be a cop."

Still touching him, I asked, "Why did you leave the force?"

He glanced at me briefly. Then he turned his attention back to the road. "A story for another time."

I wanted to ask him about Abby but decided that I'd gone as far as he was going to let me. Instead, I fiddled with the radio and found NPR, and we quietly listened to *Morning Edition* until we pulled into the driveway of a nondescript, single-story ranch with an attached garage. The vinyl siding was white but with slight shades of mold green that begged for a good power washing. The shutters along the windows had once been black, but age and sunlight had faded them to a dark gray. Waist-high shrubs, shorn of their leaves, fronted the house, but in between, windows peeked out from the foundation of the building, showing that the house had a basement.

John parked by the curb, and we walked up to the front steps. I rang the bell.

After what seemed like an interminable wait, a man opened the door. He was in his late sixties and very tall—six seven, at least. At one point in his life, he probably had been very fit and muscular. But when the body slows down, muscle often turns to rubber around the middle and in the shoulders. He wore a long-sleeved tee that showed he was around thirty pounds too heavy for his height. The man still had a full head of unkempt white hair, but it was thinning, and his scalp shone pink in the scant morning sunlight. His jowly cheeks were covered with two days of gray stubble, and he had the demeanor of a bulldog. "What do you want?" he growled.

"Are you Arthur Finn?"

"What do you want?" he repeated, gazing at me angrily over a pair of wire-frame glasses.

"I'd like to talk to you about your son, Merlin."

He grimaced and eyed John suspiciously. "You cops?"

I shook my head. "I'm a journalist with the *Sheffield Post.*"

Arthur stood just inside the doorway, but when he spit, it landed inches from my leather boots. "That's what I think of reporters."

He turned and started to close the door on us. I tried one last gambit. "Your son broke into my house yesterday."

He stopped cold, then slowly turned and studied me through his glasses. "Did he now? What did you have that he wanted?"

I cocked my head but didn't answer.

For the first time, he smiled a cold grin. "Come in. You've piqued my curiosity."

When he walked, it was in his stocking feet, and it was more of a slow, bowlegged shuffle, as if his knees were rheumatoid-ridden. We followed him into his dark living room. The heavy green curtains were closed, and a single lamp on an end table was the only illumination, save for the silver light coming from a muted large-screen television mounted on a bare wall, wires snaking to outlets below. A John Wayne movie was running without sound.

He sat down in a well-worn cloth recliner. The arms were faded and threadbare. "Take the load off. Let's sit and talk."

Other than the recliner, the only other place to sit was a plaid cloth couch. Without taking our coats off, John and I sat down.

I glanced around the room. Arthur had three framed photos on his living room walls. One was of an American eagle posing in front of the flag. The second was the iconic scene after 9/11 when the firefighters hoisted the flag over the debris at ground zero in New York. The third was of a man and a little boy with fishing poles over their shoulders.

I pointed to it. "Is that a picture of you and Merlin when he was a little kid?"

It was adorable. Like the opening scene from *The Andy Griffith Show*.

He looked up at it and sighed. "Yeah, it's a reminder that even he was a little boy once."

Newspapers were stacked up next to Arthur's recliner. The end table next to him carried an empty plate covered in bacon grease and a coffee cup with a Fox News logo.

Trying to ingratiate myself to him, I pointed to the cup. "I used to work for Fox News."

His eyes glistened. "Did ya' now? You ever meet Hannity?"

I slowly shook my head. "We worked in different places in the building."

"Why did ya leave?"

The real reason was I just couldn't stand it. Not my kind of journalism. But I lied. "Someone made a pass at me."

Arthur chuckled. "Yeah, you're a looker. I hear that happens all the time at Fox. I hear they make all their women wear little short skirts on the sets." He sat on the edge of the recliner and leaned forward, his hands claw-like, resting on the knees of his gray trousers. "So, young lady, what's your name?"

"Genie Chase."

"And now you're a reporter for a newspaper. Too bad you couldn't find decent work. Bet you woulda made a fine secretary."

I let the insult pass.

Arthur fixed his gaze on John. "And who are you? You a reporter too? You smell like a cop to me."

John only smiled. "No, sir. These days, I do odd jobs."

The old man grinned. "I gotcha. Odd jobs, you're a fixer. I understand Merlin uses boys like you in his line of work."

"What kind of work is that, Mr. Finn?"

He smiled at me enigmatically but changed the subject. "What did you have that Merlin wanted bad enough to break into your house, Genie Chase?"

I glanced at John, who shrugged.

Cat's already out of the proverbial bag.

"A notebook."

The man adopted a wide grin, and he clapped his hands together. "Jim Caviness's notebook?"

"Yes."

He chuckled wickedly. "I knew Jim Caviness. He was a dumbass. The Russians knew his brain was fried. He wrote things down in a notebook so he wouldn't screw up. I was surprised as hell when I heard that his wife killed him. I guess she got him before the Tolbonov brothers did."

I leaned in. "What can you tell me about Valentin and Bogdan Tolbonov?"

Arthur's smile turned into a sneer. "Don't ever trust 'em. Merlin treated those boys straight. He was their most loyal soldier. He ran his Brotherhood crew for the Russians and never skimmed a penny. Then, out of nowhere, Wolfline sent two assassins up to his place in Connecticut to kill him." Arthur sat back. "Only the security on that mountain is tighter than Fort Knox. Merlin killed 'em first."

John frowned. "Word on the street was that Merlin was moving in on Wolfline's drug trade. The two men he killed were low-level dealers."

Arthur shook his head. "He wouldn't dirty his hands over street thugs."

The fact that Merlin Finn had tortured the two men to death in his redneck dungeon flashed through my mind. "Why would the Tolbonovs want to kill Merlin if he was such a good soldier?"

He glanced over at John. "Like the boy here said. Word on the street. Sometimes in our line of work, bullshit trash talk can get people killed. Perception's reality. They're scared of him."

"Why?"

Arthur flashed me a grin. "He's big and he's smart and he controls the Brotherhood. They thought if they could get rid of my boy, they'd control Merlin's crew."

John offered, "But now that Merlin's out, all bets are off."

His grin grew broader. "Goddamned right, son."

John's voice was steady when he asked the question. "Did your son kill Judge Niles Preston and Abby Tillis?"

John's too invested in this.

Arthur sat up straight. "Wouldn't know nothin' about that."

I asked, "Has your son been in contact with you since he escaped from Lockport?"

More silence.

"Do you know where Merlin is?"

He laughed. "Seriously? If I knew where he was, I sure as hell wouldn't tell a reporter."

I tried again. "Have you seen him since he escaped from prison?"

Arthur slowly shook his head. "He knows that the feds are watching me. And they're keeping tabs on that cheating bitch wife of his too up at Oak Hill. Let me tell you, Miss Reporter, that once the FBI gets tired of watching her, she's a dead woman for taking up with that Karl Lerner." He grimaced when he added, "And it won't be quick."

His words chilled me. I recalled the note I found in my underwear drawer back home.

I'm going to make you model these for me.

Chapter Seventeen

"There was another fatal OD last night." Mike glanced over the top of his computer screen, focusing on John, who was seated next to me. "This one was an eighteen-year-old male, a freshman at the community college. Bryan Townsend lived in a condo at 81 Buckner Avenue. We talked with his roommate. He said he knew that Townsend was using and thought that he might have been dealing to pay for his habit. His body was found in the men's room at the Exxon Station on West Avenue. We searched his car for drugs, and it was clean. He must have either shot up his supply or someone robbed him."

"Was he dealing for someone or was he working on his own?"

Mike was still trying to figure out why John was there. "Don't know." He'd met John the day before when he'd identified Abby Tillis's body.

When we both entered his office, Mike politely shook his hand, but his face registered curiosity.

Up front, I could have explained why John was with me, but I was in a bitchy mood and still smarting from the bombshell revelation that Mike had attached himself to a pretty, young Realtor. Sooner or later, Mike would ask. I was just going to make him wait.

Mike moved his eyes from John to me. He wanted to watch my

expression when he told me the news. "Oh, and we found the dead body of a high-level street dealer last night just behind the East Sheffield Train Station. Have you ever heard of Travis Monk?"

I felt a sharp jolt of electricity snap inside my chest. I did my best not to let my face betray my shock. Travis Monk was the drug dealer I'd staked out in November on Edison Avenue. Before the "homeless" scout ratted me out, I'd taken dozens of photos of his customers and clear shots of Monk's Cadillac Escalade. I'd sent them anonymously to Mike's email. I'd assumed that since he was never arrested, Monk had moved to another town.

"How did he die?" Even I could hear the nerves in my voice.

Please let it be natural causes or an overdose.

"Foley is doing the autopsy today, but from what I could see, he'd been tortured and beaten to death."

John leaned forward, suddenly very interested. "Merlin Finn?"

Mike was still watching me when he answered. "It has his MO all over it. Plus, we think that Monk was one of Wolfline's crew."

I asked, "Have you checked to see if there's any security video in that part of town?"

Mike frowned as if I should know better than to ask that question. "Of course we have. One camera mounted in the parking lot of the train station and one security camera at the Shell station up the street. The killers dropped him off using Monk's own Escalade. The man we saw rolling the body out of the SUV was dressed in a black parka and wearing a ski mask, just like the thugs in the marina homicides. We haven't found the kid's Escalade yet."

John spoke up. "Probably at the bottom of Long Island Sound."

Mike wasn't finished. He was staring right at me. "You know, an anonymous source sent me photos of Monk selling dope over on Edison Avenue last month. We used them as leverage. We wanted him to flip on the Russians. Threatened Monk with prison time if he didn't turn snitch."

I cleared my throat. "Did he?"

Mike nodded. "There's a glut of drugs on the street right now.

I wanted to use Monk to find out where Wolfline was getting their supply."

I interjected. "I heard Wolfline's getting out of the business."

"I doubt that. Before we got anything useful out of Monk, Finn killed him. Finn would have been better off leaving him alive to snitch on the Russians."

John frowned. "With the FBI crawling all over them, it's a wonder the Russians can move anything at all."

Mike squinted at John. "I'm sorry, who are you again? You work for the Friends of Lydia?"

John smiled back. "I do odd jobs."

Interesting way to put it. It's the second time in less than an hour that I've heard him use that phrase.

Mike grimaced. "Could I have a moment alone with Genie, please?"

John adjusted his glasses and grunted. "Sure." He stood up, picked his overcoat from the back of his chair, draped it over his arm, and slowly walked out of the office.

Giving him a minute to get out of earshot, Mike leaned forward and jerked his thumb in the direction of the doorway. "What's the deal?"

There it is. The question.

I cocked my head. "What do you mean? What's the deal with John?"

He rolled his eyes. "Yes, John Stillwater. Why is he here?"

"After the B&E on my apartment yesterday, the Friends of Lydia have generously offered me a bodyguard."

Mike stared at the empty doorway. "He looks and acts like a cop."

I nodded. "He used to be."

"Okay, the offer still stands. Want to me to park an officer on the street in front of your house?"

Oh, he is so adorable.

I smiled. "No need. John will be there."

"Overnight?"

Without another word, I smiled mysteriously and stood, grabbed my bag and my coat, and started for the door.

Before I got there, I heard Mike clear his throat. "Be careful, Genie. You really don't know much about this guy. For the time being, if I were you, I wouldn't trust anyone."

—

We drove back to my place, and John parked the Mustang next to the Sebring in the driveway. We went in, and while John went through the house to make certain there wasn't anyone hiding in a closet, I dug out the extra key from the junk drawer in the kitchen.

When John came back downstairs, I handed it to him. "Here. You can come and go as you please."

"Thanks. Where do you want me to sleep?"

There's that sexual adrenaline again.

I could feel my cheeks reddening.

"Well," I stammered, "Caroline's room is probably a bit girly for you. How about I sleep there tonight, and you take my room?"

When I said the words "take my room," the sexual tension inside me ratcheted up another notch.

What is this all about? Last night it was Shana, and now it's John?

If John noticed my clumsiness, he didn't let on. He merely said, "No worries. I'll just camp out on the couch if that's okay." Then he glanced around the kitchen. "I see the coffeemaker on the counter. Mind if I make myself a pot of coffee?"

"Help yourself. Filters and coffee are in that cabinet."

"When do we leave for your office?"

I watched him pull down the coffee filters. "We don't. I'm going to be fine. I'd rather have you guarding the castle."

"Really?" He took out the plastic container of Stop-n-Shop breakfast blend. "I'm supposed to keep an eye on you."

I shook my head. "There's a difference between keeping an eye on me and being a babysitter. I can't do my job if you're standing next to me while I'm interviewing people. It was kind of awkward with Arthur Finn and Mike this morning." I scrunched up my nose, trying to be honest yet adorable.

He folded his arms and studied my face, taking measure of my resolve. Finally, he answered, "Okay, you win. But on one condition." He held up a finger indicating to give him a minute. I watched as he briskly hustled out of the kitchen.

While he was gone, I filled the coffeepot with water and emptied it into the maker's reservoir. I had only just pushed the button to turn it on when John returned.

"Here." He held out his hand.

"What's that?" It was a black plastic wafer and about the size of a fifty-cent coin.

"A GPS tracker. It's waterproof and has a five-day battery life."

I took it out of his hand and held it up to see it better. "If you had to, you could track me by using my phone. I have a tracking app already loaded. All I have to do is add you."

He shook his head. "A phone is too easy to lose or steal. Put this in your pocket. It connects directly with my laptop and cell phone."

"This seems a little James Bond to me."

"It's very James Bond. It's the only way I'm letting you out of my sight."

I slid it into the pocket of my black jeans. There was comfort that John had given me another layer of protection. But I was certain that once I was in the car, I'd take it out of my pocket and drop it into my bag. I never go anywhere without my bag. "Okay, Q. Are we good?"

"We are now. While you go out to do your newspaper thing, I'll set up my laptop here on the table and get some work done for Nathaniel."

I liked having John there, especially with Caroline in Colorado. Having someone to come home to would be nice. "I should be back here around five. I'll pick up some takeout."

He scowled. "We passed a grocery store on the way here. I'll go get a few things and make us dinner tonight."

Yes, I like this very much.

He glanced back out at the living room. "Where are your holiday decorations? I could put some up for you."

I braved a smile. "Still in the attic. Tell you what, when I get home tonight, you and I can do it together."

—

"What did you get from Merlin Finn's father?" Lorraine Moretti was sitting behind her desk, peering at me through her silly cat glasses.

I consulted my reporter's notebook. "He told me that the two men his son killed up in Brockton weren't drug dealers at all. They were assassins sent by the Russian mob to kill Merlin Finn."

"Can you substantiate that?"

I sighed. "I doubt it. Police reports claim the two men were drug dealers."

Lorraine looked at me over the top of her glasses with a grim expression. "So the trip out there was a complete waste of time."

I didn't take the bait. "Before I came in this morning, I stopped by SPD to pick up the incident reports. A drug dealer named Travis Monk was found tortured and beaten to death last night. The police think it might have been Merlin Finn."

She growled, "Well, that's something at least. Go write it up."

I started to get up but sat back down again. "Can I ask you a question?"

She'd turned her attention to the computer screen on her desk and now seemed annoyed that I would have the audacity to pull her away from it. "Yes?"

"When did you know that someone was going to build an urban mall here in Sheffield?"

She blinked, running answers through her head. Finally, she

responded. "Ah, yes, the mall. I wouldn't know what information our corporate office had or when it knew that an urban mall was being built in Sheffield. I sincerely hope you're not implying that our company did anything unethical. Galley Media's values and sense of ethics are held to a high standard, Genie. And we expect our employees to do the same."

I hadn't really expected a straight answer, and I wasn't disappointed. Wordlessly, I got up and went out to the newsroom. I wondered how Galley had known about the stealthy purchase of all the land that was required for such a massive project. They'd made the deal with Ben just prior to the developer approaching the city about permits.

How did Galley Media know?

And what idiot, in this time of online shopping, would consider investing hundreds of millions of dollars to build a dinosaur like a shopping mall? Hell, they were going the way of the newspaper. Both of us were products of another time.

And yet, someone was doing it.

As if on cue, Bill McNamara from advertising slid into the chair next to my gunmetal-gray desk. Playing with his handlebar mustache, he grinned at me. "How's it going with the new boss?"

I glanced over at her, still hunched over her keyboard. "About how you'd expect. I heard you have a new VP of advertising. How's it going with her?"

His lanky frame shuddered theatrically. "Her name is Sue Lewis. Every time she says something, every sphincter muscle in my body tightens."

I couldn't help but chuckle. "I heard some of the other sales staff saying she was a real ballbuster."

"I'm not sure all of us are going to survive the Galley transition. They have to keep us on staff for a year, but that doesn't mean we can't find other jobs."

I need to talk to Ben about taking the position at Lodestar.

I turned my attention back to Bill. "Heard anything more about the mall? Who's the developer?"

"A company called Wyatt Investments out of Boston."

"Is that who bought up all the land out there? They were really quiet about it."

Bill nervously pulled on his bow tie. "Don't know. I can find out for you. Why?"

"Just curious how Galley Media got the intel on the mall before we did."

"Oh, by the way, the project has a name, the Sheffield Meridian."

"Meridian? Doesn't that have something to do with maps?"

Bill grinned. He was about to show off. "It's a circle of constant longitude passing through a given place on the earth's surface and the terrestrial poles."

I rolled my eyes. "Yeah, what I said."

He held one finger in the air. "Furthermore, in Chinese medicine, it's a set of pathways in the body along which vital energy is said to flow."

"Great. Maybe they should call it the Zen Mall. You hear anything more, can you let me know?"

He leaned in and whispered, "You'll be the first."

A half hour later, I quietly finished the piece on the late Travis Monk and sent it to Lorraine. Then I turned my attention to the young man who had died the night before by overdose.

I did some poking around on the internet and the various social media platforms and discovered that eighteen-year-old Bryan Townsend graduated from West Sheffield High School last year with honors. According to his Facebook posts, he was close with his parents, enjoyed sailing, and was studying law enforcement at Sheffield Community College. According to his Instagram account, over the summer, he worked as a deckhand for Groward Bay Marina.

Coincidence?

I decided to pay a visit to the kid's roommate. Before I put my coat back on, I sent Lorraine a short email letting her know what I was doing. When I hit the Send button, I could feel the bile in my throat.

Changing jobs was looking better and better.

So why haven't I given my notice?

Chapter Eighteen

I pushed through the back door and stepped out onto the concrete steps leading to the employee parking lot. I'd just gotten to the driver's side of the Sebring when I heard my phone ping. I unlocked the car and slid in, started the engine, and cranked up the heater.

Then, taking my phone out of my bag, I checked to see who had sent me a text. Fear charged through my veins.

Eric Decker, Wolfline Contracting's attorney.

The last time I'd seen him was in that very same parking lot. His Jaguar had been parked behind my car, blocking me in.

Involuntarily, my eyes darted to the far corner of the lot. It was where Bogdan Tolbonov's F-150 pickup truck had been parked. It was the first time I'd laid eyes on him. His sheer size and menacing presence were frighteningly intimidating.

That was back in October, and Eric wanted to know where the Friends of Lydia were keeping Betsy Caviness. What the Tolbonovs really wanted was the notebook.

And now Merlin Finn, the Tolbonovs' enemy, has it.

The text said simply:

Please, I need to talk with you.

I thought about calling John before I replied but decided that at that moment, the ball was in my court. I typed:

When and where?

Better be someplace public.

It took a few moments, but the return text popped up with another ping.

The Aquarium here in Sheffield. Jellyfish exhibit. Fifteen minutes.

I considered calling John, but my comfort level with having someone looking over my shoulder while I asked questions was low. I put the car in gear and decided that the aquarium was public enough that I would be safe meeting the attorney there.

I took the Merritt Parkway, which at one o'clock was frustratingly crowded with traffic.

Last-minute Christmas shoppers?

At exactly a quarter past one, I pulled into the parking garage across the street from the aquarium. I got my ticket from the kiosk and hustled across North Water Street, got to the entrance, flashed my press credential, and flew past the young lady at the counter.

The aquarium is in South Sheffield, which had become a trendy neighborhood of chic shops, restaurants, clubs, and bars. The aquarium was the tourist cornerstone that brought it all together. A massive brick building, once an 1860s iron works factory, now housed sea otters, seals, loggerhead turtles, sharks, fish, crabs, and other sea life. It was also the home of the area's only IMAX theatre. Over half a million people visited the aquarium every year.

The week before Christmas, however, was a slow time. The place was nearly empty as I dashed past the touch tank and the massive room where sharks swam behind thick glass.

I nearly skidded into the jellyfish exhibit. The room was dark. The only illumination came from recessed lights in the ceiling directly above the cylindrical tank that slowly changed from a neon blue to pink and back. The lights were hidden, so it appeared that the hundreds of slow-moving jellyfish in the glass cylinder were glowing. Their slow journeys were governed by gentle flows of water within the tank.

Outside the exhibit, laughter and conversation echoed off the brick walls and glass tanks. Inside, all was quiet except for soft, tinkling, new age music that made the jellyfish's movements a delicate, slow ballet.

The only person in the room other than me was a tall man in his forties, glasses tilted back on the top of his balding head. He stood close to the glass, his patrician nose inches from the tank. His hands were jammed into the pockets of his black businessman's overcoat. Eric Decker stood slightly behind the tank, so he could observe anyone who walked into the room.

I stepped cautiously toward the tank glancing at the room's perimeter, making certain no one was hiding in the darkness along the walls.

He moved around the exhibit, hands still in his pockets. When I got close enough, he blinked at me and said, "Miss Chase, I can't thank you enough for meeting with me."

I nervously glanced around the room again, then back at the doorway. "Is Bogdan here with you?"

He raised his eyebrows and shook his head slightly. "That's what I want to talk with you about. Bogdan's missing."

"What?"

Eric took the glasses from the top of his head and put them on so he could better inspect the jellyfish. "You know, there's evidence that jellyfish evolved over 700 million years ago. They're ninety-five percent water. They don't have a circulation system, a respiratory system, or a central nervous system. So delicate, yet so durable."

Get to the point.

He continued. "They possess twenty-four eyes. Supposedly, they are one of the few animals that possess a three-hundred-and-sixty-degree view of their environment. Maybe that's their evolutionary advantage. Eyes in the back of their head, as it were."

"Tell me about Bogdan."

He tipped the glasses back onto the top of his skull. "Two days ago, he went missing. We don't know where he is."

"What was he doing?"

The hint of a sneer played on the attorney's thin lips. "He was looking for someone."

"Who?"

He hesitated for a moment. "Merlin Finn."

I'm going to make you model these for me.

Fear rolled through my extremities again. Bogdan was one of the scariest people you'd ever not want to meet.

And now there's someone even scarier?

"So why are you telling me this? Shouldn't you be talking to the cops?"

He lifted his chin and scratched his long neck. "Yes, well, the Tolbonovs and the police don't have a good working relationship."

I unzipped my parka. "I heard that the FBI has been keeping a close eye on Wolfline Contracting. Maybe the feds know where Bogdan is."

A sudden flash of anger passed across his face, and his voice grew stern. He hissed, "The FBI has an overly inflated opinion of itself. They serve no purpose other than to harass law-abiding citizens."

"What does Valentin think?"

He took a breath, calmed down. My remark about the FBI hit a nerve. When he spoke again, his usual voice was back, restrained, soft-toned. "This is all off the record, Miss Chase. And if it comes up in a court of law, I'll deny what I'm telling you."

Of course it is.

"Okay. Off the record."

"Because of the attention being lavished upon the Tolbonov brothers by federal law officials, Wolfline Contracting has been shedding all operations that might be interpreted as being outside of normal legal parameters."

"What?"

He sighed in exasperation. "Wolfline is going legit."

I frowned. "What does that look like?"

"No more escort services, no gaming, no pharmaceuticals."

"No prostitution, sex trafficking, gambling, and drugs? Is that what you're telling me?"

He slowly nodded, glancing around to make sure nobody else was within earshot.

"How about murder, extortion, and blackmail?"

Eric's nostrils flared. He answered, crossing his arms, and his eyes bore into mine. "Plus, there was always the specter of the Caviness notebook finding its way into the wrong hands. Better to be proactive."

The notebook again.

"What's their new line of work?"

"Property development. The new name of the company is Wolfline Management."

"So again, why are you telling me all this?"

He turned back to staring at the hypnotic movements of the jellyfish. "Mr. Tolbonov is convinced that his brother is dead. He knows that the new owners of your newspaper don't like you very much. He fears for your job. He knows that you're raising a teen-ager and money is important. Mr. Tolbonov is willing to pay you fifty thousand dollars if you can find his brother…or locate his remains. And another fifty thousand if you can find Merlin Finn."

How does Valentin Tolbonov know I'm having problems with Galley Media?

I hadn't yet told anyone at the newspaper that I was taking a new job.

Is there a mole at the Sheffield Post?

And even with the new job with Lodestar, a hundred thousand dollars would go a long way for Caroline's college fund.

I squinted at the attorney. "How do I know I'll ever see the money?"

Eric smiled. "Valentin Tolbonov always pays his debts."

—

He left before I did.

Not in any particular hurry, I stopped by the massive shark tank and sat down. Watching as sand tigers, nurse sharks, and sandbar sharks gracefully but slowly maneuvered in circles around the edge of the glass, surrounded by schools of grouper and other reef fish, I tried to relax and consider what had just happened.

This exhibit was much larger than the jellyfish room, and it too was dimly lit, the light emanating from above the tank. People were drawn to the big predators. The voices of the audience were hushed, the patrons mesmerized.

Whenever I'd been in that exhibit and taken a few minutes to appreciate the slowly moving tableau, the question would come up. Why don't the sharks eat the other fish in the tank?

The answer was, "Because the aquarium keeps the sharks well fed. There's no need for the sharks to attack and eat the other fish."

Yes, but what happens if the sharks get hungry again?

Eric Decker had offered me a hundred thousand dollars to find what was left of Bogdan Tolbonov and locate the murderous Merlin Finn.

I didn't say no.

This was a breach of ethics, a conflict of interest to the newspaper. But how much did I owe them now?

I didn't say yes.

By not saying anything, had I tacitly agreed to the bargain? Was I working for the Russians?

I stayed for a few more moments and then went to the exit. I was going to call John Stillwater and tell him about the meeting I'd just had with Eric Decker but decided it would be better done in the warmth of my car.

I trotted back across Water Street, used the kiosk to pay my parking fee then took the elevator up to the second level where my car was parked. I patted myself on the back for remembering the floor and the location of the Sebring. Even sober, I often forget where I park.

I pulled my scarf up over my chin and mouth. I was parked on level two, and because the garage was essentially open to the elements, the cold air off Long Island Sound whipped through the parking area like a wind tunnel. As I walked from the elevator toward my car, I could hear the sound of my boots clicking against the concrete floor and echoing off the walls.

What's that?

I stopped dead in my tracks.

There was a white square planted under my driver's side windshield wiper.

What the hell?

I quickly scoped out my surroundings. Only parked cars. Not another soul to be seen.

I stepped gingerly up to my car and with a trembling hand gently plucked the folded-up piece of paper out from under the wiper. Surprised at how my hand shook, I opened it. The handwriting was identical to the note that had been hidden in my panty drawer.

Put your nose in my business, little girl,
and I ll slice it off.

Chapter Nineteen

Something inside me snapped. I put a hand up to my mouth to keep from crying out. My eyes darted everywhere at once.

Is he hiding somewhere, watching me?

I unlocked my car and slid into the driver's seat, locking the doors.

For all the good that'll do.

Hands shaking, I reached into my bag for the phone to punch in Mike Dillon's number.

No.

I started to punch in John's number.

The phone chirped and buzzed in my hand. My heart pumped even harder.

"Genie?"

"John?"

"Genie? Are you okay?"

How does he know?

He answered my unasked question. "What are you doing at the aquarium?"

The GPS in my bag.

My words came out in a tumble. "I met with Eric Decker. Bogdan's missing. Tolbonov wants to pay me to find him. And find Finn too." I stopped for a beat.

"What?"

I took a deep breath to steady my voice. "I came back to my car and found a note on my windshield. I think Finn wrote it."

"What? When? Where are you?"

Holding my cell phone to my ear with one hand, I leaned over and rummaged through my bag, looking for the half-empty bottle of Absolut.

In my bedroom, damn it.

"You know where I am." I snapped my answer. Stress was taking a toll.

Calm down.

"I'm in my car in the parking garage across from the aquarium."

"Get out of there. Meet me someplace public."

I thought for a moment of where the best place to meet him was. "Brick's. It's a pizza place that has a bar in the back. It's just a few blocks from here, in South Sheffield. Meet me there."

"I'm on my way."

I put the phone down and backed the Sebring out of the parking spot. Just before I put the car into drive, I glanced down at the sheet of paper, open on the passenger's seat. I brushed it off like a spider onto the floor.

Then, attempting to stay calm and not gun the gas, I gently moved forward, down the ramp to the first level, heading for the exit.

Wait, get a grip.

There must be video. Security footage. I parked in a spot close to the office where I'd just paid the fee. Turning off the car and locking it behind me, I rushed toward the office in the lobby facing Water Street.

Consistent with the outer facade of the building itself, the walls were red brick, decorated with photographs of the city and Long Island Sound taken from the top level of the garage, five stories above the street. The floor in the lobby was simple black-and-white tiling. Two red kiosks were embedded in the wall where people inserted their parking voucher and paid their fee, either in cash or by credit card.

There was an anteroom where the security guard sat. I saw him behind a sliding glass window overtop a counter cut into the wall. I judged him to be in his late sixties, most likely retired from his full-time career and discovering that without at least part-time employment, his Social Security check wouldn't be enough to keep the cable bill paid and the lights on.

He was dressed in a white shirt, blue cardigan sweater, and tan slacks. Seated at a gray metal desk, he was nearly hidden behind three large computer screens. But his attention was riveted to the paperback book he was surreptitiously holding in his hands, just below the level of the desktop.

I rapped on the window.

He glanced up, looking slightly embarrassed. He shouted, "Is the kiosk not working again?"

I pointed to the computer terminals. "Do you have video?"

He stood up and blinked at me through bifocals. Moving to his side of the window, he slid it open. "What did you say?"

I saw by the badge pinned to his shirt that his name was Phil.

"Someone just left a threatening note on my windshield. I'd like to look at your security footage to see who it was."

He appraised me for a moment. "Did you ding somebody's car?"

"No, someone's stalking me. I want to see who it is."

"Well, young lady, best you should call the police. I'm not supposed to be lettin' people back here to look at the videotapes."

I crossed my arms and locked my attention on his left hand. He was still holding the paperback, a Michael Connelly mystery. "Cops are going to ask why you didn't see what happened. You going to tell them you had your nose in a novel?"

He chewed on his lip for a moment and squinted at me. "I was just takin' a short break."

"Please?"

He heaved a heavy sigh. "Okay, but let's make it snappy. Don't want somebody from the parkin' authority to walk in and see you back here. I could get fired." He reached down and pressed a button under the counter, and I heard the lock in the metal door snap open.

The office, not much bigger than a closet, was dominated by the single desk, one chair, and three computer screens sitting on the desktop. Phil seated himself, and I stepped behind him. The three screens were segmented into four rectangles each, different scenes from different locations inside the garage and on the rooftop.

"I was on Level 2. This happened about five minutes ago."

He moved the mouse until the pointer on the middle terminal rested on Level 2, then backed the video up. Time in reverse, I watched my Sebring slide from its present location going backward up the ramp, then slightly past an empty parking place, then pull in, front end first.

I was disappointed to see that the camera was on the opposite side of the wide expanse so that my car was partially obscured by a GMC Yukon. With the video still running in reverse, I could barely see myself get out of my car, glancing around the area, looking for bad guys, then read the note, put it on the windshield, and walk backward toward the elevator, disappearing behind the doors.

Moments later, we both watched as a large, black Lincoln Navigator rolled backward and parked in front of my car.

Phil made the video skip ahead so when he hit the button, we were moving forward in time instead of going backward. The Lincoln, also obscured by the GMC SUV, pulled up to my back bumper. It sat idling for a few moments, then a door swung open, and a man got out of the driver's side.

Too small to be Merlin Finn.

He was dressed in black slacks and a black winter coat, the hood pulled over his head, a scarf hiding the lower half of his face. The man glanced furtively around the garage, then quickly went to my windshield and deposited the note.

Somebody other than Finn had written it?

Then, as if to answer my unasked question, the rear door swung open, and another man stepped out of the SUV. Massive, tall with broad shoulders, he was also in black slacks, black coat, hood pulled up, dark scarf pulled up over the lower half of his face. All I could see were his dark, piercing eyes.

An uncontrollable shudder shook my frame.

Merlin Finn.

I'm going to make you model these for me.

Bastard.

He stepped to one side so that the Yukon wasn't hiding him. He knew where the camera was. He was staring dead at it. Finn ran a single finger across his throat.

Son of a bitch is warning me, threatening me.

Phil glanced up at me with a worried expression on his face. "That the guy who's stalkin' ya?"

I nodded.

Phil's voice was barely a whisper. "He's scary."

I felt my heart quicken again as fear slid through my veins. "How many exits are there in this garage?"

"Just the one."

"Is there a camera there?"

"Yes, ma'am."

"Can we see if we can get the license plate?"

He scrabbled at the keyboard, and then we went through video time-stamped from the second the Lincoln left Level 2 to the point where we watched the white-and-yellow exit gate rise and the Lincoln pull out onto Water Street.

Phil whispered, "There's no front plate. Connecticut, you gotta have both a back and front plate."

I straightened up. Finn wasn't stupid. He'd taken the front plate off, knowing that there'd be a camera at the exit.

But how did he know I'd be at the aquarium?

Either he was following me...or he was following Eric Decker.

Chapter Twenty

There are plenty of fancy restaurants and trendy dance clubs in South Sheffield, but Brick's isn't one of them. It's your basic neighborhood pizza joint with a tiny bar tucked away along the back wall. It's dark, it's quiet, and it's a good place to talk.

Plus, it's a place where it's unlikely any corporate types from Galley Media might walk in at that time of the day.

Brick's was only a couple of blocks from the aquarium and I could have easily walked there. But it was cold outside, and I wanted to get my car and myself away from that cavernous parking garage.

Where the hell is John?

I glanced at my watch.

He should have been here by now.

I breathed slowly in and out. The rough edges of the last fifteen minutes were starting to flatten out, nerves settling back down, heart pumping normally, hands steady. I raised one to signal the young man behind the bar for service.

"A little early in the day, isn't it?"

I turned when I heard the familiar voice. It was John standing behind me in his insulated leather coat, his longish hair tousled by the wind, peering at me through his black-rimmed glasses.

I answered him. "Not for me, not for what I found on my windshield." I turned to the kid behind the bar. "Vodka tonic."

"What can I get you?" The bartender directed the question to John.

"You got any coffee back there?"

"Yes, sir. We've got a fresh pot on."

When the young man rushed off, I felt slightly embarrassed that I'd ordered a drink during the middle of the day while John was caffeinating.

While he stripped off his coat and hung it on the back of his barstool, I caught his eye. "Where have you been? I was starting to think something happened to you."

He sat down and adjusted his glasses. "I circled the block a couple of times to see if anyone was watching this restaurant or your car."

"See anything?"

He shook his head. "Let me see the note."

I took it out of my coat pocket and quickly handed it to him. I hated even touching it.

He unfolded the sheet of paper, flattened it against the bar, and studied it. "Block letters. Looks like the same handwriting as the note you found in your house yesterday."

"Yup."

The young bartender came by with my vodka and John's cup of coffee. "Cream or sugar?"

"Black is fine." John held up the note and looked more closely at it. "Huh."

"What?"

"The paper."

"What about it?"

He put it down on the bar again and took a sip of his coffee. "For bar coffee, this is pretty damned good."

"What about the paper?" I took a hit off my drink.

"It's eight and a half by eleven copier paper."

I looked down at it. It looked ordinary. "So?"

He nodded toward my oversized bag, the strap hanging over my coat draped over the barstool. "What kind of paper do you have in your bag?"

I looked at him, confused. Then I rummaged and pulled out my tiny reporter's spiral notebook, holding it up for him to see. "This is all I've got. Why?"

John smiled. "Exactly. You have the world's biggest handbag and the only writing paper you have in it is your little journalist notebook. Who carries copy paper around with them?"

I thought it through. "Someone who wants to leave a note?"

"Someone who's planning ahead of time to leave a note." He placed his coffee cup back on the bar.

"You think Merlin Finn was planning to leave a note all along? Why?"

"Tell me about your meeting with Eric Decker."

I glanced around the restaurant. The young bartender was watching a television mounted over the bar. His attention was on ESPN. Lunchtime was winding down and the only other patrons were two couples. One couple was a man and a woman both in professional business attire. The other two people in the restaurant were women, dressed nicely but casually, most likely housewives or stay-at-home moms out for lunch and a glass of wine. They were all out of earshot.

"He told me a lot of what you already know. He said that between having the FBI down their necks and their concern about the notebook being in the wrong hands, they've decided to go completely legit."

John frowned. "I still don't believe that for a minute. They don't have it in their DNA to go straight."

"They've changed the name of Wolfline Contracting to Wolfline Management."

"They can change it to the Wolfline Baptist Church, but that doesn't mean they're getting out of the business."

"Decker told me that Bogdan is missing."

His eyes narrowed. Clearly, his attention was piqued. "Tell me about that."

"Decker said that Bogdan was hunting for Merlin Finn. He disappeared. Nobody's heard from him in two days."

He shrugged and eyed my vodka again. "Back when I was heavy into drinking I could go on a bender longer than that. Nobody would see me for days."

Me too.

John continued. "And to answer your question about leaving notes, he's intimidating you, baiting you. He wants to be scarier than he actually is."

I shuddered. "I saw the video of him killing the judge and Abby Tillis. He's damned scary."

Damn it. For a second, I forgot that John had been married to Abby Tillis.

He stared at the mirror behind the bar. "Have you ever heard the story about how the Tolbonovs got their start? When Valentin got into the diamond business, he was cheated out of a deal by a competitor. He and Bogdan kidnapped him and his family. Then they took them upstate somewhere, tied the guy to a tree, and made him watch while Bogdan slit the throats of the wife and two kids."

I held up my hand. "I've heard this, but when I was told the story, it was three kids. Then the Tolbonovs bury the competitor alive. Mike Dillon thinks it's just an urban legend to keep their crew in line."

"Maybe. Maybe not. But the story pops up from time to time. If you're in the business of intimidating people, it helps to be as scary as possible."

Because of his disapproving looks, I hesitated to take another sip of my drink.

Fuck it.

I took a healthy hit and put the glass on the countertop. "Where do we go from here?"

John adjusted his glasses. "Depends on what you have planned for the rest of the day."

"Before I got the text from Decker, I was on my way to talk with the roommate of the kid who overdosed last night."

"Sounds like a plan."

"What are *you* going to do?"

He sipped his coffee. "Follow you at a discreet distance."

Right that moment, those were the most reassuring words I'd heard in a long time. "I appreciate that. What about the project you're working on for Nathaniel?"

John glanced around the room. "It's nearly done. The guy this company wants to hire as CEO has three pending lawsuits against him for sexual harassment. I just need to write up the report, and I can do that tonight after dinner."

Then he looked down at my drink, nearly gone.

I upended the glass and finished it.

"Are you having another?"

What the hell is it to you?

Then I recalled an innocuous, throwaway statement he'd made just a few minutes before. "You said you were a heavy drinker once?" I asked.

John nodded. "Cost me Abby. She didn't leave me because she found someone better than me. She left because she found someone less drunk than me."

Remembering the scotch he'd had the night before at Shana's place, I asked, "Did you quit?"

He sighed. "When Abby left and the NYPD decided I should find another line of work, I'd hit bottom. I quit cold turkey. Did AA and the whole nine yards."

I reached out and put my hand on his. "How about now?"

"I have the occasional drink. I think I have it under control." He glanced down at my empty glass again. "But do we ever?"

"Shana said that, at one point, Abby was hoping to reconcile, trying to get back together with you. Shana said you couldn't trust her again."

He shook his head. "I didn't want to let her be in a position where I'd hurt her again. Sometimes it's better to be just friends."

"But you loved her once."

"I never stopped loving her, even when I found out she was sleeping with someone else while we were still married. I was hurt, but I understood why she felt the need to do it. I loved her until the day Merlin Finn killed her."

Chapter Twenty-One

Driving from South Sheffield to the north side of town, I was comforted every time I caught a glimpse of the black Mustang two or three cars behind me. As hard as I tried, I couldn't see anyone else who might be following my Sebring.

Eighty-one Bruckner Avenue was in a neighborhood undergoing a reformation. Much like the neighborhood where the Sheffield Meridian was going to be built, old homes had been purchased and knocked down. Except on the north side, in their place, luxury condominiums and apartment buildings had been constructed or were in the process of being built. Price tags for purchase or rental were outlandishly high.

With one exception. The holdout was the complex called Crystal Garden Condominiums where Bryan Townsend had lived. Two brick buildings, both two stories high, side by side, faced a small parking area. The buildings were fronted by scruffy bushes, and each condo unit had its own doorway and tiny sidewalk to the parking lot. As I parked in front of Unit B3, I noted the wreaths tacked up on the doors and the Christmas trees in the front windows of neighboring condos.

But much like my own home, there was nothing on the door or in the window of the unit that Bryan Townsend had called home.

Getting out of my car, I glanced behind me and watched the black Mustang slide silently near where the parking lot emptied out onto Wolfpit Avenue. Then I walked up the steps and rang the doorbell.

A few moments later, the door swung open, and a young man in his early twenties appeared. He was barefoot and wearing a pair of jeans and a black T-shirt that said, "Shout out to all stoners who smoke every day and still get their shit done."

"Help you?" he asked, his voice low and somber. His hair was cut fashionably short, and he had a full hipster beard that hid the lower half of his face and long neck. A diamond chip rested in his earlobe and a metal ring threaded through his lower lip. It looked painful, like a fish on a hook. His eyes were glassy.

Oh, good, he's high.

I smiled up at him. "I'm Genie Chase with the *Sheffield Post.* Do you mind if I come in and talk with you?"

He appeared momentarily confused. "Uh, his parents already handled Bryan's obituary."

"I'm not here about an obit. I'm a reporter. I'd like to talk to you about Bryan."

"The cops have already been here asking questions."

I took two fingers and crossed the front of my coat. "I promise to ask new ones."

Bet you can't even remember what the cops asked you.

He nodded his head in a vague manner. "Guess that's okay."

Then we stood there for a few awkward moments, me in the cold, him half in and half out. "So, can I come in?"

"Oh, yeah, sure." He waved me in and then disappeared into the tiny living room.

I entered and closed the door behind me. There was a laptop sitting on a sofa that had seen better days. The arms had rips in them and gray tufts of stuffing peeked out of the fabric on the sofa's cushions.

A second sofa, worn but in slightly better condition, was

pushed against the wall to my left. Through an open doorway, I spotted a small kitchen complete with counter space crowded with dirty dishes, old boxes of Chinese food, a roll of paper towels, and a box of Honey Nut Cheerios. The house smelled vaguely of mildew, rotting fruit, and weed.

I took off my coat. "Mind if I sit down?"

He motioned to the couch without the laptop, and then he sat in the other. The illumination from the computer screen coated him in an odd silver color.

I took my phone out and hit the recording app. "How about if we start by telling me your name?"

He smiled. "I'm Paul Reed."

"Awesome. Have you and Bryan been roommates for very long?"

The young man shook his head. "About four months."

"How well did you know him?"

Paul shrugged. "He was a neat freak." He nodded toward the kitchen. "Always bitching at me if I left something out in the kitchen. He kept his bedroom spotless. Ask me, I think he was wound way too tight."

"Did you guys ever hang out? Talk?"

He shook his head. "Nah, he was a little too intense for me."

"How's that?"

Paul leaned forward in a conspiratorial way. "You know he was using drugs."

This guy is really fucked up. Of course, I know he was using. He died from an overdose.

"What kind of drugs was he using?"

His only answer was to look away from me.

"Paul, Bryan is already dead. Anything you tell me isn't going to hurt him."

Paul bit his lip and stayed silent.

"Was he shooting heroin?"

The young man nodded. "Pills too. Bad shit. Oxy, mostly."

"Was he selling?"

Paul sniffled and ran his finger under his nose.

You doing coke too, Paul?

"Yeah, he was selling heroin. He'd cut it with fentanyl. I think that was the shit that did him in."

"Cops say they found his body in the men's room at a gas station."

His mouth formed a perfect o. Then he quietly responded, "I know, right? How disgusting is that? An awful place to die."

"Was he freelancing, or was he selling for someone?"

Paul leaned forward again. "Bryan told me once. He said that he was working for a syndicate called the Brothers or somethin'."

"Could it have been called the Brotherhood?"

Paul snapped his fingers and pointed at me. "That's it. The Brotherhood. Bryan said he was gonna work his way up the corporate ladder and become a crime boss. He said something about working a market some Russians left open. That's what I mean; the guy was intense."

"He give a name? You know who he was working for?"

Paul rubbed his eyebrows as he thought.

Boy has burned through some brain cells.

"A magician. Let's see, it wasn't David Copperfield. It wasn't Penn or Teller."

"Was it Merlin?"

He snapped his fingers and pointed at me. "Yeah, Merlin the magician."

The boy was thinking about Merlin the Arthurian wizard, but I didn't feel like arguing the point. "Did he say the name Merlin Finn?"

Paul nodded enthusiastically.

"Did you tell this to the cops?"

"No. The cop I was talking to, Keith somebody, wasn't very nice. Kept sniffing at me, thinking I'd been smoking something. Hell, I was straight when they came askin' questions."

Not like now.

"Did they search Bryan's room?"

"Yeah, they didn't find anything. Bryan kept his room really clean."

"Where did he keep his stash?"

Paul glanced at the window again. "In the trunk of his Toyota."

The cops searched his car. There was nothing in it.

"Can I look?"

Paul was honest about Bryan's room. As much of a roach-fest as the rest of the house was, the young man's bedroom was tidy and well cared for. Not what I would have expected for a heroin addict.

The twin-size bed was neatly made, a blue comforter folded at the foot. Framed photos were placed on the bureau—one of an older couple I guessed were his parents. The other was of a pretty girl, in her late teens or early twenties. She was laughing at the camera, her hair pinned up on the top of her head, wearing a sleeveless top and a tiny pair of Daisy Dukes.

I pointed. "Is that Bryan's girlfriend?"

He nodded. "Yeah, tragic. She overdosed a couple of nights ago."

I felt a nasty twist in my stomach. "What's her name?"

"Holly." He stopped and thought again. "Holly Dickenson. Yeah, they found her in the ladies' room at Lando's the other night. That tore Bryan up something awful."

Enough to commit suicide in the bathroom of a gas station?

Paul leaned in and gave me a whisper. "I think she was selling for Merlin the magician too."

I walked to the closet and slid open the door. His clothes were all neatly hung. Shoes and sneakers lined up all in a row on the floor. The drawers to the bureau contained what was supposed to be there—clothes, socks, underwear. No drugs. Not even a half-empty bottle of Absolut.

Bryan's bathroom was spotless.

What man keeps his bathroom this clean?

The medicine cabinet held only shaving cream, aspirin, Band-Aids, and toothpaste. Paul had been watching me all the while I searched Bryan's room. I asked, "Why did Bryan keep his room so clean?"

He bobbed his head. "I think he was kind of a germophobe."

"You said he'd cut his heroin with fentanyl. Where'd he do that?"

"Kitchen."

"Show me."

He led the way from Bryan's bedroom into the narrow hall, which gave me a peek into Paul's room. It was a sty. Rumpled blanket on an unmade bed. Piles of clothes on the floor. I didn't want to think about what Paul's bathroom looked like.

The kitchen wasn't much bigger than a walk-in closet. Four-burner stove, cheap refrigerator, microwave sitting on the counter along with dishes from last night and this morning. More dishes in the sink. Trash can overflowing.

But the table was spotless. Not even a single ring from a wet glass or coffee cup.

I motioned toward the table. "Is that where Bryan worked?"

Paul opened the refrigerator, peering absently inside. "Yeah, made me nervous when he measured and bagged up his shit. Had a ton of pills too. A little grass around the house is no big deal. The kind of drugs he had, if the cops found it here, we'd do serious time."

"Where did Bryan get his merchandise?"

Paul opened the refrigerator and absently stared at the nearly empty shelves. "The hard stuff came from Merlin the magician's guys. Bryan would get a text message, then he'd take off and come back with a new stash."

"What about the pills?"

Unable to locate anything edible, Paul closed the refrigerator door. "When he needed more, he'd hop in his car and come back with a plastic shopping bag full of pill bottles. You know, like when you get a prescription. Those tiny, brown plastic bottles? He'd have a bag full of them."

"Where did he get those?"

"Only thing he ever said was he was heading down to the candy shop. I didn't ask where that was. I didn't want to know. We about done? I think I'm going to do a Taco Bell run. I'm starving."

I glanced around the filthy kitchen one more time. I stopped when I got to the trash can. "You going to take that out?"

He frowned at me. "Yeah, I'm gonna to take it out." Paul's tone was defensive.

I recalled how the garbage had been strewn over the front lawn of the house where Holly Dickenson had lived.

Someone wanted what was in that trash.

I smiled. "I'll take it out for you."

—

I hustled down the concrete steps toward my car, popping the trunk remotely with my key fob. With one fluid movement, I heaved the heavy bag of trash into the trunk and closed it. Glancing across the parking lot, I was relieved to see the black Mustang.

Then I stood and gazed around me.

Is someone watching, waiting for Paul Reed to take out the trash?

I didn't see any sinister pickup trucks or SUVs. I opened my car door and was about to slide inside when something caught the corner of my eye.

Movement. Something above me, in the sky?

I looked up and squinted at the dull light of that afternoon, seeing nothing but stone-colored clouds.

John must have become concerned, because he got out of his car, and hand held to his forehead, shielding out some of the light, he scanned the sky as well.

Finally, we both looked at each other from across the parking lot and shrugged. An unspoken signal to get in our vehicles and get out of there.

Chapter Twenty-Two

I set the bag of trash on top of the wooden picnic table in my back yard. I didn't care how cold it was. There was no way I was going to search through Paul Reed's garbage inside my home.

I didn't know how old that picnic table was, but on that afternoon, in the frosty light of winter, it was looking sad. The wood was weather beaten and cracked, and both benches were swaybacked.

John came out of the house with a fresh plastic bag and two sets of plastic gloves. "What are we looking for?"

I untied the plastic straps of the garbage bag and took my pair of gloves from John. "I don't know. Something that tells us who Bryan Townsend's pill supplier is."

I slid on the gloves, noticing right away that they weren't made to keep my hands warm. I instinctively blew warm air on my fingers before I started.

John stamped his feet against the cold. "Yeah, let's try to make this quick."

I started picking out empty cans of Chef Boyardee spaghetti and meatballs and empty containers of Budweiser. Then I gingerly pulled out empty boxes of macaroni and cheese, coffee filters, and greasy pizza containers.

John held out the empty bag for me to drop the trash from Paul and Bryan's kitchen. He smiled. "It's a glamorous life, isn't it?"

I chuckled but then found the first of the pill bottles. I had hoped to see what pharmacy they'd come from. But the label that had been glued to the bottle had been stripped off.

"Damn it." I handed it to John, who inspected it and dropped it into the bag he was holding.

All told, I found thirty empty pill containers, all denuded of any identification as to what they were holding or where they were from. "Shit."

"Keep looking," John said quietly. "Unless the kid took those labels with him, they must be somewhere."

I rummaged some more, running out of trash. "I'll say one thing, for a heroin addict, the kid was careful to cover his tracks."

John answered. "You know, we're assuming he was an addict because he died of an overdose. Addicts make mistakes. This kid was pretty smart."

I glanced over at him. "You think maybe someone killed this kid and made it look like an accidental OD?"

"Maybe. You said his girlfriend was Holly Dickenson. She overdosed and died twenty-four hours before he did. Maybe he was pissed off that his girlfriend got some bad shit and he got into a fight with his supplier."

"Roommate said the supplier was the Brotherhood. Do you think they killed this kid and made it look like an overdose?"

John shrugged.

Suddenly, I had a thought. "Hey, can you haul out that empty box of mac and cheese?"

John leaned over and pushed a few items of trash around until he found the bright orange and blue box. He handed it to me.

The top had been torn open but not removed. Once the pasta and cheese packet had been emptied, the cardboard tab had been tucked back in.

Just like if you were storing something inside.

I opened it and ripped the tab off the box to give me an unfettered look at the interior.

"Got it." I poked my gloved fingers inside and gently pulled out a wad of torn labels, the glue on the backs of them holding everything together in a ragged, uneven mass. "Crap, these have been ripped apart too."

John blew on his hands again. "Okay, let's wrap this up and look at what you've got inside where it's warm."

We disposed both garbage bags by dropping them into my supersized plastic bin at the corner of the house. Then we went inside, shed our coats, and I dropped down at the kitchen table to pull apart the bits of paper stuck together by the adhesive originally pasting the labels to the plastic bottles.

"You want some coffee? I'll make a pot."

I looked up at John, who was studying me with more interest than I would have expected.

Are you waiting to see if I'll have coffee? Or are you waiting to see if I'll want another vodka tonic?

"Coffee sounds good." My buzz from Brick's had worn off anyhow. I pointed to the cupboard. "You know where everything is."

While John busied himself, I turned my attention to the gluey mess on the table in front of me. Slowly, carefully, I began pulling the shreds of paper apart and set them out like jigsaw puzzle pieces. "Well, if I put these two pieces together, I can see most of the word OxyContin."

He turned and arched an eyebrow. "It's a start."

I pulled away a few more scraps. Then I saw it. "These are from Flax Hill Pharmacy."

John's open laptop still sat on the kitchen table where he'd been working that morning before meeting me at Brick's. He sat down in front of it. "Flax Hill Pharmacy," he said in a voice so low I could barely hear him. He expertly hit a few keys, studied his screen, then hit a few more keys, and found what he was looking for. "Address is 1213 Flax Hill Road, Sheffield. It's been doing business since 1989, independently owned by Eric Collier. It was purchased in October of this year by a company called Corsair Properties."

"What can you find out about them?"

He tapped a few keys. "Well, they don't have a website. Let's see if I can find any ownership information with the state." After a few more moments he said, "They're a subsidiary of a much larger property company called Wyatt Investments."

I frowned. "Wyatt Investments is the company who quietly bought up all the property along I-95. They're the ones building the Sheffield Meridian."

"What's that?"

"A mall."

John chuckled and got up out of his chair and took two coffee cups out of the cupboard. "A mall, what do these people think? That we're still in the eighties?"

"Yeah, I know."

"Have you given your notice at the paper yet?"

I lied. "I haven't had a chance."

What the hell am I waiting for?

I fixed my gaze on John's face. "Do you like working for Nathaniel?"

John arched his eyebrow again. "Yes, I do. You will too." He glanced down at the pieces of paper sitting on the tabletop. "So, what didn't we find in all that garbage?"

I looked at the scraps of paper as well. "Well, we didn't find any drugs. But I'm guessing the kid had them in the trunk of his car, and someone ripped him off while he was in the restroom getting high."

"What else?"

"No written prescriptions?"

"Yeah, no scrip." John poured the coffee and handed me a cup. "If there were any, most likely he'd have them hidden along with his stash in the trunk of his car.. And it's possible that whoever is prescribing this shit might have phoned it in or sent an electronic prescription."

"That's the part that we're missing. We know where the candy store is. But who's the Doctor Feelgood who's writing the scrip?"

"Look, I'll finish this later." I put the cup on the table. "I need to run into the office to tie up a few loose ends."

He was still holding his mug of steaming coffee. "I'll be right behind you."

"I really think I'll be okay between here and there."

He repeated his words. "I'll be right behind you."

"What are you going to do, sit in my office while I work?"

"We'll go back to plan A. I'll take you to work then stop by the grocery store, pick up a few things, and bring it back here. When you're ready to come home, call me, and I'll come get you."

I pursed my lips. I knew he was right. I thought again about the two notes I've found from Merlin Finn. "You win."

He grinned. "You're a smart lady."

"But first, let's drive by the Flax Hill Pharmacy."

—

When we pulled into the parking lot, I could easily see that the building had undergone renovation. Half of it was still the Flax Hill Pharmacy. The other half was something called the Armand Pain Management Clinic.

It appeared that the building might have once been fronted by plate glass windows. But the facade had recently been altered in that it was all brick and windowless. The new facade was of a slightly redder hue than the old brick.

There were two glass doors, one leading into the pharmacy, one for the clinic. Only three cars plus ours were in the parking lot. We sat for a few moments observing the front of the clinic and the pharmacy. It was far quieter than I had expected.

A Volvo SUV pulled in, and a woman who might have been a

soccer mom got out. She was dressed in a stylish beige overcoat and boots with fur along the tops. She was in her forties, wore her dark hair in a ponytail that peeked out from under a ball cap she wore. Once out of the car, she nervously glanced around the parking lot.

She stopped when she saw us.

John uttered. "Uh-oh."

"I'm getting out."

"What?"

"If she sees us just sitting here, she'll get suspicious. I'm going to go inside and take a look around." Without another word, I got out of the car, ignoring the interest I was getting from the soccer mom.

I passed her as I headed for the clinic doorway.

"He's not open."

I stopped and turned. "What's that?"

The woman was getting her bag out of the front seat of her car. "You looked like you going into the clinic. It's closed today."

I eyed the doorway. A handwritten sign read *Closed. Will reopen again tomorrow at 9*.

The woman came up beside me. "Are you a patient?"

"It's my first time seeing a doctor at this clinic. Are *you* a patient?"

She glanced around her again. "Yes. Let me guess, you've reached the end of your eight-day supply and your doctor can't prescribe anymore."

In Connecticut, your physician, by law, can only give you an opioid supply for eight days.

I tried to give her an embarrassed expression. "It's that obvious, huh?"

She pointed at her chest with her thumb. "That's why I come here."

"Do you know why the clinic is closed?"

She reached out and put her hand on my arm. "I heard that

another one of his patients overdosed last night. That's two in the last two days. I'm worried."

"Worried?"

She took her hand off my arm and leaned in. "That the police are going to find out where they got their prescriptions and close Dr. Armand down. Wouldn't that be a kick in the ass? Are you headed into the pharmacy?"

"Are you filling a prescription?"

She gave me a faltering smile. "I got my scrip yesterday from Dr. Armand but didn't get a chance to get it filled. I had to pick my son up from his music class. He's got an electric guitar." She rolled her eyes. "Ugh."

"Do you mind if I come in with you?" I reached out my hand. "I'm Genie by the way. That's why I was coming to see Dr. Armand. I need a prescription. My back is acting up again."

She nodded knowingly and shook my hand. "Yes, the old back. For me, it's just stress. Come inside with me. I'm Jill."

Being a reporter, you get information in a lot of diverse ways. Hard work, long hours, tough questions, but sometimes it's just dumb luck. Jill was my lucky break du jour.

The interior of the drugstore was surprisingly small. When pharmacies were built in the eighties, they didn't have the same broad concept as today's CVS and Walgreens chains. Those stores carry everything from paperbacks to magazines, cosmetics to floor fans, candy to Christmas decorations, canned and frozen food to school supplies.

The store we walked into had been tiny to begin with. But after being chopped in half, there wasn't much more than a couple of aisles carrying the most basic of first aid items, vitamins, blood pressure cuffs, and what looked like used wheelchairs. Her back against the front counter, facing a display of cigarettes, the cashier, a young girl in her twenties wearing a black long-sleeved cotton shirt, sporting a spider web tattooed on her neck, was tapping out a text on her phone.

The most prominent feature in the store was the pharmacy itself in the back. "So, you haven't been in here before?"

"No, is this where I'll need to fill Dr. Armand's scrip?"

Jill gave me an earnest expression. "Here and only here, girl. Dr. Armand owns the clinic and this pharmacy. If you go anywhere else, it'll get reported to the state. They have a database to keep track of who's getting what kind of pills. It's really none of their business, don't you think?"

We started back toward where the drugs were dispensed. Jill nearly clapped her hands when she saw there was hardly anyone at the counter. "With the clinic closed today, I kind of thought that nobody would be in here."

"This place gets crowded?" I noticed the armed guard sitting in a chair off to one side, leafing through a magazine. Because he was seated, I could only guess at his size, but he looked to be a very large guy. He was wearing a security guard uniform that offered no logo or patch. Other than the gray shirt and pants, the only way you'd know he was working security was the holstered pistol attached to his belt.

Seeing my line of sight, Jill whispered. "That's Chet. He looks mean, but he's a just a big teddy bear."

I suddenly recalled how Bristol Finn had referred to her husband in a similar way when they were first married.

The man behind the counter was about five seven, in his thirties, and was wearing a white coat and blue jeans. His head was completely shaved, his pink scalp shining under the lights overhead, and he had a tattoo of the head of a pit bull on his right cheekbone.

"I don't know his real name, but everyone calls him Dodge, because he moves fast behind that counter when things are busy." She bobbed from one side to another. "You know, dodge and weave."

We stood behind a young man wearing a flannel coat, jeans, and sneakers. On his head, he wore a dark blue stocking cap with a Huskies logo. It only took a moment for him to hand over his scrip and receive a plastic shopping bag with at least a dozen vials inside.

As he turned to leave, he appraised Jill and I, looking at us up and down, followed with an appreciative grin.

When he walked away, Jill reached out and squeezed my hand. "Some of the clientele here is a little rough."

"Hi, Jill." The man behind the counter had Jill fixed in his sight. "What do you have today?"

"The usual." She handed over her slip of paper.

Dodge turned and expertly filled a plastic bag with four tiny, brown plastic containers filled with pills.

She reached into the pocket of her coat and pulled out a wad of cash. As she did, she leaned in and whispered to me, "Cash only here. No credit cards, no checks."

"Gotcha."

Dodge narrowed his eyes at me. "Who's your friend, Jill?"

"This is Genie. She's going to be a new patient of Dr. Armand's."

He smiled at me. "Awesome. Looking forward to doing business with you, Genie."

Out of the corner of my eye, I noticed the armed guard was getting out of his chair. Once up, he hitched up his belt and took a phone out of his pocket. The guard slowly lumbered to where we were chatting with Dodge.

The guard's voice was low but soft. "You're a newbie?"

I smiled at him. "Hi, I'm Genie."

Without saying another word, his phone came up, and he snapped a photo of my face.

I felt Jill's hand back on my arm. "Don't mind Chet. He likes to have photos of the clientele. Don't you, Chet?"

He nodded and ambled back to his chair.

When Jill and I got outside, I zipped my parka back up, and she did the same. I was happy to see John still sitting in the Mustang, a few parking spaces away.

"Is that your husband?"

She was looking at John, who purposely was ignoring us. I replied, "No, that's just a friend."

"Look, you seem like a nice lady."

"You too."

"I should warn you about Dr. Armand."

"What about him."

She hesitated. "Women who come to him. He may want you to do things."

"What kind of things?"

She cocked her head and sighed. "Depends how much you want the pills, girl."

Without another word, she got into her Volvo, and I walked slowly back to the Mustang.

But not before I memorized her plate number. I might have to reach out to Jill again sometime.

Chapter Twenty-Three

Mercifully, when John dropped me off at the paper, Lorraine was in a meeting with the other department heads, along with Ben Sumner and the odious Robert Vogel. No longer considered management, I gratefully sat at my newsroom desk and polished off a piece on a mugging on Spencer Avenue and an assault at the Monterey Grill. The assault was the most fun. A customer had paid for his dinner but instead of a tip, left a nasty note on the credit card receipt. The food server, a young woman, followed the man and his wife out to their car and began shouting at them. The customer's wife, overhearing the waitress, began a heated exchange that escalated to fists and fingernails. The wife was arrested.

Fun ink.

Seeing that it was getting close to quittin' time, I decided to make one last work call to Mike Dillon to see if there had been any progress on the Groward Bay homicides.

"Hey, Genie."

"Hey, Mike. Just checking in."

"Nothing new on the double homicide. But we got a missing person that you might be interested in."

I watched the conference room door open and the participants of the department head meeting come out. Nobody was speaking. Lorraine's face was colored crimson, and Robert Vogel wore the expression of someone who had just eaten a bug. A few of the others, our lead pressman, the graphic arts director, and the head of circulation, came out smiling. They were the old guard, employees who hadn't been displaced yet.

Ben was the last to exit. His countenance was stern, lips pressed together. He headed for his office.

Vogel headed for the front door.

What just happened?

I focused back on Mike Dillon and the phone call. "Who's missing?"

I visualized him consulting his ubiquitous notebook. "Leon Dempsey hasn't been seen in two days. Police were called when he failed to show up at work and there was no response to phone calls, emails, or texts."

"I'll bite. Who's Leon Dempsey?"

"Senior prison officer on duty the night Merlin Finn escaped."

My heart took an extra couple of beats. "What do we know?"

He read off the stats. "Forty-three years old, five foot nine, one hundred eighty pounds, Caucasian, clean shaven at the time of his disappearance, brown eyes, balding, no scars or tattoos, widowed, and no children. Police were called. They were let into Dempsey's house by a concerned neighbor who had an extra key to his house. There's no sign of foul play and Dempsey's car is also MIA."

"What does he drive?"

"An eight-year-old Dodge Dakota pickup truck."

I wrote while Mike talked. "Nothing fancy there. Cops check his finances?"

"He didn't make any recent cash withdrawals. But what's interesting is he made two deposits to his account. Twenty thousand dollars the week before Finn's escape and fifty thousand the day after."

I smiled. "Well, fancy that. So, he didn't take any of that money with him?"

"Nope. Cops think something spooked him and he bolted."

I took a deep breath and recalled the two notes that I'd gotten. "Finn's a spooky guy. Hey, I've got another missing person for you. Did you know that Bogdan Tolbonov is MIA?"

There was a brief silence on the phone while Mike digested that. "Where did you hear that?"

It was my turn to hesitate. "At his request, I met with Eric Decker, attorney for Wolfline Contracting. He told me that Valentin Tolbonov believes his brother is dead."

"How come he hasn't reported Bogdan missing?"

"Decker said that the relationship between the Tolbonovs and law enforcement isn't particularly cordial."

"Why did he tell you?"

How much do I let you know, Mike?

"He asked me to help them find Bogdan…or his remains."

"What else?"

"They also asked me to help them find Merlin Finn."

The silence was deafening. Finally, "I'm going to give you some advice, not that you ever take it. You never have. Stay away from these people. Is that guy John Stillwater still around?"

"Yeah, he's at my house while I'm working here in the office."

"I did some checking on him. Did you know he was a New York cop?"

"He told me."

"Did he tell you he was kicked off the force for assaulting a prisoner in his custody?"

My heart fell. I stayed silent.

"He's lucky he wasn't arrested himself or sued."

"Thanks, Mike. I'm a big girl."

"Yeah, but sometimes you make bad decisions."

"Like not committing to our relationship?"

I heard him sigh. "A conversation for another time."

He hung up without saying goodbye. I checked my watch and texted John to come pick me up. I knew it would take him a few minutes to get to the newspaper so, nosy about what had happened in the conference room, I headed for Ben's office.

The door was open, he was on the phone, and when I sat down he looked at me and rolled his eyes. He was just finishing up his conversation. "Call me back when you have something."

I collapsed in his office chair opposite him. "What's going on, boss?"

He took a deep breath. "I announced in the department head meeting that my attorney is seeking an injunction to halt the sale of the *Post.*"

"Wow."

"He thinks it's a long shot but he's using the tactic that Galley Media failed to negotiate in good faith."

"Is that a thing?"

"It's easier to prove for a seller who neglects to offer full disclosure about property and assets, but my lawyer thinks we might be able to go that route if we prove to a judge that Galley had advance information about the Sheffield Meridian, making the *Post* worth at least twice as much as they're paying."

"Do you have proof?"

"Not yet. I need for you to get on this."

Before or after I give you my three-week notice?

"I have my hands full with the investigation of the double homicide out at Groward Bay."

"Come on. Let the police handle that. I need you, Genie."

I sighed. "Let me see what I can do."

He smiled and stood up. "That's my street fighter."

"How did Robert and Lorraine take the news?"

Ben laughed. "Robert looked like he'd just taken a big bite out of a lemon." Ben stood up and mocked Vogel, "Galley's not going to like this, Ben. You got lawyers? They got more lawyers than you can ever afford. They'll bleed you dry."

I grinned. "You sound just like him."

He smiled back. "I'm not sure that's a good thing."

Getting out of the chair, I fixed Ben with my eyes. "Can you stop them?"

He shrugged slightly. "I've got to at least try. I need your help on this, Genie."

I took another deep breath. "I'll do the best I can, Ben."

—

I sat at the kitchen table, laptop open, while John negotiated his way around my kitchen. From where I sat, I could barely hear the slosh and rumble of the washing machine in the laundry room as it cleaned a small load of clothes I had in the hamper. But most importantly, it was also washing all my underwear.

Taking them out of my drawer and putting them in the hamper, I kept visualizing the hulking form of Merlin Finn fondling my panties. Touching them, smelling them.

I'm going to make you model these for me.

I shuddered.

John was putting together chicken piccata and roast veggies, and I was looking for a connection between Wyatt Investments and Galley Media. Galley was an open book. It was a publicly owned company with a board of people I'd never heard of and run by a management team that was more interested in cutting costs and increasing revenues than they were in good journalism.

Glancing up at the back of John's head while he breaded the chicken cutlets, I asked, "Did you get a chance to see if there's anything between Wyatt Investments and Galley Media?"

Without looking at me, he answered, "I took a poke at it. I'll do some more tomorrow. Wyatt has financial interests in dozens, if not hundreds, of companies. Those have financial interests in even more companies. If there's a connection there, I'll find it. Oh, by the way. Can you download a copy of the infamous notebook onto a thumb drive for me?" He quickly took one out of his pocket and handed it to me.

While I was at the laptop, I copied the file called Tucker's Veterinarian Records onto his thumb drive and handed it back to him. Then I did a search for Wyatt Investments.

The conglomerate was privately held and very opaque. The professionally designed website told me that the firm was global in scope, having offices in New York, Amsterdam, Frankfurt, Sydney, and Moscow. Their holdings were mostly commercial and residential real estate but also included "real estate private debt and direct equity investments in partnership with leading real estate operating partners, sophisticated family offices, institutional real estate owners, and leading private equity firms, in the recapitalization and acquisition of real estate assets and companies around the world. Our focus is on value-added, opportunistic, and event-driven real estate investments throughout the capital structure."

What the hell does that mean?

I saw that the Sheffield Meridian wasn't going to be their only urban mall. They already had six others in cities in the United States, Canada, Great Britain, France, and Spain.

The website was not forthcoming in who the founders or the managing partners were. Something to work on tonight from my bedroom after we finished dinner?

"Ready to eat?"

I looked up from my computer and saw him smiling down on me, spatula in hand, looking absolutely adorable. I love a man who cooks, because I can't. Well, I don't.

I packed up my laptop and stood up. "Famished."

The meal didn't disappoint. After the first taste of chicken and the roasted veggies, I said, "You're hired. Chief cook and bodyguard."

He grinned. "When Abby and I were married, I did most of the cooking. It's something that I enjoy, a good way to unwind at the end of the day. Plus, I always know that I'll be eating something I like because that's all I cook."

I took another bite of the chicken. "It's awesome."

"Not in Gerald's class, but I do the best I can." He sipped his scotch.

I grinned. "So, do Shana and Gerald hook up?"

He guffawed. "When I'm there, it's not generally a topic of conversation. But I imagine they do all sorts of things."

"Aren't you the slightest bit attracted to Shana? She's very pretty."

He studied me with narrowed eyes. "Are you?"

I cocked my head and offered an admission. "A little."

"Is it Shana you're attracted to or the lifestyle?"

I felt myself blush.

How did I let the conversation get here?

"A little of both, maybe." I suppose there should have been some embarrassment in admitting that, but I'd recently turned forty. The last time I'd been with a man was back in October, and I'll be the first to admit that I have a healthy libido. I know that menopause waits for me somewhere down the trail. What about things I haven't tried yet?

Like chains and whips?

I glanced at John and noticed how ruggedly handsome he was. And how he was smiling at me in a playful way. "After dinner, do you want to get your Christmas decorations out?"

I immediately thought about Caroline and how when this was over, John would head back to New York and I'd be alone again. I replied, "Not tonight. Tomorrow for sure."

—

"Hey, baby."

"Hey, Genie. How was your day?" Caroline's voice was upbeat and bubbly.

"You know, work, work, work. How was yours?"

"You know, ski, fall, ski, fall." She laughed.

"It's a tough life. Have you had dinner?"

"We just finished. Went to a barbeque place called Aspen Hickory House. The ribs are to die for. What did you do for dinner? Bring home takeout?"

"Yeah." I lied. I didn't want her to know that I had a man staying at the house as my bodyguard. "You know me. What else did you do besides skiing?"

"Aunt Ruth took us shopping. They have some of the cutest shops here."

Aunt Ruth was knocking the ball out of the park. Coming home was going to look like jail time after this trip.

"You'll have to show me what you bought when you get home."

"I bought some really pretty tops and skirts."

"Awesome. Is Aunt Ruth close by?"

"She's right here. Have you put up any Christmas decorations yet?"

I closed my eyes and rubbed my forehead. "Tomorrow, after work. I promise."

"I worry about you, Genie. It's almost Christmas. Are you going to be okay?"

I chuckled. "I worry about me too, baby. But I'm going to be just fine."

She handed the phone off to Ruth. "Hello, Genie."

"Hey, Ruth. I've been concerned. Do you still think you're being followed?"

"Not that I can see. After what you and Caroline went through in October, I might just be a little paranoid. One of the Aspen cops actually stopped by to meet with us. He told us that they'd be keeping an eye on our neighborhood while we're in town."

God bless Mike Dillon.

I sighed with relief. "That's good news, Ruth. Keep everyone safe."

—

Before I turned in for the night, I wanted to make sure John had everything he needed. He'd chosen to camp out on the living room couch instead of sleeping in Caroline's room.

I guess it's too girly for him.

I usually sleep in the nude, but on that evening, I had on a pair of flannel jammies over which I wore a fluffy pink bathrobe. Barefoot, I left my bedroom and padded down the carpeted steps as quietly as possible.

It was dark as I descended to the living room. The only illumination came from the streetlight outside, muted from the closed curtains.

I let my eyes adjust to the darkness and saw the indistinct outline of the couch and what appeared to be a snoozing John Stillwater.

Guess he doesn't need anything.

I sighed and wondered silently why I had come downstairs at all. I had assembled a pillow, sheets, blanket, and a comforter for him before I'd headed for bed.

One last look at John?

"Can I help you?"

His voice behind me nearly made me pee.

I turned, my heart pounding.

He smiled. "Sorry if I startled you."

"Jesus Christ, you scared the crap out of me." I took a breath and noticed that he was naked except for his black boxer shorts. I reached out to the wall next to me and flipped on the light.

When I did that, I saw that John's face reddened. I also saw his muscular chest, tight tummy, and that his shoulders and biceps were like granite.

The boy is in shape.

And that he was holding something behind his back.

A handgun.

Seeing that I had spotted the weapon, he brought it out and went to the couch, putting the gun into its holster, laying it carefully on a cushion. Then he took the comforter and draped it over his shoulders, covering himself. "Didn't mean to scare you."

"No worries. My heart rate will be back to normal in an hour or so. Look, I just wanted to make sure you had everything you need."

"I'm good."

Yes, you are.

"Okay, then. If you need anything, let me know."

Go to bed, Genie.

—

I had just settled into bed, covers over me, Tucker snuggled up next to my rib cage. I began reading chapter three of Sue Grafton's last novel.

My phone pinged. Someone had just sent me a text from a number that was blocked.

Pulling my phone down from next to the vodka, I read it. Fear turned my fingers to ice and oxygen caught in my throat.

Did you like my notes?

I dropped my phone onto my bed, my hands shaking. If that text was from Merlin Finn, then a monster was on the other end of the line.

Should I get John?

I reached out and picked the phone back up. Taking a deep breath, I pecked out:

Who is this?

After a few seconds my phone pinged again and the answer appeared on my screen. My fear turned to horror.

Come on, Genie. You know who this is. If you like my notes, you'll love what I left you at Groward Bay.

Chapter Twenty-Four

We drove up to the marina's front gate in the Mustang. John was at the wheel, his Glock holstered under his leather coat. He slowed to a stop and pointed. "It's all dark. The security lights should be on."

He was right. The place was a black hole. The only illumination came from our headlights.

In the pale twin beams, we could see the gate was wide open.

Someone wants us to come in.

"Think someone cut the power?"

He stopped the car. "I don't think Finn wants any more video."

"Why would he stop now?"

John peered into the darkness. "Don't know." He glanced at me. "You ready?"

I looked back at him. "Think we should call the cops?"

"We don't know if there's been a crime committed." He attempted a half smile. He turned off the headlights and the dash lights, and we sat quietly while the engine idled.

"What are we doing?"

"Letting our eyes adjust to the dark."

The sky was overcast, the stars and moon obliterated. The inky night seemed impenetrable.

Yet as I sat in the car, vague, black shapes slowly appeared like malignant shadows.

He put the car in gear and pressed gently on the gas and we rolled forward, driving through the gate and along the dark, narrow lane, the black hulking shapes of expensive boats on jack stands lined up on either side of us.

I cracked my window open and listened. All I heard was the crunching of the tires against the gravel and ice. I rolled the glass up again, warding off the bitingly cold air muscling its way into the car.

At the end of the lane, we drove onto the parking area. The huge dry-stack boat storage building loomed like a monstrous beast off to our left, the pale concrete pier stretched out in front of us. I strained to see into the inky black of that night to see if the massive forklift was parked outside again, with its prongs underwater.

I saw nothing.

John parked the car and cut the engine. Then he reached under his seat and pulled out a flashlight. "Stay in the car."

"No way." My words were false bravado. I was scared right down to my thermal underwear.

The air blowing in off the bay slapped my exposed face like an icy insult. Pulling up my scarf to cover the lower half of my face, I mumbled, "Jesus, it's cold."

"Shh."

I stopped in my tracks, my ears tingling, straining to hear what was spooking John.

It took me a moment detect it, the wind alternately whistling and growling around us, the occasional clanging of sailboat riggings against metal masts. But when I heard it, the blood in my veins turned as cold as the water in the bay.

An engine. Grumbling, low and steady.

We crept forward onto the concrete pier. John was slightly ahead of me, his gun in his right fist, pointed ahead of him, the flashlight, still off, in his left hand under the Glock.

Slowly, the shape materialized in the darkness. Big, black. It was a pickup truck.

Jesus Christ, it looks like Bogdan Tolbonov's Ford F-150.

John, low in a crouch, moved cautiously forward.

Doing the same, right behind him, I smelled the acrid exhaust pumping from the dual tailpipes. We moved around to the passenger's side, inch by inch.

I grimaced every time I heard the soles of my boots crunching against granules of ice.

Suddenly, John's flashlight came to life, and he had the beam angled so that the reflection on the glass was minimized.

There's no one in the cab.

He turned the beam onto the bucket seats. "There's a wallet on the console." He tried the door. "Locked."

Wanting to confirm that the truck was Bogdan's, I took another step toward the front of the truck and saw that it had the jutting black, aftermarket bumper guard that gave the vehicle its intimidating appearance. Like a battering ram.

Something glittered in what light came from John's flashlight.

What the hell is that?

"John," I whispered. "There's a chain attached to the front bumper guard."

He stepped up quickly, getting between me and the front of the truck, his gun still drawn and ready. Seeing the length of chain, he ran the flashlight along its links until the beam was in the roiling, black water of the bay.

It took me a minute to understand what we were looking at, what was floating on the surface, attached to the end of the chain.

A blackened body, chain around its neck, vaguely human, bobbing in the dark, swirling water.

You'll love what I left you at Groward Bay.

—

The cops cleared John and me off the pier while they taped it off as a crime scene again, the second time in three days.

Before doing his job, Mike admonished the both of us, "Don't even think about going anywhere until I get a chance to talk to you."

While we sat in the Mustang, listening to late night NPR, we made small talk, consulted our phones, and watched the police come and go. First, they brought in divers to go into the water and inspect the body. Then they brought the dead man up on a lift and, after a brief inspection by the medical examiner, tucked the body into an ambulance.

I was almost relieved when Mike walked with deliberation up to where we were sitting. We both got out of the car at the same time.

Without greeting, Mike started. "Do you want to tell me how the two of you came to be out here?"

"About forty-five minutes ago, I got a text." I held my phone out for him to look at.

He squinted as he read the message. "What's this about notes?"

I took them out of my bag and handed them to Mike.

He opened them, and pointing his own flashlight, he glanced at what was written. "Where did you find these?"

I hesitated. I knew Mike was going to be pissed. "The one about modeling was in my underwear drawer at the house the afternoon Finn broke in."

He gave me an incredulous expression. "How about the second one?"

"On my windshield when I was parked across the street from the aquarium."

"What were you doing at the aquarium?"

"I told you, I was meeting with Wolfline's attorney, Eric Decker." I nodded toward the empty Ford pickup truck, now silent but crawling with cops looking for clues. "Is that Bogdan Tolbonov?"

"We haven't positively identified the body yet."

I frowned. "Why not?"

He glanced at John, who had been standing wordlessly next to me. "The body's in pretty bad shape. Looks like he was burned substantially, facial features disfigured. Some of the teeth appear to be missing." He looked back at me again. "Off the record, I'd say someone had tortured the victim for days. Possibly with a blowtorch and pliers."

My stomach twisted. "Jesus Christ."

For the first time, John spoke up. "There was a wallet inside the cab of the truck."

Mike narrowed his eyes. It was clear that he didn't care for John Stillwater. "Once again, this is off the record. The wallet belongs to Bogdan Tolbonov. So does the truck."

For whatever reason, a feeling of relief washed over me like warm bathwater. Two months ago, Bogdan Tolbonov had scared me, terrified me. He'd threatened me and Caroline. He'd followed me in that truck for days, trying to intimidate me.

I had no doubt in my mind that given the right circumstances, he would have killed me.

But now he's dead. Rendered harmless.

But there's an even worse monster out there, Merlin Finn.

And I'm in his crosshairs.

Chapter Twenty-Five

"I'm having a drink before I go to bed," I told John. "Do you want one?" It was nearly one in the morning and I was way too sober to go to sleep.

"Sure." He sat down at the kitchen table.

The only light on was the one over the sink, which offered dim illumination for the entire room. I didn't feel like turning on the ceiling light. "Pretty gruesome."

"You mean what they did to Bogdan?"

Taking the glasses out of the cupboard, I went to the refrigerator and opened the freezer. "Yeah, what they did to Bogdan."

John had his hands folded on the tabletop. "I don't have much sympathy for the Tolbonovs. They've killed and tortured, swindled life savings from families, blackmailed judges. Dozens of people have died from the drugs they've put out on the street. And the children's lives they've ruined through sex trafficking? I know for a fact that Shana and I have rescued well over a hundred underage kids from the life. I know what kind of trauma that can have on young minds and bodies. That will haunt them for the rest of their lives."

I dropped ice cubes into both of our glasses and waited for him to finish his thought. When he didn't continue, I turned and looked at him.

He was gazing back at me, his jaw firm, his teeth clenched. "So whatever happened to Bogdan Tolbonov, he had it coming."

I went back to the cupboard and poured our drinks. "So, what happens now?" I handed him his glass.

He took a healthy swallow. "In this case, the enemy of my enemy is still my enemy. Merlin Finn is every bit as bad as Bogdan was. Maybe worse. I owe him for killing Abby."

"Shana told me that you were married for seven years."

He nodded. "We met while we were both on the NYPD. When we got married, she quit and became a private investigator, a darned good one. Her company had as many as ten investigators working for her."

I sat down at the table opposite John. "Were you happy?"

After a moment, he answered. "I was. She wasn't. I was working all hours. She was doing investigative work for some pretty large corporations. When I wasn't looking, the CEO of Brookmeyer Pharmaceuticals swept her off her feet." John flicked his glass with a finger. "Plus, it was when my drinking was out of control."

I understand how that can be a relationship killer. I've been married three times.

"How long were they together?"

"Only a year or so. It didn't take her long to catch on that the guy was an asshole."

I snapped my fingers. "Brookmeyer Pharmaceuticals. Isn't that the company that jacked up the price on that cancer drug by a thousand percent?"

He gave me a sour grin. "Plus, the government caught him misleading investors. That son of a bitch is still tied up in litigation purgatory. He belongs in jail." He added, "And, for what he did to my ex-wife, Merlin Finn deserves to be dead."

Suddenly, Mike's warning to not trust anyone popped into my mind. How well did I really know John Stillwater? He was an ex-cop who, for some reason I still didn't know, got kicked out of the NYPD. What did Mike say? That he beat up a person he had in his custody?

I know that his work with the Friends of Lydia was sometimes, if not often, just outside of recognized legal boundaries. I know that he carries a gun.

And now I'd just seen an ugly flash of anger. Angry enough to kill?

Before I'd gotten the text telling me that something had been left for me to find at Groward Bay, I'd entertained lusty thoughts about Mr. Stillwater.

Sitting in my kitchen, talking about his ex-wife's homicide, there was nothing romantic about the moment.

My phone pinged. I reached behind me and fished it out of my oversized bag hanging from the back of my chair. The text was from Mike.

Call me in the morning.

I glanced at John. "It's from Mike Dillon." I wasn't about to wait until morning to find out what he wanted, so I punched in his number.

"Hey, Genie. I didn't think you'd still be awake."

"Still wound up. Are you at the office?"

"I'm just getting ready to head out. We reached out to Valentin Tolbonov and asked him to come in tomorrow to identify the body. He didn't want to wait, so he came in with dental records and gave us a positive ID. It's definitely his brother Bogdan."

There's that sense of relief again.

"He needed dental records?"

I heard Mike hesitate. "What you saw in the water only scratched the surface."

The icy grip of fear overtook my relief from what I was about to hear. "Can I put you on speakerphone?"

Mike's voice dropped into a soft growl. "Is your bodyguard there?"

"Yes." Without explanation about John, I put him on speaker. "Okay."

"The reason we asked Valentin to bring in dental records was there wasn't much left of the body to identify. I'm waiting for Foley to do an autopsy, but it appears that Bogdan had been tortured with a blowtorch for days. Nearly every inch of his skin had been burned. His fingerprints were gone and someone had removed his eyes."

I felt my stomach turn. "What?"

Mike skipped another beat. "Gouged them out."

John spoke up. "What else?"

"It looks like whoever it was started pulling Bogdan's teeth."

I couldn't help myself. My stomach clutched. "Dear God."

Overkill.

I thought back to the video of the homicides at the marina. Using the forklift to kill Judge Preston and Abby Tillis was a statement. Two bullets to their heads would have been simpler and faster.

No, Merlin Finn was making his statement.

John asked, "Were there enough teeth to make an ID?"

"Yes, Bogdan had some extensive crown work done. It was enough to make an ID."

I asked, "What was Valentin's reaction?"

"Stone-faced, grim."

"Are we looking at the beginning of a gang war?"

"I wouldn't be at all surprised. Get some sleep, Genie."

I said goodnight to John and trudged upstairs. I was still wired from the discovery at the marina and the phone call from Mike, so I sat down at my desk and knocked out a piece for the *Post*'s website. It was way too late to make the morning paper. The press was already running, and the circulation crew was already taking bundles out to be distributed. But my story would be loaded first thing in the morning online, and then I'd do an updated version for the newspaper for the following day.

My lead was "Suspected gangster found brutally murdered in Groward Bay."

Then I hit the button and sent the piece to both Ben and Lorraine Moretti. I wasn't a hundred percent certain who was in charge of the newsroom. I was pretty sure it was Ben.

Then I added a note to both of them. "It's nearly two a.m. Getting some sack time, and I'll be in midmorning."

I knew that Ben wouldn't mind.

Lorraine Moretti would have a cow.

Chapter Twenty-Six

I rolled out of bed at nine and was greeted by the mouthwatering scents of hot coffee and bacon. Taking a quick look at myself in the mirror and seeing bedhead hair and a hangover mask of crow's feet and bloodshot eyes, I jumped in the shower and fixed my face in less than a half hour. A record for me.

By the time I swept into the kitchen, John had whipped up a batch of scrambled eggs and bacon and toasted a couple of slices of whole wheat bread. "Good morning."

He smiled at me. "Good morning. How did you sleep?"

I shook my head. "Ghosts and nightmares, all night. How about you?"

"Your couch is surprisingly comfortable."

He was dressed in jeans and a button-down shirt, rolled up at the cuffs. He was adorably barefoot.

"Where's Tucker? You didn't cook him, did you?"

John jutted his jaw toward the door to the backyard. "The way he was whimpering and dancing around, I figured he needed to go out."

I took a quick peek out the window and saw the little guy, nose in the snow, snuffling along the back fence. "Good call."

He put the plates on the table. "Dig in."

We both sat down and started to eat. Neither of us brought the events of last night up.

Finally, John began the conversation. "What's your schedule look like today?"

"First thing I'll need to do is pick up the incident reports at the station house."

"Check."

I picked up and bit off the end of a slice of perfectly fried bacon. "Then, I want to visit Dr. Feelgood at the Armand Pain Management Clinic."

"Okay," he mumbled while chewing a mouthful of eggs.

"I still need to see if there's a connection between Wyatt Investments and Galley Media. My boss is convinced that Galley was tipped off about the Sheffield Meridian."

"I'll give you a hand with that. Do some online sleuthing."

"That would be helpful."

"What else?"

"The supervising officer at the Lockport Correctional Facility the night of Merlin Finn's escape is missing. I think I'd like to go out there and nose around."

"How far is it?"

"Not far, about half an hour if the traffic's not bad."

When we got to the police station, Mike was already on the road, so I picked up the incident reports at the front desk. While we sat in the parking area with the Mustang's engine running and the heater cranked up, I thumbed through them.

A smash and grab, a mugging, two DUIs, a domestic dispute, and two more ODs, both nonfatal.

I glanced at the time on my smartphone. It was almost 10:30. I should have headed into the office, but instead I turned to John. "Let's go see if the pain clinic is open."

We pulled back into the lot that served both the pharmacy and the pain clinic and immediately noticed there were more cars parked there than yesterday. People were coming and going from both doorways.

"Same as yesterday? You wait here? I see what's what."

John gave me a sour expression and reached into the inside pocket of his leather coat. He took out an envelope and handed it to me. "Take this with you. They won't take credit cards or checks. They'll only take cash."

I took the envelope and peeked inside, then silently counted five one-hundred-dollar bills. "Think it will be this expensive?"

"Nah, but you never know. Watch your back in there."

"Looks a little like Grand Central Station. I can't imagine anything is going to happen. I don't know how long I'll be in there."

"I'm not going anywhere."

The temperature had risen since yesterday, and the gray ice that had covered the parking lot was now a sloppy sludge. I stepped out of the car, hung my bag from my shoulder, and minced across the way, trying to keep my boots from getting wet and dirty.

Nearly every chair in the waiting room was occupied. There were at least a dozen people of all ages from early twenties to a woman who looked to be in her sixties. They were dressed in anything from blue jeans to expensive business attire. The room reminded me of the area at the pharmacy next door. Facial expressions and body language ranged from bored to anxious.

Compared to the outside, the lobby felt uncomfortably hot and stuffy.

I stepped up to the front counter and, expecting to see a female attendant, was slightly surprised to see a white male, dressed in dark-blue polo shirt with the Armand Pain Management logo over his heart. In his twenties, he was clean-shaven, with a full head of sand-colored hair. He studied me with deep blue eyes. He wore a name badge that said Dan. As an additional accessory, he carried a pistol in a black leather holster attached to his belt. "Can I help you?"

"Yes." I glanced back at the crowd in the waiting room. "I was hoping to see the doctor."

"Have you been here before?"

"No."

He handed me a clipboard and a short questionnaire. "Fill this out and bring it back to me."

I sat down in one of the few empty seats and looked at the questions. Basic stuff, it asked for name, address, and phone number and if I'd ever been afflicted with any of a short list of medical conditions. Then at the bottom of the single sheet of paper, it made certain that I knew I'd be responsible for payment at the time of the office visit. It also asked if I was qualified for either Medicaid or Medicare.

Oh, you just know this place is scamming the federal government.

Using the name Matty Walker and a fake address and phone number, I hoped the armed man behind the counter wasn't going to ask for ID. If I had to use a fraudulent moniker, I would often defer to Matty Walker, the murderous character played by Kathleen Turner in the movie *Body Heat.*

It makes me feel sexy.

I got up out of my chair and handed the clipboard back to Dan, who gave me a brief smile. "The doc will see you now."

I frowned and glanced around at the crowd in the waiting room. Clearly, I'd been the last one through the front door. "Really?"

He hit a button under the counter, and I heard a soft buzzing sound coming from a door off to my left. "Through that door."

A woman in a lab coat and jeans met me. She was only about five four, had a mop of curly brown hair, and wore pink framed glasses. Her cherubic face was a mass of freckles. "Follow me, please." Her voice told me that she was disinterested and bored.

We stopped midway up a short hall. Pointing to the scale, she said, "I need to get your weight."

I felt slightly disoriented. It was as if I was in a parallel universe. It was a doctor's office, but everyone in it was half-assing their way through the day. They were only going through the motions.

I started to take off my winter coat.

We don't need to weigh this.

She held up her hand. "Not necessary. Leave your coat on."

I stepped up on the scale, and the woman reached past me to adjust the large counter weight but never tinkered with the smaller one. She wrote something down on her clipboard and then she repeated, "Follow me."

She led me into a small examining room complete with the green leather table covered with a two-foot-wide strip of paper. The sink and countertop had all the right things, glass containers with cotton balls, wooden tongue depressors, and gauze. A blood pressure cuff hung from the wall.

As we entered the room, I asked, "How did I jump to the front of the line ahead of all those people in the waiting room?"

She looked me up and down and gave me a mysterious smile. "Take off your clothes and put on the hospital gown. It ties in the back."

Red flags immediately went up. An actual exam wasn't in my game plan. I was just going to see if I could score a prescription for Vicodin. Then I'd take it next door, turn it in, and I'd have a solid piece to write for the paper. Expose this place for the pill mill that it was.

Getting naked wasn't on my radar screen.

The nurse, if that was what she was, closed the door behind her, and I was alone.

Strip?

How bad did I want this story?

What had Jill warned me about yesterday? *How bad do you want your pills, girl?*

I took a deep breath and quickly hung my coat up on a hook

on the wall, sat down on the examining table, and pulled off my boots and insulated socks. Then I unbuttoned my blouse and slid out of my jeans. I left my bra and panties on while I put my arms through the threadbare gown and did my best to tie the strings behind my neck and back.

I pulled my phone out of my bag and texted John.

Waiting for an examination. Not sure if this place is legit or not.

He immediately texted me back.

Is there an armed guard there?

Yes.

Pill mill. Did you say you're waiting to be examined?

Yes.

They might be checking you to make sure you're not wearing a wire.

Of course.

Make sure I'm not a cop?

Before I could receive John's answer, a man wearing a white lab coat walked into the room. He was in his fifties, balding, had a curly salt-and-pepper beard. His eyes were bloodshot, and broken veins mottled his cheeks. He was very tall, six five, and slightly overweight. Seeing my phone in my hand, he barked, "We don't allow cell phone usage in the clinic."

I reached over and dropped the phone into my bag. "Sorry."

He perused the information on the clipboard. "I'm Dr. Armand."

"Nice to meet you."

I was still standing barefoot on the cold tile floor as he stepped up to me, studying my face. "What's the nature of your visit today?"

I attempted a smile. "I was in a car accident years ago, and I'm still having back problems. I need something for the pain."

He glanced down at the clipboard he was holding. I could see information on it that was in my handwriting. "Matty Walker. Pretty name for a pretty lady."

"Thank you."

"Turn around. I want to take a look at your back."

I did as I was told and stood facing the examination table.

"What kind of pain medication did your regular physician prescribe?"

"Vicodin, 10 milligrams."

"You still have your bra and panties on," he snapped. "Take them off."

From the way his voice sounded, he was pissed off. Still facing away from Armand, I reached around behind me and undid the clasp of my bra, snaking out of it, placing it in my bag. Then I pulled on the elastic of my panties and shimmied out of them, painfully aware that my bare bottom had been momentarily exposed to the doctor's eyes.

"I assume that your physician had exhausted the amount of medication he can prescribe for you?"

"Yes."

"I'm just going to examine your back."

I felt him untie the lower set of strings and pull aside the fabric of the gown. Then with the fingers of both hands, he delicately touched my shoulder blades, then ran his fingers down either side of my spine until he got to the top of my butt. "Pretty skin. No scarring. Your injuries were internal?"

"Yes."

"Turn around please."

I did so and looked up into his face.

"Are you presently employed or associated in any way with a law enforcement agency?"

"No."

"How bad is the pain for you, Matty?" His eyes were narrowed. "Use a number from one to ten, ten being extremely painful."

"Eight."

"You need the pills, then."

"Yes. Will you prescribe them?"

He licked his lower lip. "I have to complete your examination first."

"Do you do this with all your patients?"

"Only the pretty ones." He pointed to my neck. His voice got low. "Untie the strings on the gown and let it fall to the floor."

This guy ain't no real doctor.

I shook my head slightly. "No."

He cocked his head. "I have to finish the exam. I can't prescribe your pills until we're done here."

What's he mean—until we're done here?

"I can't finish the examination until you disrobe."

I took a deep breath. How bad did I want this story?

"Okay." I reached both hands behind my neck and undid the strings. With no effort of my own, the gown slid down the front of my body and fell in a heap on the floor. I stood before Dr. Armand completely naked.

He didn't say a word. I could feel his eyes slowly move from my face to my neck, to my breasts, to my tummy, to the soft tuft of curly blond hair between my legs.

The man's breathing became deeper as he slowly stepped forward, his gaze locked onto my boobs. His hands shook slightly as he reached up and gently touched my nipples.

"No!" I slapped his hands away.

Rage colored his face a deep purple. "You'll do what I want, or you get no pills."

"How many women have you abused here in this room?"

"That's none of your fucking business." He reached out again to fondle my breasts.

I slapped at him again. "I said no."

Armand's jaw set, his lips tight, his eyes narrowed slits. He took a half step back and pulled aside his lab coat, reached down, and unzipped his pants. Then he took out his penis and began to fondle himself. "Get down on your knees, Matty. You want your pills, you have to work for them."

I stood with my hands on my naked hips. "Kiss my ass, doc. I'm getting out of here."

"Don't want your pills, then?"

I turned and reached for my panties.

His big hand was on my shoulder, twisting me around to face him, pushing on me to get down on my knees.

Then I did it without thinking.

I balled up my fist and punched him hard on his nose.

—

I've taken a couple of rudimentary self-defense classes, and one thing I learned was that a person's nose is very sensitive to pain. Also, there's no bone in the nose, only skin, blood, tissue, and cartilage. It's really easy to break someone's nose. And if you strike someone squarely in the proboscis, the pain is blinding, literally. It will bring tears to your eyes, and your vision blurs immediately.

The crowning touch? It bleeds like a son of a bitch.

John was where I'd left him, in the idling Mustang on the other side of the small parking area. When he saw that I was being escorted angrily out of the building by the armed guard, John quickly got out of the car and trotted over to meet me. "What's going on?"

I could hear the anger in my voice. "No story, that's what's going on. No story, no drugs, no witness to crimes being committed."

"What happened in there?" He opened the passenger's side door of the car.

"Dr. Feelgood tried feeling me up and then wanted a blow job in exchange for the drugs."

"I'm guessing you didn't do it?" I slid into the car, and he held the door open, waiting for my response.

"No, I broke his nose instead." I scrunched up my face. "It was a real mess."

John took a look at the guard who stared back at him and shrugged. He echoed my statement. "It was a real mess."

Chapter Twenty-Seven

John dropped me at the office, and he went back to my place to do some work on his laptop. I hung my coat up on the department coat tree and glanced in at the editor's cubicle. It was empty.

I dropped my bag on the floor next to my desk chair in the newsroom and headed back to Ben's office. The door was open, so I knocked on the doorframe. "Can I come in?"

For the first time since the transition started, I saw Ben grin. He extended a hand and motioned me to sit down in one of his upholstered office chairs. "Come in, sit down. What have you been up to?"

"You saw the piece I put together last night about finding Bogdan Tolbonov's body?"

He turned his laptop around so that I could see the screen. He'd been looking at it, admiring it. The headline screamed, "Reputed Mobster's Body Found at Graveyard Bay."

I shook my head and made a tiny tsk-tsk sound. "Graveyard Bay? You too?"

His grin grew broader. "Lorraine Moretti started it, didn't she? But now, a third stiff shows up out there? I think we all should be calling it Graveyard Bay. Are we in the middle of a gang war?"

"Kind of looks that way, Chief. The Russians look like they're getting their asses kicked by the Aryan Brotherhood."

"I thought those guys liked working together."

I glanced around the office. Ben had put some of his sailing photographs back up on the wall. "Right up until Merlin Finn killed two of Wolfline's drug thugs. By the way, Finn's father contends that the two men Finn tortured and killed were assassins sent to murder Finn in his own home up in Brockton."

Ben leaned back in his chair and linked his hands behind his head, obviously relaxed. "Well, somehow they got into a serious pissing match. Have you found a connection between Wyatt Investments and Galley Media yet?"

I don't have enough on my plate?

"Not yet."

He frowned and glanced away from me.

"But..."

I got his attention again.

"There's a pill mill over on Flax Hill Road. I think that's why we've seen a rise in opioid overdoses in Fairfield County. I was just there and nearly scored a prescription from the Armand Pain Management Clinic that happens to be in the same building as the Flax Hill Pharmacy."

"Nearly scored?"

I leaned forward, my stomach still queasy from my lewd encounter with Dr. Armand. "All I had to do to seal the deal was perform an act of oral gratification on Dr. Feelgood. I broke his nose instead."

"A pill mill? You know, it wasn't that long ago there were more of those in Florida than there were McDonald's franchises. I thought Connecticut had made it harder for them to operate."

I spread my arms. "Yet here we are. Everything old is new again."

Ben raised his eyebrows. "What's this got to do with Wyatt Investments?"

"They have a subsidiary called Corsair Properties. They own the building where the pill mill is operating."

Ben scowled while he thought. Finally, he mumbled, "Keep digging."

Tell him, Genie.

I cleared my throat, fidgeted in my seat for a moment, then began. "Look, Ben, there isn't any good way to tell you this, so I'm just going to say it. I'm giving my notice."

I thought I could see his unnaturally tan face go pale and the corner of his lip twitch. "What? Why? Is it because of Galley Media?"

"At first, yeah. They want to cut my pay."

"Because if it's Galley Media, you have to understand that they're history, Genie. I'm tossing them the hell out of here."

"I got a job offer at more than double what we pay reporters here."

He leaned forward. "I'll keep you at the editor's salary."

"I'm not sure that a judge will keep the sale from going through."

"There's no way I'm letting Galley Media buy this newspaper."

Ben wasn't fighting the sale because the buyer was being a prick to the employees. He wanted the newspaper back because once the Sheffield Meridian was built, the *Sheffield Post* would be reaping the benefits of new, well-funded advertisers.

Ben was certain that he'd been cheated.

I clasped my hands in my lap. "I'm sorry, Ben. You know I've enjoyed working here."

His jaw jutted at me, his eyes ablaze. "I don't have to remind you that I was the only one who would bring you on staff. Your career was in the toilet."

Ouch.

I blinked, feeling the sting of tears glazing my eyes. "I know that, Ben. I'll be forever grateful. But I have my mojo back. This is a real opportunity. I need for you to be happy for me."

He blinked and considered for a moment, quiet, thinking.

"Okay, I never want to stand in someone's way if they can better themselves. When's your last day?"

"January fourteenth."

Ben nodded and stood up, coming around the desk.

I stood up, and we hugged. He stepped back and winked at me. "It's all going to be okay. I'm going to stop this sale."

As I turned to leave his office, I pondered what he'd said. Did he think that if he kept ownership of the newspaper, I'd change my mind? It also occurred that he'd never asked where I was going.

I had just sat down at my desk in the newsroom when my phone rang. I picked it up and heard Leslie at the front desk say, "Hey, Genie. I saw that you were out of Ben's office. There's someone here to see you."

I went through my mental calendar but didn't recall any appointments for that day. "Who is it?"

"A Mrs. Tomasso."

The name sounded vaguely familiar. "Give me a minute and then send her back here." I quickly riffed through the incident reports that I'd gotten from the cops earlier in the week. When I found what I was looking for, the name jumped out at me, Charlie Tomasso, missing for over five days.

The woman who came into the newsroom was in her thirties, slim, about five five in height, with black hair cut in a cute pageboy style complete with bangs. Her eyes were a dark chocolate-brown and the way they were red and bloodshot, I guessed that she must have been crying. She wore a brown fur coat that I thought might be mink. I'm not a fur person.

"Mrs. Tomasso?"

She gave me a hesitant smile. "Geneva Chase, thank you for seeing me without an appointment."

"Would you like to take off your coat?" I glanced at the department coat tree, which seemed woefully inadequate for such an expensive piece.

She shed her fur and draped it across the desk next to mine.

Marty Graff, our business writer, was out interviewing a new brewery that was opening up in South Sheffield. He kept his desk in meticulous order, and there was plenty of empty space to accommodate her coat.

Without invitation, she sat down in the plastic chair next to my desk. I sat down as well. "How can I help you, Mrs. Tomasso?"

She knitted the fingers of both her hands together and rested them on her lap. "I read your online story this morning about finding the body of Bogdan Tolbonov."

She got my attention. I didn't reply, instead waiting to see what else she had to say.

The silence was discomforting. She was obviously struggling with something. Finally, "My husband worked for him, worked for Wolfline Contracting."

"What does your husband do for Wolfline Contracting?"

"Did." She glanced around her to see if anyone was within listening distance. "This has to be off the record, okay?"

I wasn't sure what I was going to hear, but I agreed. "Okay."

"To be clear, I love my husband very much. He's a loving man, and there's nothing he wouldn't do for me or Frank."

"Frank? Is that your son?"

She smiled shyly. "Frank is our Labrador retriever. Charlie and I don't have kids, so Frank is our baby."

I nodded to let her know that I understood and she should continue.

"But Charlie is a big, tough guy with a temper. He was Wolfline's muscle. Charlie collected money from people who didn't want to pay. He intimidated people into doing things they didn't want to. Sometimes, he beat people up."

Sounds like Bogdan Tolbonov.

"You said he *was* muscle. Not anymore?"

Her head moved from side to side slightly. "Before he was with Wolfline, he was working for the Brotherhood."

"Merlin Finn's crew?"

"Before I met him, Charlie did two years in Lockport for assault. He joined the Brotherhood while he was in prison. When Charlie got out, he got a job working for Merlin Finn."

"Then Finn went to jail for murdering two of Wolfline's men."

She nodded nervously. "With Merlin gone, everybody in the Brotherhood took a job with Wolfline. Charlie worked directly under Bogdan Tolbonov. But then Merlin Finn busted out of prison. Charlie told me that he wanted back into Finn's crew again. That's what we argued about the night he took off."

"He's still missing?"

She leaned in, tears gleaming in her brown eyes. "The police aren't doing anything."

I wasn't entirely surprised. Charlie Tomasso didn't sound like a very nice guy. "How can I help you?"

"When I read your story online about finding Bogdan's body, I felt like you must be really well connected. Maybe you know where Charlie is."

I didn't even know what he looked like. All I had was the description in the police report. "Do you have a picture of Charlie?"

She bobbed her head and dug around in her brown Dooney & Bourke handbag until she found what she was looking for. When she handed me the photo, I noticed the Cartier watch on her wrist.

Being muscle must pay well.

I took the picture from her and studied it. It was from their wedding. "How long have you and Charlie been married?"

"Two and a half years."

The man smiling next to the bride was very tall and broad in the shoulder. His chest filled the tuxedo shirt and strained the buttons on his coat. His hair was buzzed tight to his scalp, his cheeks were rosy under the lights, and he was smiling into the camera. For a bad guy, Charlie had a baby face. A gold tooth glimmered in the camera flash.

"Has Charlie ever been gone this long before?"

"No. He's gone off on a bender a couple of times but only

for a day, maybe two tops. He'd always come back with a killer hangover and with his tail between his legs." She smiled. "And he'd always bring me a present. One time, it was a new Corvette."

I sat back in my chair. "Do you have any idea at all where Charlie might be?"

Her hands clasped and unclasped in her lap. "I called one of his old Brotherhood buddies who's still working for Wolfline. I asked if he knew where Charlie might have gone off to. He said that Merlin Finn was lying real low, picking off members of the Wolfline crew one at a time." She was dead silent for a moment, collecting her thoughts. "I think Charlie wanted to get back into Finn's gang again. He was willing to do most anything. I think Charlie might have killed Bogdan Tolbonov."

Chapter Twenty-Eight

Since Lorraine Moretti was at least temporarily out of the picture, Ben asked if I would take on some of the editing duties. I stayed busy punching up the two pieces that Marty Graff turned in. One on that new brewery and the other on the annual story of Christmas sales in Sheffield spiking this year.

"Did anyone touch anything on my desk, Genie?" Marty had asked when he came in out of the cold.

I grinned internally as I recalled seeing the mink coat draped over his desktop. "I didn't see anybody touch anything, Marty. Are you missing something?"

He stared at his pens and files and started fussing with them. "No, but everything is askew."

"Askew," I mumbled under my breath and punched up Mike Dillon's number.

He recognized my number. "Hey, Genie, what's up?"

"Anything more on finding Merlin Finn?"

"No, but it looks like the FBI is doubling their efforts."

"Because of what he did to Bogdan?" I would have thought they would have been grateful for the helping hand.

"Partly. By the way, they told me they're convinced the Tolbonovs are getting out of the business."

So, Decker was telling the truth.

"The FBI claims they're pulling back on surveillance on the Wolfline operation and focusing exclusively on Merlin Finn."

"But?"

"They don't have a clue where he is."

"Makes it hard to keep an eye on him, now, doesn't it?"

"Is that guy still shadowing you?"

"John Stillwater? Yes, he's still on me." I purposely used the double entendre. I was still stinging from his new relationship with the Realtor.

After half a beat, Mike said, "Stay safe."

I glanced at the clock on my computer screen and it, along with my rumbling tummy, told me that it was nearing lunchtime. Knowing that I didn't have my car parked out back, I entertained the notion of ordering a corned beef and rye from Pete's Deli. Their sandwiches were kick-ass and they delivered.

As if on cue, my phone pinged. I picked it up off the desk and glanced at who had just sent me a text.

Eric Decker.

It read:

> Mr. Tolbonov has respectfully asked for your presence over lunch. He said to bring Mr. Stillwater if you like.

I hesitated. If there was one person who frightened me more than Bogdan Tolbonov, it was his older brother, Valentin.

How does he know John's been looking out for me?

I met Valentin last October while I was searching for a missing high school girl, Bobbi Jarvis, one of Caroline's best friends. I dropped in on him unannounced at his place of business in Greenwich, Valentin Diamonds, an exclusive, hyperexpensive jewelry shop catering to the one percent. Locked doors, no windows, armed guards all over the place.

He had denied that he was directly involved with running Wolfline Contracting. By the time our conversation was finished, however, I was convinced that he was the capo running the Russian mob in the tristate area.

He's inviting me to lunch?

This scared me right down to my pantyhose. But how could I say no? If there was one man in the world who knew what the game was in this part of Connecticut, it was Valentin Tolbonov.

I texted back.

When and where?

The reply:

Quattro at 12:30.

I started to punch in John's phone number when I saw how badly my hand was shaking. I took a breath and made the call.

"Hey, Genie. Do you need a ride somewhere?"

"Yeah." Even I could hear the nerves in my voice. "You and I are meeting with Valentin Tolbonov in about a half hour."

He was silent for a few moments as the news sunk in. "I'll be at your office in ten minutes."

I sat at my desk and worked to control my heart rate and my breathing. I wouldn't be any good to anyone if I couldn't at least appear not to be frightened. I emailed Ben that I had a lunch meeting.

He emailed me back. "With who, your new boss?"

I didn't respond. Instead, I threw on my coat, hung my bag from my shoulder, and marched deliberately to the back of the building. Pushing open the door, I stepped out on the concrete landing and saw that the black Mustang was sitting at the foot of the steps, idling.

I slid into the passenger's seat, and John asked, "Where?"

"Quattro. It's a chichi restaurant in Westport."

"Know how to get there?"

"Hop onto the Merritt, get off on the Westport exit, turn onto Route 1 until we take a left on Main Street."

"Who sent the invitation?"

"Decker. Have you ever actually met Valentin Tolbonov, face-to-face?"

John kept his eyes on the road and slowly shook his head from side to side. I saw him glance at me. "Are you nervous?"

"A little."

"Are you afraid?"

I lied. "Nah."

"If you were smart, you'd be afraid."

—

I'd never eaten at Quattro. It was much too pricey for a newspaper salary.

Quattro was a stand-alone building with large windows fronting a brick facade. A quaint, green canvas awning offered the doorway protection from the elements. As we pulled into the parking lot, I saw that the window blinds were shuttered.

There were three other vehicles in the parking lot in addition to ours, all black, a massive Chevy Suburban and two Escalade SUVs parked on either side of it.

John and I looked at each other. He asked, "Ready?"

"No."

Then he opened his door and got out.

I did the same. As we both walked up to the front door, there was a sign in the doorway that proclaimed, "Closed—Private Party."

As we stepped onto the front porch and under the green awning, the door swung open, and a man emerged wearing an ankle-length, black leather coat. He was tall, trim, and clean-shaven, and his hair was cut military style tight to his head.

As we stepped past him, we were greeted by two more men, nearly identical to the first. The taller of the two stared at John. His voice was crisp, businesslike. "Are you carrying?"

John nodded and pulled open his coat, showing the shoulder-holstered Glock.

The second man pointed at it. "I'll need to hold on to that for you."

John shook his head. "No thank you."

The three men glanced back and forth at one another, unsure what to do next. The one who had opened the door for us wordlessly walked past us though the dark, empty dining room until he disappeared through a doorway in the back of the building.

We all uncomfortably waited in awkward silence.

I took the opportunity to study the dining area. There were about twenty tables all covered with deep-blue tablecloths and centered with glass vases of fresh flowers. In the doorway of the kitchen, a man stood, wearing a white chef's jacket, with his hands held loosely behind his back. Another man, in his twenties, wearing a red apron over a white shirt, stood motionless behind the well-stocked bar.

The restaurant was ready for a lunch crowd that wasn't coming.

I took a look at the two remaining thugs and silently wondered what kind of firepower they had hidden under their long leather coats. I'd be willing to bet it was massive.

Finally, not abiding the silence anymore, I spoke up. "So you eat here often?"

The man closest to me cracked a smile and rolled his eyes.

The third thug came back through the empty dining area and fixed John with his eyes. "You can keep the weapon, but you'll have to stay out here."

John bobbed his head. He understood. "I'll stay out here, then."

I suffered a brief panic attack. "Can I have a word with my associate?"

One of the men gestured that we could adjourn to the corner of the room, out of hearing range. We slid behind one of the four-top tables, and I hissed at John. "What do you mean you'll stay out here?"

"I'm not giving up my gun."

"What are you going to do? Something goes wrong, you gonna shoot it out?"

He leaned in. "I keep my gun, it's less likely something goes sideways."

"So I'm facing Tolbonov down by myself?"

"You did it once already."

"And I said I'd never do it again."

"Look, you're a reporter. You'll know what to ask and what to say. He's less likely to talk honestly in front of me anyway. I've been dogging him for a couple of years now. We're both looking for a reason not to sit down at the table together."

I stepped back. He was right, of course.

I can handle this.

"Wish me luck." I waved my hand at the thug who had told John he could keep his gun but needed to stay in the dining area. "Lead on."

I followed him through the dining room, around the many tables and chairs, until we got to the open doorway in the back of the restaurant. We entered a much smaller dining room with four tables, each with four chairs. One of them was occupied.

Valentin Tolbonov was seated at the table by himself. When he noticed that I'd walked into the room, he stood up. He was tall, had a full head of curly red-and-gray hair. He was in his mid-forties and was trim.

His face was all angles, high cheekbones, and a sharp, patrician nose softened by a closely cropped beard, which, like his hair, was rust-colored with hints of silver. Thick eyebrows accented his piercing, dark-brown eyes.

His attire was immaculate—black slacks cut perfectly to his ankles and waist, a white shirt, and a subdued blue tie. I noted that a matching suit coat was draped over the back of the chair where he'd been sitting.

There was a solitary drink on the table along with his cell

phone. When I'd come in, he'd been scrolling through something on the screen.

Although Valentin was at his table alone, he was far from being the only one in the room. Once my guide left to go back to the front entrance, I counted four more men in the room. They were all dressed in gray slacks, white shirts, and black sports coats. It was easy to spot the shoulder holsters they all wore.

When Valentin spoke, it was without a trace of any accent. "Miss Chase, I'm told you were the one who found my brother. I believe I owe you fifty thousand dollars." His voice dropped. "I always pay my debts."

Chapter Twenty-Nine

Glancing behind him, Valentin barked, "Dante, please get Miss Chase's coat."

One of the gangsters stepped forward and helped me out of my coat, draping it over his arm.

Valentin shifted his eyes, looking at the bag over my shoulder. "I'm sorry, Miss Chase, but Pavel needs to search your bag."

I felt a tiny nugget of anger swell in my chest. "Why? You asked me here. Don't you trust me?"

The hint of a smile played on his thin lips. "You? Yes. Your bag? No. Please indulge me."

Feeling my face redden, I handed my shoulder bag to a second man who stepped forward.

Good luck pawing through that, dumbass.

Pavel simply upended the contents of my bag onto the table in front of Valentin. I was appalled when out spilled pens, car keys, tissue, wallet, assorted cosmetics, lipsticks, breath mints, tiny chocolates, my cell phone, my recording device, two airplane-size bottles of vodka, tampons, and loose change.

Christ, how embarrassing.

The thug poked through it all and checked to make sure my recorder and phone weren't listening in on our conversation.

He cocked his head at his boss. "Looks clean."

Valentin said nothing. He stared at the contents lying naked on the top of the table. Finally, he reached out and picked something up. "What's this?"

Heaped on top of my anxiety at meeting with Valentin, I now had an additional kick of adrenaline. I didn't answer.

Pavel took a quick peek at what was in the Russian's hand. He answered. "GPS tracker. We use them all the time."

Valentine put it back in with my loose change. "Is that so Mr. Stillwater can keep track of you?" His eyes strayed to the doorway.

I remained silent again.

He nodded to his henchman and waved his hand in the air. "Help Miss Chase put all of this back."

I picked up my empty bag. "I'll get it." Then I held my bag at the edge of the table, and with my hand on its side, I swept everything back into it, unmindful of where it all fell. I took a breath. "So how can I help you, Mr. Tolbonov?"

He gestured to a chair. "Please, let's sit down. Pavel, get Miss Chase a drink, Absolut and tonic."

As the man left our room, heading for the bar, Valentin and I sat down. I started. "I'm sorry about your brother." Part of that statement was true. Part of it was a lie. I was relieved because a very scary man was dead. But they were brothers, and no matter how bad these guys were, another member of the human race was grieving.

"Thank you." He reached behind him and fished an envelope out of the inside pocket of his suit coat, which he placed on the tabletop. "Everything I'm going to tell you must be off the record." He glanced again at the doorway. "You can share our conversation with Mr. Stillwater and Miss Neese, if you like, but it must never become news."

"Off the record."

Pavel returned quickly and placed the drink in front of me. Then he took his place behind Valentin with the other three men and remained motionless, as if part of the furniture. They were four silent, attentive statues, one still holding my coat over his arm.

"Would you like something to eat?" Valentin offered. "I know the owner. The food here is very good. The roast duck is the chef's signature dish."

I noted that he had nothing in front of him except a glass of red wine. "Are you eating?"

He sadly shook his head. "No appetite."

"I'll pass."

Valentin took a swallow from his wineglass and began the discussion. "Bogdan and I were half brothers. I was older than him by twelve years. Both of my parents were pediatricians in Moscow. Russia was still part of the Soviet Union, and by standards at that time, we had a good life. Plenty of food, a nice apartment, a car.

"However, my father resented authoritarianism and was quietly critical of the party. That was a very dangerous thing back then."

My finger drew a line in the condensation on the outside of my glass. "From what I understand, being critical of the Putin regime still is."

He fixed me with his dark eyes. "When I was only eleven, a man quietly broke into our house in the middle of the night while we were sleeping, a party official, a neighbor, a brute. He stabbed and killed my father, then shoved my father's body off the bed and raped my mother."

I was stunned into utter silence. The matter-of-fact way he was talking gave me the creeps.

"I heard my mother's screams. At first, I was paralyzed, frozen with terror under the covers of my bed. Then I couldn't stand hearing her entreaties anymore. I ran to the kitchen and found the meat cleaver she had used that evening to cut up the lamb my father had purchased in the market. I ran with the cleaver into my parents' bedroom. There I found my father's body, lying in his own blood, on the floor and a strange man, a big man, pants down around his ankles, grunting on top of my mother like a farm animal."

He stopped talking for a moment and stared off into space. I glanced at the four men standing behind him. I didn't know if they'd heard this story, but their faces registered total disinterest. They were focused only on the doorway behind me that led to the outer dining room.

I whispered, "What happened?"

His eyes snapped back to me. "I severed his spinal cord with the cleaver. It was instinct. I didn't know how to properly kill a man. He didn't die immediately. But his body ceased moving. His brain couldn't talk to his body. The man's head was cocked to one side, so I slowly crept up, still clutching the cleaver, so that I could look into his eyes. I was both horrified and fascinated. His lungs had stopped accepting air, and his heart, separated from the brain, had stopped pumping. The man was dying."

He took a healthy swallow of his wine. "I watched his eyes go from terror, knowing he was about to die, to acceptance, and then his life drained from his body and his eyes became empty."

"How did you feel?"

A tiny smile played on his lips. "I learned at that early age just how much I enjoyed revenge."

I was nearly overcome with a shudder of revulsion. I stifled it with a swallow of vodka. "Is that when your mother smuggled you out of the Soviet Union?"

He nodded in acknowledgment. "Nine months later, Bogdan was born, a child made from that unholy union between my mother and Satan. My mother raised him as she raised me. And to me, he wasn't my half brother. He *was* my brother."

His face turned deadly serious. "That's why it's most important for you to find Merlin Finn." He pushed the thick envelope he'd taken from his suit coat and pushed it across the table.

I looked down at the simple white package. I didn't touch it. "What's that?"

"Fifty thousand dollars in cash."

"For what?"

He was silent for a moment. Then, "For finding my brother's remains."

I shuddered again, took a sharp intake of air. "I can't accept that."

He scowled. "Of course you can."

"It wasn't anything that I did. Someone texted me where..." I stopped in midsentence. "Where...?"

His face softened. "Where Bogdan's body had been left."

I nodded.

"Was it Merlin Finn? The one who sent you the text."

"Yes."

He considered that for a moment, then continued. "Nonetheless, you were first on the scene. The money is yours to do with as you please. It will come in handy raising a teenager, yes?"

The envelope remained untouched on the table in front of me.

Yes, the money would come in handy.

Valentin leaned forward. "I'm upping my offer to a hundred thousand dollars."

"What? I'm sorry, what? Did I miss something?"

"That's what I'm willing to pay you to find Merlin Finn."

I let that soak in, thinking about what that kind of money could do. Help send Caroline to college. Buy a new car.

When's the last time you took a vacation, Genie?

I put that aside and asked another question. "Do you know a man named Charlie Tomasso?"

Valentin slowly sat back. "Why do you ask?"

"His wife came to see me this morning. She's worried about him. She said he used to work for Wolfline."

"An unsavory employee who Wolfline recently laid off."

"He's been missing for five days."

He eyes narrowed. "When Mr. Finn found a way to escape from his incarceration, Mr. Tomasso smelled a business opportunity and sought employment with the Brotherhood. Last I heard, Mr. Tomasso is running drugs and prostitutes in New Jersey."

I wanted to ask if Valentin thought Tomasso had anything to do with the death of his brother. But I was hesitant, worried that Tolbonov might wonder how much Mrs. Tomasso knew.

"Eric Decker says you're going legit."

Valentin raised an eyebrow. "Officially, my interests in Wolfline Contracting have always been legitimate, in spite of what the FBI thinks. I was never involved with the day-to-day operations."

"Mr. Decker says the new name is Wolfline Management."

He slowly nodded. "We're changing the corporate policy and expunging any unsavory individuals who might have been employed by Wolfline Contracting."

"Keeping your diamond business?"

A small smile played on his lips. "Yes, it will always be my passion. But I will need to focus on Wolfline's newest endeavor."

"What's that?"

"An urban mall. We're building the Sheffield Meridian."

I felt a shot of adrenalin pulse through my limbs. "Wyatt Investments hired you to build their mall?"

He placed his hands flat down on the tabletop. "It's a six-hundred-million-dollar project. As you can see, I will be very busy for at least two years, just on this project alone."

I glanced back down at the untouched envelope in front of me.

Valentin saw that my attention was drawn to the money hidden inside. "One hundred thousand dollars, Miss Chase. In addition to what's in that envelope. Find Merlin Finn."

I looked back up into Valentin's dark eyes. "And then what?"

His face clouded over, and his heavy eyebrows knitted together. "Justice, Miss Chase. Justice."

Chapter Thirty

"Did he buy you lunch?" John peeked over at me while he drove.

Initially, when we slid into the car in the parking lot of the restaurant, neither one of us said a word, waiting until we were well underway and the restaurant was in our rearview mirror.

I replied, "He offered. I don't think either one of us was hungry."

"How about now?"

I could use a drink.

"I should eat. There's a Burger King on the way. Stop at the drive-through?"

"Ugh. Can't we do better than that?"

"Penny's Diner is on the way back to the newspaper. Want to stop there?"

"Sure, Penny's Diner. Sounds like a plan." He took a left onto Route 1 and asked, "What are the takeaways from your meeting with Tolbonov?"

"You first." I wanted to hear his impressions. Even though he hadn't been in the room with us, I knew that John had a keen sense of observation.

"I don't know if you can ever call someone like Tolbonov frightened, but he's clearly rattled."

I listened as we passed businesses decorated with bright

holiday lights and holiday sale signs in their windows, stores filled with shoppers readying themselves for Christmas morning.

John continued. "He held the meeting at Quattro, a restaurant that Wolfline owns."

"You looked that up before we got there?"

"While we were there. Tolbonov's goons thought I was checking my Twitter feed. And I'm sure you noticed that there were no windows in that building except in the front, and those blinds were closed."

"I noticed."

"Three guys, heavily armed, met us at the door. How many in the room with you?"

"Four more."

John took a right onto East Avenue. "Tolbonov isn't taking any chances."

I shuddered, recalling the charred remains of Bogdan Tolbonov floating in the dark waters of Groward Bay. "He had to identify what was left of his brother. Nobody wants to take any chances. The diner is just up the street."

"What did the two of you talk about?"

"There, pull into the parking lot. He repeated what Eric Decker had told me. That Wolfline is going legit."

I glanced over just in time to see John roll his eyes. He smirked. "I wish I could believe that." John pulled in and parked between two SUVs. "If they're not killing people or cheating them or selling them, then what's Tolbonov planning to do?"

Before I opened my door, I said, "For starters, he's been contracted to build the Sheffield Meridian."

John shook his head in disbelief. "What's the price tag on that?"

"Six hundred million."

He cocked his head. "I don't know. It doesn't feel right."

We both got out of the car at the same time, went up to the restaurant's doorway, and let ourselves in. Immediately, we were immersed in the warm atmosphere and soft sounds of diners clinking cutlery against their plates and subdued conversation. The place smelled of bacon, frying hamburgers, onions, and coffee.

We were led to a booth by a woman in her fifties, hair done up on her head with bobby pins, dressed in denim skirt, white blouse, blue apron, wearing a tiny replica of a holiday wreath pinned to her chest. She handed us menus and asked if we wanted something to drink.

John ordered coffee.

I hesitated. Seeing John's face, I asked for coffee as well.

"What else did Tolbonov want to talk to you about?"

"He tried to give me an envelope stuffed with fifty thousand dollars cash."

"Why?"

"For finding Bogdan's body."

He stared at me for a moment, judging me.

"I didn't take it."

He rested his chin in his hand, elbow on the tabletop. "Journalistic integrity?"

I shook my head. "I know a lot of reporters who subsidize their newspaper paycheck by working as private investigators. Mostly background checks. Kind of what you do for Lodestar?"

He gave me a mysterious grin. "Then why didn't you take the cash?"

"It's blood money, John. One person I don't want to climb into bed with is Valentin Tolbonov. Going legit or not."

He looked relieved.

I added, "He wants to sweeten the pot. He offered me another hundred thousand if I find Merlin Finn for him."

"Are you going to do it?"

I watched as the waitress carried two steaming cups of coffee up the aisle, heading in our direction. "If I find Merlin Finn, I'm telling the cops where he is."

John's face clouded, and I suddenly recalled how Finn had

tortured and killed his ex-wife. John growled, "Not if I find him first."

—

As we finished up our lunch and I stabbed the last chunk of blackened chicken from my Caesar salad, John's phone rang. He glanced at the screen. "It's Shana. I'll just be a minute."

I watched as he slid out of the booth and headed for the alcove at the front door, away from folks who might overhear his conversation. It gave me a chance to wonder what kind of man he really was. What did I really know about him?

He was once a New York cop and now worked for Lodestar Analytics doing opposition research for politicians, and political parties and doing background checks on CEOs. Here, he's my bodyguard.

What else does Lodestar do?

Something I should know more about before I take the job with them.

I knew that John did pro bono work for the Friends of Lydia. I found that dangerously attractive.

And he was.

Dangerously attractive.

I recalled seeing him standing in the dark living room last night wearing only his boxer shorts. His body was chiseled and muscular, his chest moderately hairy, his waist trim.

I sighed.

In another lifetime, perhaps?

The last time I'd been with anyone, it was a one-night stand with a sleazy actor. My sexual appetite, usually very healthy, had been at a low point after that.

Maybe a romp in the hay with John Stillwater is just the thing I need?

But the look on his face when he talked about having first crack at Merlin Finn was startling. Was he capable of taking matters into his own hands and exacting revenge for the death of his ex-wife?

Isn't that a normal reaction?

I sipped my coffee and watched him walk quickly back up the aisle, his phone in his hand. He sat back down. "Change of plans. I'm going to have to leave you on your own. One of Shana's snitches said that Merlin Finn is personally supervising a shipment of guns and drugs coming up from Philadelphia. She and I are going to check it out. Since Finn is nowhere near here, you should be okay without someone hovering over you."

I smiled, both relieved and a little anxious. Merlin Finn scared me plenty, but having John around 24/7 was getting on my nerves, no matter how cute he was wearing only his boxers. "So you won't be camping out on my couch tonight?"

"Nope. Mind if we swing by your place so I can get my overnight bag?"

"If I'm going solo, I'm going to need my car anyway."

He surprised me when he reached out and took my hand. "Look, if we weren't sure that Finn was nowhere near you, we wouldn't leave you on your own. Don't go anywhere without your phone and your GPS tracker."

At the mention of the tracker, I recalled the curious way Valentin Tolbonov had studied it.

Anything Valentin Tolbonov does creeps me out.

Still feeling the warmth of John's hand atop my own, I asked him a question. "What are you going to do with Finn once you catch up to him?"

I was chilled by his words.

"Justice. All I want is justice."

The similarity and irony in the words and tone with what Tolbonov had said only an hour before weren't lost on me.

Chapter Thirty-One

It only took him a few minutes to pack, and then, just as he was getting ready to leave, it felt awkward. We'd been through a lot in a very short time. Shake hands? Hug?

John picked up his small suitcase, and then, clasping my shoulder, he leaned in and kissed me on the cheek.

Sweet.

"You need me, call."

I smiled. "You too. Good luck."

And then John and the Mustang were gone.

My ten-year-old Sebring was like an old, comfortable friend, but as I slid behind the wheel, I missed the new leather smell of Shana's car. The same leather smell I noticed in her dungeon. Sexy. Thinking about it gave me another tiny sexual thrill.

I put it out of my mind and started for Lockport, about a half hour away.

The town's main industry was the prison. It housed five hundred inmates and, with over one hundred and fifty men and women working there, it was the town's largest employer. It was a high-security facility holding some of the worst of the worst in the entire state.

Which was why when Merlin Finn found a way out, it threw the town into turmoil.

Federal and state investigators crawled in like cockroaches, asking questions, doing background checks, questioning everyone from the guards to the customers of the coffee shop just up the road from the main gate.

Merlin Finn had somehow managed to punch through a wall, climb up through a narrow air vent using ripped bed sheets as rope, and then impossibly cut through four layers of metal grating to reach the roof. He climbed down the outside of the building, chopped through the perimeter fence, and disappeared into the night.

The investigators were convinced that Finn had help getting the tools he needed and the time required to make his escape. How had he managed to elude the security cameras? Where did he get the cutting tools?

Speculation fell immediately to the guards. When questioning them proved fruitless, it fell to peripheral employees—members of the teaching, medical, and kitchen staffs.

That was a dead end.

Was the Brotherhood so powerful within the walls of Lockport Correctional Facility that it could produce or steal everything needed to bust out their leader?

That was what the investigation concluded.

But now, there I was on the road going east along the coast of Long Island Sound, nearly to the border of Rhode Island, because the supervisor the night of the escape, Leon Dempsey, was missing.

Maybe Finn's escape wasn't as clear-cut as everyone thought. While I drove, I broke the law and called the prison using my cell phone. I was amazed when I was able to score an appointment with the warden, Paul Fisher. To his credit, he wanted to get out ahead of any publicity fallout that might come from the guard's disappearance.

We met at his house, not at the correctional facility. I didn't mind, because prisons make me feel claustrophobic. And if I'm anywhere near the general population, even though we might be separated by bars, their leering eyes and lascivious expressions and catcalls give me the heebie-jeebies.

You can't blame them. They're men, and many of them haven't been with or seen a woman in a very long time. A tall blond with long legs, even though covered up in a parka, jeans, and boots, is a lovely, teasing novelty.

Fisher lived in a two-story Tudor about a mile from the facility. The expansive lawn was completely covered with snow, but I could still spot landscaping and shrubbery around the periphery of the house.

He must have been waiting for me, because he opened the door just as I was trudging up the stone steps. "Careful. I put some salt down, but those steps are still slick."

I smiled and held out my gloved hand. "I'm Geneva Chase with the *Sheffield Post*."

He frowned momentarily. "Oh, I thought you were with the Hartford newspaper."

I cocked my head. "If we do this right, the Associated Press will pick it up, and it will run in every newspaper in the state."

He nodded, back on track. Paul Fisher was slightly taller than me and, at one time, had the build of a football player. But that time had been thirty years ago, and now he was big in the shoulders and in the gut, and the gray knit sweater he wore stretched tightly over his chest and stomach. "The missus has coffee in the kitchen. Can I take your coat?"

I slipped off the parka and handed it to him. He turned and hung it in the hall closet, then waved at me to follow him. The house was warm and comfortable. The wall-to-wall carpet was off-white as were the cloth couch and two easy chairs. The living room doubled as a library as there were floor-to-ceiling bookshelves along the walls filled to the brim.

The kitchen was a soft coral color, the appliances were stainless steel, and the table was covered in a green-and-red holiday tablecloth. A woman dressed in brown slacks and a black, long-sleeve top was fussing at the counter when we came in. "Hi, I'm Barbara." She held out her hand, and I shook it.

This is a much better reception than I had hoped for.

"Can I pour you a cup of coffee?"

"Yes, please, black."

All three of us sat at the table with steaming cups in front of us. Paul started. "I presume you're here about Leon Dempsey."

"I am. Apparently…"

He interrupted me and held up his hand. "Before we start, let me explain why I'm giving you my time."

My eyebrows arched, and I listened.

"Two weeks ago, when Merlin Finn walked out of my facility, the press tore us apart. That was on top of the federal and state investigators crawling all over us."

I took a sip of coffee. "Yes, sir."

"I'm talking to you because I'm confident that Leon had nothing to do with the escape, and I'm hoping you'll write it that way."

I blinked at him. "We both want the same thing, Mr. Fisher. We want the truth."

"That's all I'm asking."

I glanced at Barbara, who nodded back at me. "Tell me about Mr. Dempsey."

Paul said, "He's a good man. I've known him for over fifteen years. I've been his boss for the last seven. He's never missed a day of work, never been accused of an infraction, and more importantly, the inmates respect him. He's a man of his word, and when he tells you something, he means it."

"Clearly, he has your respect."

"He does."

"Any thoughts about where he might be?"

Before Paul could answer, Barbara reached out and put her hand on my wrist. "Let me tell you a little more about Leon."

"Okay."

"He was married for nearly twenty years to his wife, Nancy. She died just this past October in a horrible car accident."

"I'm sorry to hear that."

Barbara continued with a sigh. "They'd been having troubles for months. Nancy would confide in me that Leon was just going through the motions of being a husband. It's so difficult to stay in love when you've been married for so long, isn't it?"

I wouldn't know. My record for a relationship was with my third husband—four years. In my case, that was about three years too long.

"Were they thinking about divorce?"

"Leon was," Barbara confided.

I glanced at Paul, who was clearly uncomfortable with this discussion, but it apparently had been agreed upon before my arrival that this was the direction it needed to be.

"His wife wasn't?"

"She wanted to try marriage counseling. He didn't. I think he just wanted his freedom."

"You said she died in a car accident?"

Barbara nodded. "It happened on Halloween night. It was raining here in Lockport that night. Her brakes failed going around a curve. She hit it going too fast and ran head-on into an oak tree."

For a moment, I remembered my beloved Kevin. He too died on a rainy highway, slamming head-on into a brick overpass on the Merritt Parkway. The wound, over a year old, still hadn't scarred over.

"How did Leon take it?"

Paul leaned forward. It was his turn to talk. "Even though they'd been having some rough spots, it hurt him deeply. He sat in my office and cried. They'd been married for twenty years, and now she was gone. He wanted out of the marriage but not like that."

I took another sip of my coffee and hesitated before I asked my next question. "The police have said that two deposits had been made to Leon's checking account. Twenty thousand dollars and another deposit for fifty. One before Finn escaped and one after."

Paul put his hands on the tabletop, palms down. "Life insurance payments. This is why we consented to this meeting. To get the truth out. Investigators have been on this since the escape. They concluded that the Brotherhood conspired to get Finn the tools he needed to get out. None of my men had anything to do with it."

"Where do you think Leon is?"

Paul rubbed his eyes. "He and I spent a lot of time talking after Nancy died and then again after the escape and we all were under suspicion. The stress was killer. Leon wasn't handling it well. He was drinking, not on the job, but when he wasn't at the facility, he was in Jack's Bar and Grill. One night, the bartender called me to come get him and drive him home."

I waited. Sometimes a reporter's best friend is silence. Nature abhors a vacuum.

Paul continued, "I think he just said fuck it. The cops searched his house. Didn't find anything missing, but it looks like he might have packed a bag when he left. I think Leon will turn up when he runs out of gas or beer money. I'm just afraid that his stellar career in corrections is over."

My conversation with Paul and Barbara hadn't offered me much other than an excellent cup of coffee.

Chapter Thirty-Two

I drove to Leon Dempsey's place and parked in the driveway. The house was a single-story ranch style home on a small lot in a cramped neighborhood. Everything there looked like it had been built in the mid-eighties. A cookie-cutter neighborhood, all the houses were remarkably similar to one another.

I sat gazing at the house through my windshield. The curtains were drawn, and I was the only vehicle in the driveway. I saw multiple tracks in the snow where the police had come to look through the house.

I got out of my car, zipped up my coat, turned to my right, and trudged across the snowy lawn of the house next door. I recalled Mike Dillon telling me that a neighbor had a spare key to Dempsey's place and had let the cops in to look around.

Maybe I'll get lucky and the neighbor will let me snoop around as well.

I pushed the bell and waited until the door swung open and a Hispanic woman in her forties appeared. She was wearing slacks, sneakers, and a blue sweatshirt with a white logo that said Loving Touch Caregivers. "Can I help you?"

"Hi, my name is Geneva Chase, and I just met with Paul Fisher, the warden at Lockport Correctional? He asked me to stop by and check on Leon Dempsey's house, what with him being gone and all. He said one of Leon's neighbors had a spare key. Would that be you?"

It wasn't a complete lie. I had just met with Paul Fisher, and we had talked about Leon Dempsey. Checking on the house was my idea.

The woman's eyes involuntarily darted toward Dempsey's empty house, then back to me. "Henry...Mr. Byrd...had a spare key. He gave it to the police so they could look through Mr. Dempsey's house. The police kept the key."

The disappointed look on my face must have been obvious, because then the woman quickly said, "Would you like to talk with Mr. Byrd? He and Mr. Dempsey were friends."

I smiled. "Sure. As long as you think Mr. Byrd won't mind."

She leaned in and gave me a stage whisper. "I think Mr. Byrd is bored out of his mind. He'll like a visitor."

I went in and luxuriated in the warm living room. It was a small space with a leather couch, recliner, faux wood coffee table stacked with a small pile of *Sports Illustrated* magazines, and a big-screen television, currently tuned into a program of football highlights. In the center of the room sat a silver-haired man in a wheelchair.

"Mr. Byrd, you have a visitor."

The man in the wheelchair twisted around and studied me. His hair was white and wispy, his scalp easily seen underneath. He was wearing a green flannel shirt and brown slacks. One leg was encased in an off-white cast from his ankle to his thigh.

Upon seeing me, he managed, with effort, to turn his wheelchair to face me. "And such a pretty visitor."

"Hi, I'm Geneva Chase." I walked over to shake the man's hand. His skin was dry and his grasp was gentle. I had the distinct impression that if I squeezed his hand too hard, his fingers might break like the bones of a bird.

"I'm Henry. Would you like some coffee?"

I held up a hand. "I've had my quota for the day." I gestured back at the woman standing behind me. "I understand that you and Mr. Dempsey are friends."

He smiled. "Did Rosa tell you that?"

The woman shrugged.

"We weren't friends so much as we liked talking about the Patriots. We're both big fans. Ya know, it ain't the Cowboys that are America's team. It's the New England Patriots."

I gave the man a big grin. "Amen to that, Henry. Do you know where I can find Leon?"

"Nope. Tell you what I told the cops. After his wife died, he just always seemed like he was on edge. Like he was lookin' over his shoulder all the time. Worried. It wasn't like Leon to be worried all the time."

"What do you think he was worried about?"

Henry appeared thoughtful for a moment. When he answered, it was with a quick shrug.

Rosa, the caregiver, spoke up. "I think it was the little blond who followed him home one night from Jack's Bar."

Henry's face went serious. "Rosa."

Her voice was sharp. "Mr. Dempsey's poor wife isn't cold in her grave, and he started cavorting around with a younger woman. It's disrespectful to Mrs. Dempsey."

"Was she Mr. Dempsey's lover?"

Henry's tone was harsh. "Rosa. None of our business."

"Do you know the woman's name?"

Rosa offered Henry an angry stare. "Two weeks after the funeral, that woman showed up."

Henry, surrendering, held up his hand. "Leon told me her name was Anna and she was from Hungary or some damned place like that. Pretty girl, blond and tall like you. Younger, maybe in her twenties."

It was a compliment right up until the age thing. "Did he mention a last name?"

"I'm sure he did, but I don't recall it, and even if I did, I couldn't pronounce it."

"Wouldn't happen to have a photo, would you?"

He shook his head. "Sorry."

"Do you think that when Leon took off, this Anna woman went with him?"

Henry's eyes turned sad. "No, just as fast as she came into Leon's life, she went right back out again. She kinda vanished right after that guy broke out of prison. Poor Leon caught all kinds of shit for that, and he didn't have nothing to do with it. It was them damned skinheads in there."

"Any idea at all where he might have gone?"

Henry thought for a moment. "My guess is that he'd just had enough of everything. Had a nervous breakdown, maybe. He got in his car, started driving, and just kept going. I just hope he's going to be okay."

I said my goodbyes to Henry and Rosa and hopped back in my car. Before I did, I looked up the directions to Jack's Bar and Grill on my phone.

It was four in the afternoon when I walked in. I felt right at home. The air was thick with stale beer. The smell of cigarette smoke, illegal for many years inside a Connecticut pub, still clung to the walls. A Budweiser neon sign hung behind the bar, lighting up dozens of bottles sitting on shelves. Another neon sign brightly pronounced that "It's five o'clock somewhere".

Also, behind the bar was a flat-screen television showing muted images from the Fox News station. Below that hung a Rudolph the Reindeer sign, complete with a red light bulb for a nose. The words on the sign said, "We say Merry Christmas here."

Two old-timers sat at one end of the bar, drinking Miller Lite and talking quietly, taking no notice of me at all.

However, the tall guy behind the bar gave me a grin that rivaled the neon hanging on the wall.

I took off my coat, hung it from the back of a stool, and sat down. I ordered an Absolut and tonic.

He quickly splashed it together and brought it to me almost before I'd finished asking for it. "I haven't seen you in here before. I'd remember someone as pretty as you are."

It's been a while since I've been hit on in a bar.

I answered by looking at him and holding my glass up in a mock toast. Then I took a healthy gulp, feeling it love me all the way down.

He took a bar rag off his shoulder and started wiping down the wooden surface just off to my right. "New in town? I'm Will, by the way." He held out his hand for me to shake.

"I'm Genie. I'm from the insurance company that had the policy on Nancy Dempsey. I came to follow up with Leon Dempsey to make sure he was satisfied with how we handled things."

His brow furrowed. "I don't think he's pleased at all. When I last saw him, he was still looking for a check from you people."

It was my turn to look confused. "According to my records, we've already sent Mr. Dempsey two checks."

Will shook his head. He was in his midthirties, short brown hair, brown eyes, and bartender cute. The more you drank, the better he'd look. "Last time I saw him, he was bitchin' because he hadn't seen a nickel from the life insurance on his wife's accident."

"Huh." I took another hit of my vodka. I might be tempted to have a second one of these before leaving to go back to Sheffield. "Does Mr. Dempsey come in here a lot?"

"Oh, he was a regular. Most of the prison guys come in here after their shifts. I haven't seen Leon for days now. Word is that he hopped in his car and just started driving. People blamed him for the escape a couple of weeks ago. Did you hear about it?"

I looked up at him, hopefully in an adoring manner. I'd gotten off on the wrong foot by pretending to be with the insurance company. If those two deposits into Dempsey's account hadn't come from his wife's life insurance, where did the money come from? "Tell me."

Will leaned down, his arms crossed in front of him on the bar, his face inches from my own. "The top guy in the Aryan Brotherhood broke out of prison. He busted out a wall, climbed up an air vent, cut his way through wires, climbed back down again, and chopped through the outside fence."

I put a hand up to my mouth. "How did he manage that?"

He nodded knowingly. "Cops wanted to blame Leon because he was the supervisor on shift that night. But after all the questions were asked, the feds said that the Brotherhood put it all together."

"Are they that strong up there in Lockport Correctional?"

Will gave me an incredulous look. "Oh, yeah. Those are some dangerous dudes."

"How about the guy who got out?"

"Guy by the name of Merlin Finn. The worst of the worst. Killer without a conscience. Got two tattoos, Aryan symbols, one on either side of his face." He pointed to one cheekbone, then the other.

"Well, I feel bad about Mr. Dempsey. Here I thought we'd done a good thing by him. Now I've got to go back and check with our financial department."

"I'm sure he'll turn up. You can make sure he gets his money then, right?"

I held up my glass. "Absolutely right. Can I get a refill, Will?"

"Absolut you can," he said, grinning, taking my glass, and grabbing the bottle of vodka off a shelf. I could tell he was pleased with his half-ass joke.

"In the meantime, does he have family here in town I can talk to about getting him his check?"

He poured a healthy dollop of vodka into my glass. "No family. He had a girlfriend for a while."

"He did?"

"Yeah, she was in here by herself one night about a week after

Nancy's funeral. That was the night she and Leon met. Next thing you know, they were going out."

"Was it serious?"

"It was for Leon. I understand why. She was a looker. Tall and blond, in her late twenties, early thirties."

"How old was Leon?"

"In his forties, I guess. I never thought of him being a player, but I guess I was wrong."

"They broke up?"

"I think that might have been one of the things that finally snapped for Leon. He thought she was really special."

"You know her name?"

"Anna something. Foreign-sounding name. From Austria I think. She was almost as good-looking as you." He handed me the icy cold glass.

"Why thank you, sir. Do you know of any way I might be able to reach this Anna?"

He slowly shook his head. "Sorry. She left Leon and disappeared. It was like she was never here. It broke Leon's heart."

I sipped my drink and wondered what I should do next. I'd hit a wall.

"Hey, want to see a picture?"

My heart skipped a beat. "You have a picture?"

Will pulled his phone from his pants pocket and scrolled through some other photos in his screen. "Yeah, Leon's birthday was about three weeks ago. She and him were in here knocking back shots that some of the other guards were buying them." He stopped scrolling. "Here."

Will held up the phone, and I took it from him to get a better look at the photograph on the tiny screen. I assumed the man I didn't recognize was Leon Dempsey. A regular-looking guy, hair slightly mussed, eyes half shut from drinking too much, gazing loving at a young blond sitting in a booth next to him with her arm around his shoulder.

I immediately recognized the woman, though. Her name wasn't Anna.

It was Eva Preston.

Chapter Thirty-Three

On my way back to Sheffield, I wrestled with what I knew.

It was looking more and more like Leon Dempsey had been paid to help break Merlin Finn out of prison. Twenty grand before and fifty grand after.

Then what? He got cold feet? He thought they were going to reopen the investigation into who helped Finn get out of jail?

The theory that he had a nervous breakdown, got into his Dodge Dakota, and took off for parts unknown with no money in his pocket didn't sound right to me.

How did Judge Preston's wife fit into it?

All along, she said that the judge had been having the affair. Eva Preston had told me that more than once. But had it been her having the affair with Leon Dempsey?

Had she been the one who paid Dempsey to help get the head of the Aryan Brotherhood over the wall? Why?

She must have known that if Merlin Finn got out of prison, he'd be coming to kill her husband.

Or was that the reason? That she wanted Judge Preston out of the way?

What did I know about her? Basically, what Shana and John had told me. That when she came to the United States, she was working as a hooker for the Tolbonovs. When the judge became a widower, the Russians gave Eva to Niles Preston as payment for his ongoing services in the courtroom.

And to keep an eye on him?

When Judge Preston had heard that Finn was free, he knew that he had a target on his back. According to John, the judge had asked the Tolbonovs for protection, and when they refused, he contacted the Friends of Lydia to hide him.

The night that Abby Tillis was supposed to take him and his wife, Eva, to Hartford to hide in a safe house, both Abby and Judge Preston were brutally murdered by Merlin Finn.

Did Eva tell Finn where Abby and Niles were going to meet?

Did Eva facilitate Finn's escape from Lockport?

It made no sense. Eva Preston was supposed to be a Tolbonov operative.

The setting sun had been in my eyes as I drove west toward Sheffield, right up until I turned north on Route 7 and headed to Wilton. It was dark and nearly six o'clock when I pulled in front of the Preston house.

Just before I pulled onto the cul-de-sac where the house was located, I passed a cop going the other way. I watched my rearview mirror to see if he'd switch on his blue and whites, turn around, and bitch at me. The last time I'd been out to see Mrs. Preston, a cop had told me to leave her alone.

I parked my car at the curb in front of the house and glanced around me. It was dark and silent.

From the interior of my car, I looked through the large bay window into the living room. It was holiday festive. The Christmas tree was lit with hundreds of multicolored lights. Before I went up the steps, I checked my bag for my phone and for my container of Mace.

Then thinking about John, I took out the tiny GPS device he'd given me and pushed it into the pocket of my jeans.

I didn't anticipate any trouble, but I wanted to be ready.

When she opened the door and saw me standing on the porch, her face registered confusion. "Geneva Chase? From the newspaper?"

"I'm sorry to bother you. Can I come in and ask you a few questions?"

Her wide cobalt-blue eyes blinked twice. She forced a smile. "Of course."

Walking into the warm house, I could smell cinnamon and the aroma of something roasting in her kitchen oven. "It smells really good in here."

Her smile became genuine. Her long blond hair was pinned to the top of her head, and she was wearing a baby-blue sweatshirt, designer jeans, and slippers. Clearly, she hadn't been expecting guests. "Yes, a small ham casserole. There's a potluck dinner at my church tomorrow night, and I like making these things ahead of time so I can just heat it up before I take it over. I mean, who wants to cook on Christmas Eve?"

For a moment, I was caught off balance. Tomorrow was Christmas Eve? I'd lost track of the calendar. And she belonged to a church? Hardly what I would have guessed if she had engineered the betrayal and death of her own husband.

I noticed for the first time a drink in her hand.

She saw me glance at the glass. "Can I get you something to drink? Something festive?"

"Coffee sounds pretty festive." I was sorely tempted to ask for a cocktail, but I needed to stay sharp.

Eva smiled at me again. "Follow me into the kitchen."

Her entire house had an old New England feel to it. The brick walls were painted white, the cabinets were blue, and the glass in the doors showed stacked dishes stored inside. The flooring was black and white tile, and the floor-to-ceiling windows gave a view of the backyard. Floodlights illuminated the snow covering landscaping behind the house.

While I stared out the windows at the winter wonderland

behind her home, she poured my coffee into a mug festooned with Christmas trees and handed it to me. She held up her own glass and said, "Cheers and happy holiday."

We clinked. "Cheers."

We sat down at the table. "You said you had some questions?"

I put my phone on the table and hit the recorder app.

She held up her hand. Her smile was gone. "I'm sorry. Everything we talk about must be off the record."

I blinked. "You don't know what I'm going to ask you yet."

"I'm sorry. I'll be happy to be as honest with you as I can be, but I don't want anything recorded."

Disappointed, I put my phone back in my bag. "Okay, tell me about your relationship with Leon Dempsey."

She jerked as if she'd just gotten a tiny electric shock. "Leon Dempsey?"

"You met Mr. Dempsey in a bar called Jack's in Lockport. You met him there shortly after his wife was killed in a car accident. What was the nature of your relationship?"

Before she could answer, I heard a cell phone go off in the living room. "Excuse me." She left the kitchen, and I fought the urge to follow her. Instead, I sat where I was and strained to listen to her end of the muffled conversation.

When she came back into the kitchen, she seemed mildly relieved. "You were asking about Leon."

"Yes." I was surprised that she used his first name.

"We were lovers."

I was shocked that she was so forthcoming. "How did you meet?"

She took a drink from her glass, and I sipped my caffeine. "You said yourself. I met him at Jack's."

"Did you meet him by chance, or did you know he was going to be there?"

A tiny mischievous smile played nervously on her lips. "I was supposed to meet him there."

"You were told to meet him there?"

She nodded.

"By who?"

She was silent.

"Why?"

"Why do you think?"

"Did you pay Leon Dempsey to help Merlin Finn break out of prison?"

She upended her drink and drained her glass. She stood up and grabbed my half-empty cup and went to the counter to refill them. "Yes."

"Why? You must have known that once he was out, he'd come to kill your husband."

She handed me the mug, now full, and gave me a grin. "Of course."

"Is that why you did it? You wanted your husband dead? Certainly, the Tolbonovs didn't want that. Your husband was on their payroll."

She held out her glass again. "Cheers."

I frowned but reached out and touched her glass again. "Cheers." I took a sip and placed the cup on the tabletop. "You once worked for the Tolbonovs."

"I still do."

That admission made me sit back in my chair. "Did they know that you helped get Merlin Finn out of Lockport?"

She remained silent.

"Did you kill Leon Dempsey's wife, Nancy?"

Eva stared out the back window. "Me? No."

"But someone killed her?"

"It was part of the plan. She had to be out of the picture."

"Leon wanted his wife dead?" I blew on my coffee and took another sip.

"Leon never knew that his wife's accident hadn't been an accident at all."

Why was this woman telling me all this?

I recalled what Chet the bartender at Jack's had said. Leon hadn't received a penny of that money yet. "He never got the life insurance money."

She shrugged.

It was truth or consequences time. "Is Leon alive or dead?"

"I don't know. It's none of my business, and it shouldn't have been any of yours."

I was suddenly exhausted. I didn't know if it was because I was talking to this hard-hearted bitch or it was realizing that it was almost Christmas or that I had stumbled onto an Alice in Wonderland scenario. I put my coffee cup back on the table. "Who killed Judge Preston's wife, Claudia?"

She looked at me with sad eyes. "That genuinely was an accident. Niles was heartbroken when she died. I came into his life just at the right time. I made him very happy."

"Until the man you helped break out of jail killed him."

I was suddenly so sleepy. My words were slurring.

Eva chewed her lower lip. "Niles lost his faith in the Tolbonovs. He never should have reached out to the Friends of Lydia."

"He was scared of Merlin Finn."

Just before I put my head down on the table and closed my eyes, I heard Eva say, "There was nothing to be afraid of. Merlin Finn is dead."

Chapter Thirty-Four

It was dark.

And cold.

So cold…

I couldn't move my arms or legs. My mouth was dry, buzzing rattlesnakes in my head.

Bad hangover.

Where am I? I can't move.

Suddenly, I panicked, trying to move my arms and legs. I was in a chair, but I couldn't stand up. My arms behind me. My legs tied to something.

My bare feet were cold, flat on the floor, felt like cement.

I suddenly wondered, did that bitch drug me and then tie me up in her basement? Cool air on bare skin.

Do I have clothes on?

"Hello?" I said it tentatively, not certain if I wanted someone to hear me or not.

Where am I?

"Hello?" A little louder that time, hearing it echo softly off a hard wall.

Mouth so dry. Tongue thick. I tried moving my arms again. No luck.

"Hey!" I shouted that time.

Fear gripped me when I heard movement, like a door opening.

A bright fluorescent light came on overhead, and I was momentarily blinded. I couldn't move my arms to shield my eyes.

I saw who it was.

Holy mother of God.

Bogdan Tolbonov.

Nearly seven feet tall, shoulders filling the doorway, head like a cinder block atop a short, thick neck. Hair cut close to his scalp, stubble shading the lower half of his face, square chin, thin lips, tiny pig-like eyes.

You're dead, you motherfucker.

Terror crept over me like a thousand cockroaches.

He grinned at me like an ape. "I told you you'd model those for me."

I glanced down. Dressed in only my black bra and pink panties, I was tied, nearly naked, to a wooden kitchen chair.

My horror multiplied when I saw where I was. I wasn't in Eva Preston's basement.

I was in Merlin Finn's torture dungeon. I was in the stone house on Oak Hill, far from where anyone would hear me scream.

He had on a black T-shirt, tight to his muscular body, and his bare arms were like tree limbs. He wore jeans and heavy, steel-toed work boots. The kind you could kick a man to death with.

Bogdan stepped to one side. Valentin came in behind him, wearing a dark-blue button-down shirt, slacks, shoes polished to a high gloss. When he saw me tied to the chair, he took a breath. "How did we get here, Geneva? I never wanted this for you. It's much more fun having you out in the world, chasing clues, writing your newspaper stories. Thank you, by the way, for the piece you wrote about Bogdan's untimely demise. It was very helpful to us."

Bogdan left the room for a moment, then came back in with a chair just like mine. He set it on the concrete floor directly in front of the one where I was placed.

In yet another surge of horror, I realized my chair was directly over the drain used to catch body fluids as they leaked out of the dungeon's victims.

Valentin took a handkerchief from out of his trouser pocket and wiped the surface of the chair clean before he sat down. He motioned behind him. "So, look, Bogdan's still alive."

I glanced at the man, hulking, grinning next to the doorway, leering at me.

I cleared my throat and found my voice. "Eva said that Merlin Finn is dead."

Valentin glanced back at Bogdan. "He was dead minutes after he escaped from Lockport Correctional Facility. Shot in the head."

"Eva helped break him out."

Valentin pointed at me. "If you hadn't discovered that, we wouldn't be here. You'd be home preparing for your holiday."

"Why did Eva break him out?"

"We have people inside the prison who keep track of things for us. Finn was obviously pissed off about being inside for two consecutive lifetime sentences. He and his Brotherhood were making noises about Finn escaping and organizing a gang war, coming at us. I thought it was best if we help engineer the event and manage it ourselves. That way, once Finn set foot outside the prison, we'd know where he was and finish what I'd wanted to do months ago."

"The two men he killed in this room weren't drug dealers. They were your assassins."

"Finn was picking away at the edges of our operation. He needed to be contained."

The way Bogdan kept staring and licking his lips, I was painfully aware of how exposed and helpless I was. "How about you untie me, give me something to wear, and we can finish this conversation over a nice glass of red wine."

He cocked his head sympathetically. "A nice offer. Let me consider it."

Keep him talking.

"Finn caught your boys before they could kill him."

"There was a spy working for me at the time. I didn't know who it was until we let everyone think that Finn was out of prison and getting his crew back together. A man by the name of Charlie Tomasso told Finn when my men would come for him."

"Charlie Tomasso. Where is he?"

Valentin sat back, thinking for a moment. "In our line of work, we need to hire men of a certain physicality." He motioned back to where Bogdan was standing. "My brother is a good example. Tall, strong, brave, preferably loyal. Bogdan, Merlin Finn, and Mr. Tomasso all have similar builds. Mr. Finn lies in a grave out in these woods. The body you found that night at the marina, that belonged to Mr. Tomasso."

"His skin burned beyond recognition, his fingerprints destroyed, I get that. Why take his eyes and pull his teeth?"

"Bogdan's eyes are brown. Charlie's eyes were green. And Charlie had a gold tooth, right here." Valentin pointed to one of his own molars. "If we only pulled the one tooth, it might be too obvious that his killer was trying to hide something. And printing dental records? Child's play. You can create anything on your computer these days."

"Why didn't you just use Merlin's body?"

Valentin grinned. "Merlin was already dead. If Bogdan is going to disfigure someone, he prefers to do it to a person who's still alive."

Jesus Christ Almighty.

When I visibly shuddered, Bogdan's grin grew broader.

"Why pretend that Bogdan is dead at all?"

Valentin held up a finger. "Now we're getting to the good part. This past summer, the FBI started taking an unhealthy interest in Wolfline Contracting. It was slowing things down to a painful level. That was bad enough."

He leaned in as if sharing a secret with me. "Then in October, Jim Caviness was murdered by his wife. He left her a notebook with all his appointments and tasks and contacts. Mrs. Caviness handed it off to someone she trusted while she went to jail. The deal was that person would never go to the police with the notebook as long as Mrs. Caviness stays healthy."

The fucking notebook.

Valentin's lips broke into a grin. "I always suspected it was you who had it, Genie. But we didn't know for sure until we caught you staking out one of our drug dealers back in November."

Shit, shit, shit. Is he saying that I precipitated all this?

"By now, you realize that it was Bogdan who searched your house and took the notebook from your freezer. While there, he searched your hard drive on your laptop and didn't see where you made a copy. However, last night when we brought you here, we found this thumb drive in your bag and a copy of the notebook in the file cleverly labeled Tucker's Veterinarian Records. Bogdan told me that you own a tiny dog."

Poor Tucker. Who would walk Tucker? It's been hours.

Valentin held up the thumb drive. "Does anyone else have a copy?"

I lied and shook my head no.

John Stillwater has a copy.

"In time, Bogdan will find out if you're telling the truth. Makes no difference really. Between the FBI and the stupid notebook, I knew I had to do something drastic. Make it look like we were getting out of the business, going legit."

"Not true?"

He clapped his hand and chuckled. "Far from it. We're in expansion mode. But the feds aren't chasing after us anymore. They're too busy trying to find Merlin Finn. From the perspective of law enforcement, the Brotherhood has taken over all the illegal operations that Wolfline Contracting once ran."

"The drug dealer from that night. Guy by the name of Monk. You killed him?"

He shrugged. "Loose end. He was in the notebook. Plus we found out he was a snitch."

"What about Judge Preston?"

"Another loose end. He got a case of the nerves when he heard Merlin Finn was out. We told him he had nothing to worry about, but he didn't believe us. Wanted to cut a deal with the Friends of Lydia. Thankfully, Eva was there to intervene."

"Do you honestly think you can fool everyone into thinking that Bogdan is Merlin Finn?"

Valentin twisted dramatically to look at his brother. "We only need to take him out and show him off when we think it's necessary. Like when he killed the judge and that woman. It was Bogdan's idea to wear the bondage mask."

I considered the video for a moment. I'd been convinced it was Merlin Finn. The cops were convinced it was Merlin Finn. "In the video that night at the marina, Bogdan was asking Preston and Tillis a question. They both kept shaking their heads. What was the question?"

Valentin turned his attention back to me. "He was asking the judge if he'd already given any information about us to the Friends of Lydia. Bogdan was certain he hadn't. He'd already tortured them both. But the best motivator can be the fear of death. He thought it prudent to ask one last time."

"You're not handling the day-to-day operations and Bogdan certainly isn't. Who's going to run the show?"

He winked at me. "Good question. We needed someone the Brotherhood will respect and fear. Merlin's long-suffering wife, Bristol, has stepped up to take the lead, and her right-hand man will be Finn's old lieutenant, Karl Lerner. They will continue to live here in this house, even though Corsair Properties officially purchased it from Bristol. Bogdan wants to have easy access to this room. It'll bring him hours of enjoyment. You'll be his first guest here. He had to use one of our warehouses in Bridgeport to entertain Mr. Tomasso, Niles Preston, and Ms. Tillis."

I tried to keep my growing horror in check. "How are you associated with Wyatt Investments? How did Wolfline get the contract to build the mall?"

"The money flowing through Wyatt comes from Moscow and illegal operations all over the world. The investment company launders billions of dollars on a global basis."

"Who's Corsair Properties?"

"Corsair is a subsidiary of mine, bankrolled with Wyatt's money. That pain clinic and the pharmacy next to it, by the way, are incredibly lucrative. I know you were in there. The guard at the pharmacy sent me your photo. Just so you know, we're going to open pain management centers all over the tristate area."

One more question. "How did Galley Media know about the mall? How did they know before we knew at the newspaper?"

He squinted at me. "Galley is one of my legitimate investments. I own a great deal of stock in it. Wyatt Investments also holds a great deal of stock in Galley. They told the CEO of Galley that your newspaper would be a good acquisition. Your boss was ready to sell cheap."

Goddamn. Ben was right. Galley knew beforehand.

I took a breath. I was out of questions.

But Valentin had more to say. "So now we come to you, dear Geneva. As I said before, if only you hadn't driven out to Lockport. I don't know how you found out that Eva was linked to Finn's escape. She was very careful to keep her identity a secret while she seduced Mr. Dempsey and persuaded him to make Finn's escape a reality."

Except for that one drunken photo taken by the barkeep.

He continued. "When you drove to Eva's house last night, a friendly cop spotted you. One who you'd met earlier in the week. He let us know you were there. Then I called Eva and instructed her to tell you everything she knew. You weren't going to be able to use the information anyway."

The cop who'd passed me as I pulled into Eva's cul-de-sac. The bastard's working for the Russians.

He leaned back in his chair. "Right now, you are the newspaper headline."

I blinked at him in confusion.

He glanced at his watch. "It is just a little before nine o'clock in the morning, December twenty-fourth." He showed me his teeth. "Christmas Eve."

I'd been unconscious for fifteen hours? "What the hell did Eva slip into my coffee?"

He explained, "Yesterday, I duped Mr. Stillwater and Miss Neese into what I'd hoped was a trap we'd set for them, using Merlin Finn as bait. Unfortunately, we had to shift gears when you showed up at Eva's house. We couldn't have you there with your GPS device, so we devised another plan."

"I don't understand."

"At about ten o'clock last night, your car was discovered abandoned by the side of a road just inside the city limits of Danbury. It was found by John Stillwater, who received a frightening text from you and tracked you using the GPS device we took out of your pocket and put back in your bag, which we left in your car. Once he and the police found your vehicle, there was no sign of you. However, on the passenger's seat, they found your bag with the usual contents, of course, but with one addition, an envelope with fifty thousand dollars in cash. Oh, and your cell phone is missing, along with your thumb drive, of course."

I had the sudden, horrible realization that Caroline must be worried sick. I hadn't called last night, and now the police were searching for me.

He grinned at me, all teeth. "The two-word headline in this morning's *Sheffield Post*: 'Reporter Missing.' Delicious being part of the news instead of writing it."

I felt my heart pounding. "What was the text you sent to John?"

"He received a text message from you saying *Help me, John. Finn has me.*"

Valentin slapped his knee and laughed. "That darned Merlin Finn. Always one step ahead of everyone."

He pulled my phone and the battery from his coat pocket.

As long as he keeps the phone off and the battery out, they can't track me with it.

"In a day or so, using your phone and text messages, we'll lure him into another trap. And finally, he'll be out of my hair. If I'm lucky, we'll get Shana Neese as well." He handed the phone and battery to Bogdan, who placed it on the shelf holding the masks and bondage hoods.

I struggled with the ropes tying my wrists together. My ankles were anchored snugly to the legs of the chair as well.

"So now to you." He leaned in so close that I thought he was going to kiss me. "You are my Christmas present to Bogdan."

My eyes involuntarily darted to Bogdan's face. He was nodding with approval.

"I'm going to be leaving tonight on vacation. My wife, my son, and I are flying to the Caribbean for the holiday. Once I'm out of this room, Bogdan has my permission to unwrap his gift and play with you as he wishes."

He reached out and snapped the side strap of my bra, chuckling. He waved his hands around the dungeon. "I think you'll keep Bogdan amused until at least the New Year. I'm afraid this is the last time you and I will chat."

Terror gripped me. My voice was stuck in my throat. When I finally got the words out, it was a tiny warble. "Please don't do this."

He stood up and pushed his chair back. Turning to Bogdan, he growled, "I know you're anxious, Brother. But limit yourself to an hour for this morning. You have other things to do. Then you can come back and spend whatever time you want"—he glanced back at me—"doing whatever you want with her. Merry Christmas, Miss Chase."

He opened and closed the dungeon door with a solid thud. My horrified eyes surveyed the room—the whips, blowtorch, chains, collars, hoods, clamps, electrical devices. I strained to look behind me at the wall I knew was there. Hanging from leather straps were knives of all sizes, surgical blades, bone saws, stainless-steel bone spreaders.

I'm going to throw up.

In a voice so low and gravelly, it sounded like words echoing from a crypt, he said "You're shivering. You're afraid."

My body was shaking uncontrollably.

Bogdan pulled up the same chair his brother had been sitting in. He sat down, leaned forward, and placed his big hand on my left inner thigh, touching it lightly. Then he placed his other hand on my right thigh. He felt and squeezed the skin, gently at first, then more roughly. He made as if to push my legs further apart but realized that my feet were tied to the chair. My legs were splayed as far as they would go.

He pulled a switchblade out of his jeans pocket and flipped it open. "We're going to have such fun." Bogdan leaned forward and cut the ropes loose from my left ankle, then did the same with the right.

I kicked at his face as he was leaning forward.

Expertly, he caught my ankle before it reached its target. He smiled. "That's the spirit. I love it when they put up a fight."

The lights went out.

We were back into total darkness.

I felt him drop my ankle.

He growled like an angry dog. "Fuck."

From outside the dungeon door, someone shouted, "Someone cut the power."

Chapter Thirty-Five

It was pitch-black again, and I heard Bogdan rush out of the dungeon.

I didn't hear him close the door.

Why should he? You're tied up.

But my feet and legs weren't. And my arms weren't tied to the chair, were they? I couldn't see, but it felt like my wrists were tied behind the back of the chair, not to the chair itself.

The seat of the chair was too wide for me to put my legs on either side of it and try to stand. I'd have to maneuver my shoulders high enough to get my arms over the chair back.

I pushed up with my right leg, leaned forward, lifted my right shoulder into an unnatural position, felt a sharp pain in the socket. Chair back too high.

Try again.

Straining, unnatural stance, right leg cramping, lean over, lift shoulder.

Sockets straining.

I can't do it, damn it.

I sat back down. Panic growing, eyes straining to see in the dark, heart pounding.

Try again, goddamn it.

Pushing up with my right leg, lean over, lift shoulder. Sweat dripped into my eyes.

Right leg shaking, pain stabbed me in the shoulder like a hot needle.

Harder, try harder.

Arms went over chair back. I stumbled forward, nearly collapsing on the floor.

Slick with sweat, I tussled with the ropes on my wrists, hoping to slip out of them.

Tied tight.

Panic swept over me again like a black wave.

Stop, breathe, breathe, slow down.

I shut my eyes and tried to control my breathing.

Calm, Genie. Stay calm. Visualize the room.

Whips, floggers, chains, collars.

Cutting tools! Knives, bone saws, scalpels.

Where? They were behind me somewhere. I couldn't use my hands to reach out and feel a wall in the total darkness. I turned and shuffled forward, trying desperately to recall what impediments might be between me and the knives. I remembered a spanking table and a St. Andrew's Cross. Where were they?

Slowly, deliberately, I moved forward, hesitant, careful not to bark my knee or feet on anything, worried that if I walked too quickly into the wall, I'd stab myself with something sharp hanging from the wall.

When I hit it, it was hard enough to push air out of my chest. I turned again, my back to the wall, and felt along behind me for anything to cut the ropes.

My fingers found something metallic and cool to the touch. I carefully wormed my fingers along it and found the blade.

Damn it.

Sharp.

Did I slice open a finger?

The blade had to be incredibly honed to cut through my skin so easily.

More carefully, then, I lifted the knife by the blade until I felt it slip from the hook on the wall that had held it. Then as quickly as I could, I began to saw at the rope binding my wrists, careful not to cut into an artery.

Sweat on my forehead, dripping into my eyes. Heart pounding in my ears.

Cut, you son of a bitch. Cut!

The rope went slack.

Arms free.

My phone, the battery, on the shelf by the door.

Still holding the knife in my left hand, I went back across the floor, my right hand in front of me, shuffling blindly, moving like a manic zombie.

I surprised and angered myself when I stumbled into the chair where I'd been tied, catching my toes.

The sharp agony made my eyes water. But I didn't make a sound.

My hands found the far wall, and my fingers scrabbled until they found the shelf. Knocking over leather restraints, I found the familiar rectangular device and battery. I quickly slid the battery home and prayed for power to be left and a signal.

Taking agonizing seconds to power up, I saw I had fifteen percent power left and one bar.

Enough?

I pulled up my phone flashlight app and hit the button. A tiny but intense light helped illuminate the horror show where I was standing.

Then I punched up John Stillwater.

"Genie?" His voice sounded fearful.

My words came out in a breathless tumble. "John. I'm in Finn's old house on Oak Hill in Brockton. I'm in the dungeon in the basement. It's the Tolbonovs. Finn's dead. Bogdan's alive."

"Hush. Find somewhere to hide. We're here."

Here? Where? Here? How?

"The SWAT team is getting into position. Find somewhere to hunker down. I'm afraid it's going to get hairy in there."

The line went dead.

I beamed my light around the dungeon.

No place to hide in here.

I glanced at the door.

Bogdan had been in such a hurry. He didn't close the door?

Heart hammering, I pushed the door open. It had been painted to look like it was heavy and solid wood. But I saw that it was just like any door, composite wood exterior, hollow core.

Shivering, I shut it behind me.

I stepped out into Merlin Finn's cellar, a warehouse where he'd filled shelves with bottled water, canned food, clothing, and weapons.

Karl Lerner had called it preparations for a race war.

I found my jeans and sweater wadded up and tossed into a pile on the floor along with my boots.

I tried my best to stop my hands from shaking and put the knife on a shelf filled with cans of beef stew. Then as quickly as I could, I slid into my jeans and threw on my sweater. Before I could get my boots on, I heard someone upstairs shout. "They've got a fucking army out there."

A woman screamed, "Get to the tunnel."

The doorway to the basement flew open, and a flashlight beam cut through the darkness.

I doused my cellphone light and slid it into my jeans pocket. Then I crept behind the metal shelves of canned food and crouched down as low as I could onto the cellar floor.

Led by Bristol Finn, a dozen sets of feet tramped down the wooden steps, rushing across the floor, not three yards from where I hid. On the other side of the cellar, packed tight with shelving full of disaster supplies, a throw rug was pulled back, and a trapdoor was opened.

Then, one by one, I saw black figures illuminated in the ghostly beams of their flashlights disappear down a ladder into an escape tunnel. The last two people to come down the steps were Valentin and Bogdan.

Reaching the basement, Valentin gave his brother an order. "Kill the girl and then follow us. Kill her quick. No time for anything else."

Still holding his switchblade, Bogdan grunted, and Valentin and his flashlight disappeared down the hole.

Bogdan strode purposely to the torture chamber door, opened it, going in.

Heart thudding, holding my breath, I rushed to the dungeon door, pushed it shut, and locked the deadbolt.

I heard his muffled shout. "Fuck!"

In less than a second, the door shuddered as Bogdan rammed his shoulder into it.

A second attempt, most likely from a kick of his steel-toed work boot, managed a long crack in the composite wood exterior.

Door's not gonna hold.

I looked down at my hand. I was still holding the knife I'd gotten from the dungeon wall to cut myself loose. It wasn't much more that an extremely sharp, serrated steak knife.

I ran, flying up the steps to the kitchen, trying to recall what I could of the house.

In the kitchen. Plates of scrambled eggs and toast, breakfast still on the table.

Nowhere to hide here either.

From below, in the cellar, I heard the door to the dungeon explode in a burst of cracking wood and flying splinters.

I shut the door to the cellar and locked it.

This won't last any longer than the one downstairs.

As if to say I was right, the door shook when Bogdan gave it a kick.

Shining my tiny flashlight into the living room, I eyed the front door to the front porch. Through the windows, I could see dozens of flashing blue and white lights, about fifty yards down the dirt road.

Cops, safety.

Wait a minute.

I go running out there, how many trigger-happy cops have their rifles pointed at this front door? How much adrenaline is pumping out there?

I explored the living room. There was the front door, the door to the kitchen, and a stairway leading upstairs to the second floor.

Do you want to get trapped up there, Genie?

The door to the kitchen ripped open. I turned my tiny light to the kitchen door in time to see Bogdan charging across the linoleum, switchblade in his hand.

I glanced down at my own knife.

Fuck that.

I unbolted the front door, threw it open, and ran out onto the porch and into the blinding glare of powerful searchlights. I flew down stone steps, bare feet barely touching, to the snowy ground.

I heard Bogdan's heavy steps behind me as he hit the porch.

Run.

Legs pumping, footsteps behind me.

Run.

Closer now.

Ghostly words over a loudspeaker. "Drop your weapons, put your hands in the air, and get down on the ground."

Do it.

I let the knife slip out of my hand, put my hands in the air, and fell to my knees in the snow and the ice, then dropped face-first into the snow, sliding forward.

Pounding feet thundered behind me.

I glanced back, a huge shadow closing fast.

Dear God, I'm going to die.

The air exploded with gunshots.

Too many to count.

Deafening.

Oh my God, they're shooting at me.

There was a thud close behind me, as if a heavy log had fallen.

The gunshots stopped, but the sound still echoed in my ears.

I managed to move my face just far enough to see.

Bogdan, lying still, eyes open, blood staining the snow and the slush and the ice.

Dead.

For real this time.

I looked back down the hill and watched as the cops crept up toward me in slow motion, guns drawn, focused on whatever danger waited for them in the house.

I wanted to shout out to them but couldn't find my voice.

They're all gone. They've escaped into the tunnel.

Suddenly, multiple gunshots, muffled, distant, too fast to count, like the finale of a fireworks display, echoed through the dark woods.

The cops kept coming, slowly, wary, while weapons exploded, unseen, farther down the hill.

I turned back to look at Bogdan's body again, his dead hand outstretched, almost touching my bare foot.

I was horrified.

Bogdan's eyes blinked.

Chapter Thirty-Six

Every cop car on that hill was either Connecticut State Police or FBI. Except for one.

I sat wrapped in a blanket in the backseat of the only Sheffield Police cruiser on Oak Hill. Mike Dillon sat next to me, holding my hand while I did my best to stop shivering and hyperventilating.

"The EMTs are going to take you to the hospital here in Brockton just to check you over. You'll be out in a couple of hours, and then I'll take you home."

I leaned over and put my head on his shoulder. "Thanks, Mike."

"You know that once we're certain you're up to it, the FBI is going to want to spend a few hours asking you questions."

"A few hours?"

I felt him shrug. "It's FBI. It's how they work."

"How did you know I was here?"

There was a knock on the window. John's face appeared on the other side of the glass.

Mike pointed and hollered, "Get in the front." Then he leaned in close and said, "I'll let this guy tell you."

I felt the momentary flash of cold when John opened the passenger's side front door.

I was pleasantly surprised when Shana Neese, wearing the

same style insulated leather coat as John, slid into the driver's seat of the cruiser. There was a wire cage separating the front and back seat of the cruiser. They both peeked at us through the black grid.

Shana smiled at me. "How you doing, baby?"

"Peachy. Mike was just telling me that John's the one who figured out I was here."

He pursed his lips and nodded. "When Shana and I got what we thought was your text, we found your car last night in Danbury using the GPS. Then we went back to your place. I still have a key, by the way. Oh, and I walked Tucker last night and again early this morning."

"Did you feed him?"

"Yeah, but he didn't have much of an appetite. I think he misses you."

"Thanks."

Shana spoke up. "You have a lovely home, Genie."

All I could manage was a weak smile.

John continued. "I pulled out my laptop and went through the Caviness notebook, page by page. There were several notations on a regular basis that referred to this house and Merlin Finn. I looked up the owner, and right up until this week, the house was owned by Bristol Finn, Merlin's wife."

Mike spoke up. "The feds had this place under surveillance right up until the place was sold. With the money they got from the sale, they left for Myrtle Beach."

I said, "I've got a news flash for you. After they left here, they moved right back in, like termites you can't get rid of."

Mikes eyes got wide. "They were in there?"

"I saw Bristol myself. She was leading everyone into the escape tunnel her husband had built."

John nodded and continued. "I looked up who bought this place. It was Corsair Properties."

"Who also owns the pill mill," I mentioned.

"And is a subsidiary of Wyatt Investments."

I cleared my throat. "Corsair and Valentin Tolbonov are one in the same. And Wyatt Investments is laundering money for the Russian mob on a global level."

"Connecting the dots, Corsair, Wyatt Investments, Wolfline Management, the Sheffield Meridian, I concluded the Tolbonovs were in this up to their necks."

Mike squeezed my hand. "Somehow, John got my home number and convinced me to get a DNA sample rush ordered from what we were certain was Bogdan Tolbonov's body. I burned through a lot of favors getting it done in the middle of the night."

I shook my head. My voice was still little more than a whisper. "You found out it wasn't Bogdan."

John gestured with his thumb toward the stone house. "Obviously."

I was starting to warm up from the car's heater and the shared body warmth from Mike Dillon's proximity. I told them, "The body we found was Charlie Tomasso."

John nodded appreciatively. "I recalled what you'd said about Bristol Finn not closing up this dungeon, even though she'd suffered mightily in it. It made me think that the buyers wanted it for something. I figured this would be where the Tolbonovs would bring you."

I could have given him a kiss right on the mouth just then if we hadn't been separated by the wire mesh.

Mike said, "At first light, feds put drones in the air and took an aerial look at this property, saw all the vehicles, were able to run some plates. Most of them belong to Wolfline."

"You got the address from the notebook," I whispered. "The fucking notebook."

John smiled. "It saved your life."

Recalling the footsteps in the dark basement and the tunnel door being thrown open, I said. "How many bad guys did you get?"

Mike answered. "All of them. The drones spotted the tunnel entrance in the side of the hill before we moved into place. SWAT was waiting for them when they came out."

"Arrested?"

Mike shook his head. "They came out shooting. Seven were killed. Five are in critical condition, in custody. We're still sorting out IDs."

"What about Valentin?"

John spoke up. "Caught in the crossfire. He's dead. I identified him myself."

Shana whispered, "Good riddance."

A sense of relief washed over me like warm bathwater. Recalling his blinking eyes, I asked, "What about Bogdan? He's dead too, right?"

Mike, John, and Shana all exchanged glances. Finally, it was John who answered. "He's still alive."

Dear God, no.

Mike continued. "Critical condition. He's on his way to the hospital as well. We're not sure how many bullets he took, but when he left here, he was still breathing, barely."

I was suddenly gripped with dread. I heard myself groan.

John saw my distress. "Genie, we're not sure if he's going to pull through. Even if he does, EMTs say his spinal cord was shattered. He'll be a paraplegic for the rest of his life."

Shana hissed. "In a wheelchair, in prison. With the Aryan Brotherhood knowing that he killed Merlin Finn. His own private hell."

—

"Genie!" Caroline must have been waiting at the front window, because when Mike dropped me off, she came running out of the house. She practically threw herself at me in the driveway. "I was so scared for you."

I clung to her. “Me too, baby. Let’s get inside.”

Once we were in our living room, I shed my coat, picked up Tucker, and we went into the kitchen. “Mike told me on our way here that you guys flew back early.”

“Once we heard you were missing, Aunt Ruth immediately booked our flights back.”

I never thought I’d say this.

God bless Aunt Ruth.

“Gotta love her. Did she get over the feeling that someone was following you?”

Caroline grinned. “Somebody really was following us. Or Ruth, anyway. Someone who saw her in the restaurant the first night we were in Aspen. His name’s Andy Savarese. He owns a wine shop in town. And he’s incredibly shy. He wanted to meet Aunt Ruth but couldn’t get the courage up while we were at dinner.”

“So he followed you?”

“Kind of romantic.”

“Kind of creepy.”

“Anyway, he finally got around to introducing himself. Ruth is thinking about going back to Aspen for a long weekend.”

“Good for her.”

Without saying anything, Caroline went to the cupboard and pulled a glass out. Then she went to the freezer and took a chilled bottle of Absolut, opened it and poured some, then dropped in three ice cubes. “Here.”

“What’s that?”

Her face was serious. “With what you went through, I thought you could use this.”

I took it from her and sat down at the table. “Where’d you get the vodka?”

“I had Aunt Ruth stop on our way from the airport and pick it up. I thought that if you were alive, I wouldn’t ever bug you about your drinking anymore.”

I pushed the drink away from me, got back up, and hugged her again. "Don't you ever stop bugging me. I love you so much."

"Hey, it's Christmas Eve. Want to open the presents we gave to each other?"

"I'd like that."

She dashed upstairs to her room to fetch the present I'd given her before she left for Aspen. The gift she'd handed to me still sat on the counter next to the toaster oven where I'd put it the day she left.

I went to get it and poured my drink down the sink.

When Caroline came back into the kitchen, she was holding the small box I'd wrapped. "Now?"

"Yeah, you first."

She sat at the table, Tucker at her feet, tail wagging as if the present was a treat for him. Caroline opened it. "A locket?"

"Open it."

She cracked open the gold heart. "It's Daddy."

I'd purchased the gold locket on Black Friday after Thanksgiving. The photo was of Kevin smiling into the camera.

She took the locket, undid the clasp, and placed it around her neck. "Thank you, Genie. I love it. Now open yours."

It was about the size of a small book wrapped in green-and-red paper with a scarlet bow. I carefully opened in and saw that it was a framed photograph. It was of Kevin and me. He was in a suit, frayed at the cuffs and worn from too many dry cleanings.

But dear God, he was handsome in it.

I was in a black dress that showed off my cleavage and my legs. I wanted to be sexy without being slutty.

I was trying to impress him that night.

I muttered, "This is from the first time I met you. Right here in this kitchen. I was driving your father and me to a fundraiser that night."

The photo appeared to have been taken from the kitchen doorway, surreptitiously, while Kevin and I were talking in front of the refrigerator. It wasn't a professional photograph by any stretch of the imagination, but it was the only photo in the world of the two of us when we were together as a couple.

Tears streamed down my face, and I started to cry.

Not just a little.

Full out shoulder-shaking sobs.

Caroline came up and hugged me. "Why are you crying?"

The stress on Oak Hill, nearly being killed, the escape, the gunshots...all caught up to me.

And then the photo I never knew existed.

"It's just that I love you so much."

—

I came downstairs on Christmas morning and found that sometime during the night, Caroline had been in the attic and brought down some decorations. We didn't have a tree, but she'd hung ornaments on the shades of our table lamps and hung lights in the front window.

John had promised to help me decorate. We just didn't get the time.

I thought about him. I liked having him around.

Would we be working together at Lodestar Analytics?

I made us breakfast, and then I sat down and wrote the story about Oak Hill at the kitchen table. Then I sent it to Ben with a note saying, "Here's your Christmas present. By the way, you were right. I have proof that Galley knew about the mall. Ho ho ho."

What I didn't tell Ben was that John Stillwater, while he was trying to figure out where I was being kept, discovered that Wyatt Investments was a majority stockholder in Galley Media.

Confirmed by Valentin Tolbonov.

I sent Ben that file as well.

My cell phone rang, and I saw that it was Mike. Before I could say anything, he barked, "There's a rumor going around that you're taking a new job."

"I gave my notice two days ago."

In a softer tone. "I'm going to miss you."

"I'll still be around. Just won't be doing the police beat for the *Post.* It's not like I'm moving away."

"Good. I like having you here."

I didn't know what to say, so I didn't say anything.

He added, "Let's grab dinner some night."

Really?

"What about Vicki?"

He hesitated. "I'm not sure how that's working out. You know... the age difference and all."

I smiled. "Dinner sounds good, Mike."

Right after we said goodbye, I got a text from Shana Neese:

I'm having a little get-together on New Year's Eve. I'd love it if you could join us. It's always a very special party.

I'll bet it is.

Oh, and I think John might be looking for a date. Got any thoughts?

I smiled to myself.

I love Christmas.

ACKNOWLEDGMENTS

I'd like to thank my publisher, Barbara Peters, and my editor, Annette Rogers, from Poisoned Pen Press, who were there to help me make this book a much stronger story. You ladies are terrific to work with, and I value your input more than you'll ever know.

I'd like to thank my fabulous agent, Kimberley Cameron, for pulling me out of the slush pile and matching me with a wonderful publisher. Through your incredible patience, grace, and friendship, you've changed my life. I'll always be grateful!

I'd like to thank Judie Szuets and Debra Hanson, two wonderful people I used to work with back in my newspaper days. Your voices continue to be inside my head when I write dialogue for Geneva Chase.

I'd like to thank Dawn Brock from Coastal Press who, when I needed yet another hard copy of the book to work from, would drop everything and print a copy.

Thank you, Allie Miller, for the author's photo and making me look good.

And a shout-out to Bucky Oliver at the Boathouse at Front Street Village in Beaufort, North Carolina, who let me scramble around his marina's massive forklift and take it for a spin (with an experienced driver, of course).

I'd like to thank my incredible wife, Cindy Scherschng, for her love, encouragement, and patience. You give me the confidence and the space to keep on writing.

ABOUT THE AUTHOR

Thomas Kies has had a long career working for newspapers and magazines, primarily in New England and New York. He lives and writes on a barrier island on the coast of North Carolina with his wife, Cindy, and Lilly, their shih tzu.

Photo by Allie Miller Photography